the Joining

SCENES OF WEDDING TERROR

EDITED BY
JACOB STEVEN MOHR

Crystal Lake Publishing
Where Stories Come Alive!

www.crystallakepub.com

WELCOME
TO ANOTHER

CRYSTAL LAKE PUBLISHING
CREATION

Join today at www.crystallakepub.com & www.patreon.com/CLP

Contents

GUESTS

OF THE

BRIDE

T.L. BODINE

Perfect Union

AGAON IS DEAD. HAS been for months, but now he looms like a specter, his memory haunting every conversation. She reassures herself:

You love Chris. You would have married him no matter what.

But she's not sure she believes it.

At her elbow, Chris does his best to make small talk with his future in-laws, filling in the gaps where she should be talking, covering the awkward silences whenever her mind wanders. She drifts in and out of conversation, sometimes listening to what he's saying, sometimes to the idle chatter further down the table, the usual mix of cousin gossip and screaming children. There are a lot of kids here, a whole crop since the last time she visited, and she's shocked by how grown-up the oldest among them are, the ones she knows best. Has it really been that long?

Agaon's widow is here, too—Celeste, one of her young cousins, and that's the least surprising bit because she's always been Carica's rival, always zeroed in on her discard pile, whether it was clothes or boys. She's so pregnant that her swollen belly forces her to sit pushed back from the table. Carica's eyes keep straying to it, every glance like pressing down on a bruise.

Carica and Agaon had been an open secret. Everyone knew they were together, but they went through the motions of hiding it just for the thrill. She'd sneak out of her room at night, wriggling out the window to meet him in the orchard, summer wind kissing their bare skin as they explored each other's bodies—just hands and mouths, careful not to transgress against the boundary of the marriage bed, because some acts were still best to hold sacred, because rejecting them was its own kind of rebellion.

"You ever think about what bullshit it is?" Agaon would say, when they were satisfied, lying back against the soft earth and staring up at country-bright stars peeking between the fig leaves. "The expectations. Like our whole lives are mapped out for us before we're even born, and we're just supposed to follow along, even knowing life is a death sentence."

He was always saying things like that, variations on the theme, and she was always nodding along, his edginess endlessly profound. She pretended every time that this was a new revelation, so he'd keep talking, because she loved to get lost in the sound of his voice.

"You're born and you grow up and you get married and you father your kids and you die and they grow up to do it all over. And for what? What's the point of any of it?"

"Just the advancement of the species," she teased.

He fixed her with a hard look. "Doesn't it bother you? The way they figure your whole life is just holding your breath for your wedding night? Like the most important thing you can do is get pregnant. Like you'll never do anything as important until then, or ever again."

"Of course it does." She felt his anger, genuine and boiling and intoxicating, so much so that she wanted to wrap herself around him, like maybe she didn't care about virtue or rebellion. Like maybe the tug of instinct was so strong that she could take all of him—and damn the consequences.

But she didn't. She swallowed down the hunger of her lust and lay unmoving beside him, letting his anger run its course.

"You want more from life, don't you?," he went on. "Didn't you want to go to college? There was something you wanted to study."

"Entomology."

"Right, that's it. You've always been a bug girl."

That struck him as funny, and he laughed, a little giggle that undid the power of his anger and brought home how young he was, how young they both were. Just children, really. She laughed, too, because it was funny, and because they were free, punch-drunk on love and hot summer air and the cicadas singing up to the stars on a night when nothing could go wrong.

"Promise me you'll get out of here," he said. "You'll go to college and study and become a famous scientist and I'll... I'll find a band and become a rock star. You'll know I made it when you turn on the radio and hear me touring all over the world."

She laughed and kissed him and promised. By the next summer she was college-bound, and they drifted apart, her not coming home for summers anymore, finding work and reasons to stay away becomes coming home felt like a trap she couldn't climb back out of.

And all this time, she'd assumed he was doing the same, had comforted herself with the idea that he was on his own path, his own escape trajectory, and if he was out there making the most of himself she could do the same. Because if he could leave, then she could leave, and that gave her the courage to try.

But now Agaon was dead and she was hours away from getting married and all of it had been for nothing at all.

———

After dinner, they're shuffled away from the long tables at one end of the barn and over to the opposite corner, where straw bales have been piled up in a square for seating. A small, tidy stack of gifts sits on a low makeshift table, wooden crates flipped over. It's all very quaint, very country, in case she's forgotten where she is. By morning, the aunties will have swarmed over this space, rearranged everything, hung it with streamers and flowers and boughs brought in from the orchard, folding white chairs lined up in neat rows for guests.

Carica takes a set near the presents and pats the straw next to her. Chris is a little wobbly, limbered by the champagne from dinner, beaming at the novelty of each new ritual. He's been endlessly fascinated by the farm since they arrived, even getting a tour from Uncle Torymus—the family weirdo, a lifelong bachelor with an earring and a tendency to talk too much about his interests. Everybody knew you didn't talk to Torymus if you could help it, but Chris had followed him around like an eager puppy, drinking in every fact about figs her uncle could share.

At one time, Torymus had been a favorite relative, a model for Carica's rebellion. But once she'd grown up a little, she could see how they all treated him, understood intuitively that there was a *wrongness* about him that kept him separated from the group. He could stay, but he wasn't one of them, not really. And anyway, things were different for men.

They work their way through the stack of gifts. It's the usual mix: bone china, a block of carbon steel knives, a crystal bowl for fruit. Home-jarred fig jam and fresh honeycomb. A set of dish towels hand-embroidered with wasps. A lacy split-front negligee, delivered by an older cousin with a wink.

Her fingers hesitate over the paper of her mother's gift, now that a corner is open, now that she's glimpsed the insides. A cold feeling, somewhere between shame and dread and frustration, washes over her. She's half-tempted to set it aside, to deny everyone the satisfaction of seeing her open it.

But then Chris is there, helpfully peeling off the paper for her, and she exhales a measured breath and tries to keep her expression neutral. Like she doesn't understand the significance.

"Egyptian cotton!" Chris exclaims, ooh-ing over the crisp white sheets.

"Lucky," Celeste mutters, and actually sounds jealous. She touches her belly like she can't keep her hands off it, like every sentence needs to be punctuated with a reminder of her pregnancy, of Agaon's seed germinating in her belly. "We only had linen."

It's impossible to know whether she means that as a twist of the knife. She might actually be oblivious. But Carica bites at the inside of her cheek, blinks back the sudden frustrated, embarrassed tears that threaten to spill over.

She knows what these are for, as well as anyone who grew up here. Knows that she'll spend her wedding night in the guest house of the family farm, and come morning her family will gather outside to watch and see the bloody sheets unfurled like a banner, crass evidence of the consummation. An old tradition—tasteless, barbaric, intrusive.

"You're welcome to keep these for yourself," her mother says, as if that were the problem. "And use the ones in the guest room. Our home is your home now."

Like it's a foregone conclusion she's come back to stay. Like everyone knows this is her last visit, that her wandering is over and she's come home at last to lay down roots. Why else submit to the indignities of the traditional wedding, go through all the proper rituals of marriage and consummation, if not to admit that she'd been wrong all along about leaving this place forever?

———

She hasn't been with Chris all that long. A year, or a little less. They met her senior year of college, when she was gearing up for finals and he was working as a lab assistant. The day he first asked her out for coffee, he'd been carefully wiping down the outside of a terrarium, looking with open adoration at the specimen inside, and she maneuvered closer to see what enraptured him so.

"*Latrodectus hesperus,*" she said, when she saw.

"Isn't she lovely?" he said, and then glanced up, seeing Carica, briefly drinking her in. He looked at her the same way as he'd looked at the spider, and the smile he flashed was dazzling, earnest.

"The name is kind of a misnomer," she said, offering a shy smile in return, ducking her head a little to look through her eyelashes. "They only eat their mates when they're in captivity. In the wild, the males often escape. The scientists keeping them locked up are the real killers."

"There are lots of species that perform sexual cannibalism, though," he said. "Sometimes even willingly. Enthusiastically, on part of the male. Like the redback spider in Australia, or the dark fishing spider. They sacrifice themselves, even jumping into their mates' mouths."

"Some people have a death wish," she joked.

"I think there's something kind of romantic about it," he said, and met her eyes. "I'm thinking of making it my specialty when I get into grad school. What about you? Are spiders your thing?"

She shook her head. "Pollinators." She hesitated, self-conscious. "Fig wasps in particular. My family... where I come from, figs are kind of a religion."

He laughed. "Weird religious families, I've got one of those too. Well. *Had*. We don't talk much anymore. But I promise they were absolute weirdos, snakes and faith-healers. The whole bit."

Her heart stammered. She'd never believed in love at first sight, wasn't even sure she believed in love anymore, but here he was like a miracle, like somebody had made him just for her.

And who was she to deny such a gift?

They stand together before the Maker and all of her family—aunties, cousins, her mother front-and-center watching with hungry approval. Nobody from his side, but no surprise there. They probably wouldn't have come for even a mainstream wedding, but certainly none of Chris's set would travel out so far for what they'd likely see as a backwater pagan ritual. If they hadn't disowned him before, they almost certainly would have once they saw the kind of family he was marrying into.

For the best, she thinks.

The priest stands between them, wearing his ceremonial garb, the crimson hood, the lace wings embroidered carefully on the back. He drones on, his vow of chastity somehow making him the *de facto* authority on relationships. Carica half-listens. She's witnessed enough weddings that she knows the steps by heart. She watches Chris's face instead, reads the lines of his expression, tries to guess his thoughts.

"Love is like the wasp drawn to the budding fruit," the priest intones. "Intoxicating and all-consuming at first, but the prelude to an eternal commitment. We stand today as witness to the perfect union of Carica and Chris and remember the holy sacrifice of the fig wasp, who surrenders its body to nourish the fruit."

Chris doesn't flinch, just beams at her, happy as can be, like she's the most beautiful person in the world and he's the luckiest man to be standing across from her. She lets herself get swept up in that, tries to block out everything else. Tries not to think about Agaon standing there in his place, or any of the other countless lifetimes she might have lived instead. The versions of herself that stayed behind, or stayed gone. But they're fantasies, all of them.

There is only here and now—and she's made her choice.

"As the bud opens and accepts its pollinator, do you, Carica, accept this man to be your lawfully wedded husband, bound to you for eternity?"

"I do."

"And as the wasp surrenders to the fig, offering its body and life for the growing fruit, do you Chris accept this woman as your lawfully wedded wife, to nourish and protect for eternity?"

"I do," he says, without hesitation, and she swoons with affection so intense she nearly wants to call it all off right there, wants to cancel the proceedings and send him home because she is a sham, she is a liar. She doesn't love him half as much as he loves her and she never can, never will, but then he's kissing her, and she's kissing him back, and they are wed.

The new sheets are cool and crisp against her skin.

"It's not too late to run away," she says, snuggling against Chris's chest, her face turned away. She's joking, but only halfway, and she tunes her senses to the language of his body, feeling for the tension of hesitation or uncertainty. "Last chance to make a break for it."

But he's as calm as can be, his fingers idly tracing down the long seam of puckered flesh that runs from her breastbone to her pubic mound, kissing her bare shoulder.

"It's what I've been looking for, forever," he says, propped up on an elbow. "When I left the church... if I'd known what it really meant to turn my back on them, that it meant losing everything and everyone, that they meant it when they said I was dead to them. I wouldn't have left. But now I have you. Now I can be part of something again."

"You could go back," she says, twisting in his arms to look him in the eye. "We can sneak out right now, and you can go back to them, apologize, get your family back."

"It doesn't work that way," he says, gently, sadly. Kisses her forehead. "And even if it did. What would that mean for you? Then you'd be the one who could never come home. And coming home has to mean something to you, because otherwise, why are we even here? Why did we save ourselves this whole time if not for each other?"

Chris, the romantic. So different from Agaon, with his sharp edges and cynicism. Agaon, who had railed time and again against fate and conformity and following the righteous path. But he had been a liar in the end, just as she's a liar right now.

Agaon was never going to escape. And she was never going to let Chris go.

Chris rolls over her, plants his knees on either side. Draws her up against his body. He holds her close as he kisses and probes, clumsy, unpracticed, but eager, and she leans into his earnest touches and wriggles into place beneath him, guides him gently inside.

Passion flares, instinctive, engulfing like fire, and she arches her hips up against him, panting in time with his heavy breathing. She's thought about this moment a long time, a lifetime, and never knew how it would really feel. But now she knows it's too late to stop, knows something has been breached that cannot be undone.

She opens her bud to him, pubis to throat, petals unfurling. They're shot-through with red, engorged with blood. The double rows of serrated barbs on each side rotate like sawblades.

"Wait—" he gasps, when they dig into his skin, his thrusting hips going still, his body suddenly rigid with pain. "Hang on. I—"

But there's no going back. No stopping what has been put into motion.

She uses her arms to pull Chris down into the warm, wet cavity of her body. Her thorns grind against his flesh, hook in, hold him fast, pull him deeper. She wraps her arms and legs around him, envelops him wholly, and as she subsumes him, he struggles weakly, an insect in a sticky trap.

———

The fig wasp loses its wings and antennae after entering the fruit.

It crawls blindly forward, its body bringing pollen, and it dies there, trapped inside, its body decaying, dissolving into the flesh it has enabled to grow. The fruit grows, engorged around the seed, until nothing of the wasp remains, its legacy the only proof of its existence.

Did she leave Agaon because she wanted to see the world?

Or is it only that she loved him too much, so much she couldn't bear to lose him, so much that she wanted him to live whatever the cost? Has she chosen Chris because she loves him or because he is easy—no family to mourn him, so eager to give himself up, to hand himself over?

Does it matter anymore?

In the morning, she will wake to the family's approval, and really—isn't that what she's always wanted? Wasn't the arc of her life inevitable, always fated to this trajectory? It's so hard to toil at rebellion. So impossibly exhausting to make every choice for yourself, to go against every grain.

It's so much easier to surrender. So much simpler to follow the script laid out by her ancestors, generations of forebears who established the pattern, beat the trail for her weary feet.

This is the way of things. The natural order. *And it feels so right.*

Chris screams. He writhes inside her as she swallows him down.

"I—" he gasps, but he's choked off with a grinding slurp as the last of him is pulled inside, leaving her to wonder what his last words to her might have meant.

I never thought it would hurt like this.

I changed my mind.

I love you.

She hopes it's this last one. She whispers it back to him, feeling him fill every part of her even as he dissolves, her body shuddering as absorption begins. Her bud seals again, the barbs sheathed, the petals hewing shut, so close they don't even show beyond thin, puckered seams.

In the morning, she runs the crimson-splashed sheets out on the clothesline, a flag.

Later, there will be more ceremony, rituals of mourning and celebration that stretch into the night and unfold, giving structure to the weeks and months that follow, the whole path laid before her.

She touches a hand to her belly, knowing even now that he's in there in some part, fertilizing what's growing inside. That she will grow heavy with young, and his life will pass forward into them, and one day they too may leave the nest.

But eventually—they will come home. They always come home.

T.L. Bodine is the author of *These Kids Are Not Alright, Neverest*, and many other tales of horror. She's interested in uncanny, fantastic things, and the way average people with human problems interact with them. When not writing, she can usually be found watching horror movies, playing story-heavy video games, or experimenting in the kitchen. She lives in New Mexico with her husband and two small dogs.

J.A.W. MCCARTHY

Severed Blessings

LATELY, ALL OF THE brides have been cake: precarious tiers of chiffon and silk, buttercream and ganache. Crafted for consumption. The heels, the exquisite beading, the layers upon layers of delicate lace making it impossible to slip unnoticed into a closet or hotel kitchen pantry. A bride can't take a piss without attendants and admirers and gossipers tracking her every move, a flutter of hands at the ready as she tries to squeeze all that fabric and flesh into a banquet room toilet.

No one notices if a bridesmaid disappears.

I'm the only one watching her. The perfectly pleasing bridesmaid, not too pretty but not too plain, the one who fit perfectly in the height-arranged lineup of polyester ruffles flanking the bride. She was handed a spare bouquet and squeezed into the frame by the photographer, and the rest of the wedding party folded her in because her smile matched theirs. Later, when the bride and groom examine the photos—if the groom survived—they will ask each other if they know her, if she's a distant cousin or family friend pressed into service by a mother-in-law, name forgotten and relation overlooked in the frenzy of wedding planning. Neither will recognize her, but they won't question it any further, not when her features are so pliable, easily interchangeable with the faces of the other bridesmaids. She'll become a chimera in a glossy photo, a wistful "whatever happened to...?" for those who pretend to know her. Even if someone remembers her at the wedding—carrying the bride's train, dancing in a dark corner with a drunk groomsman—they will not be able to describe her face.

The only thing they might remember with any clarity is how odd it was that this bridesmaid always kept one arm pressed tight against her side. How she turned her body so no one could see how the pale pink bodice of her dress caved in, betraying an impossible arrangement of carved-out flesh and missing bone, the hole in her side enough to elicit a flurry of whispers and gasps if anyone had taken their eyes off the bride.

If anyone besides me had noticed the bridesmaid.

———————

This cake bride is dancing with her father. He's as tall and thin as a maypole, twirling her around like molten white chocolate ribboning across the dance floor. Guests clap and snap pictures from their audience of tables draped in the bride's chosen pale pink and butter yellow. Those not watching are dancing themselves, already drunk on champagne. They cluster in little groups, maudlin conversations about the scarcity of true love stacked as sloppily as the dirty plates littering every table. Someone asks me how I know the bride; they don't even listen to my mealy-mouthed story of a bookstore or bakery or coffee shop meet-cute.

The bridesmaid taught me that a shy smile and demure stance can polish vague details into facts.

She moves with the kind of grace that comes from years of tempered necessity. Stepping into a shadow when caught in the camera's eye. Slipping away from a circle of conversation with a polite nod and an empty glass. "Bridesmaid duties," someone infers, and no one can argue with her swift exit. When a guest asks her to dance, she skirts along the outer edges of the dance floor so as not to mar the bride's spotlight. She deflects with a compliment when asked about the frayed white string dangling from her wrist. She corrects him with a flirtatious admonishment when his fingers roam to the satin-shrouded hollow on her side.

Then her hips nudge him toward the door.

This is when I follow. I'm not as graceful as the bridesmaid—not when, unlike her, I was unable to retain my youth—but I'm nearly invisible in the shadow of the bride.

Applause bursts at my back, over the music, everyone cheering on the happy couple's first dance as I slip out of the banquet hall. The bridesmaid and her dance partner are kissing in the hotel hallway now, under twinkling fairy lights. She winks at me as she lifts his hand from her unnaturally narrow waist. A caterer comes by with a cart full of clean white dessert plates and the bridesmaid takes this as her cue to usher her paramour into the nearby ladies' lounge. We didn't get a room this time.

Again I follow, locking the door behind me. It's an expansive space, divided into sitting areas with plush chairs and couches, vanities with Hollywood lighting, fresh roses in the bride's colors and silver-wrapped mints dotting every surface. The bridesmaid and her partner are already on one of the couches, her on top, smothering him in a sea of ruffles. As they writhe together, their limbs blend into her dress's pale fabric so that they look like a singular mass of nude flesh syruping over the cushions. The treacly tang of champagne breath and musk blooms around them, mingling with the bathroom's stale symphony of air freshener and shit.

I'm checking the toilet stalls in the next room when I hear the man's happy little grunts turn wet.

It's the rasp of saliva catching in his throat, a choked back moan, the cold realization that pleasure has crossed the line into pain. The bridesmaid has gotten more impatient lately, now that she's so close to being done. Her partner gurgles a mouthful of polyester satin and black hair, his hands desperately slapping against her body, echoing off the bathroom tiles. I wait until the man's noises fall away and all I can hear is the smooth, juicy violence of the bridesmaid's fingers and teeth.

She perches atop his legs, wiping her mouth and hands on the couch and her dress. The man's ribcage is pried open like a cabinet, bones split into a wide bowl, cradling a mess of unidentifiable viscera, dark wet organs and muscle pulverized in her frenzy. Covered in blood, it'll be a challenge to get her out of here—so we wait until the part of the reception where everyone's drunk and slinking away with their own indiscretions.

When she looks up and sees me standing in front of her, she smiles. Then her faces goes pale and I can see it—the wave that rolls from her throat to stomach, the measured breath that flares her nostrils and fails to mitigate her body's inevitable rejection. She presses her lips into a strained, wavering line, but it's not enough.

The bridesmaid turns just in time to unleash a torrent onto the floor between us. Undigested organs ride waves of bile and blood across the carpet. Slick bulbous shapes fat as infants force their way out of her mouth, slide down her chin, streak her face with pink-tinged saliva. Chewed-up lungs and a heart settle under the coffee table. A liver and length of intestine stop short at my feet. A single pristine kidney slaps the opposite wall with the heavy smack of failure.

She looks to me for reassurance with wide, wet, hopeful eyes. I brace myself for more of the man's organs to pour from her mouth—wasted fruits of another fruitless effort—but when she gags again, all that comes out is a dribble of chunky blood. She sits back, a satisfied calm unspooling over her body as she nods at the floor. She wants me to look again.

Just one kidney. Only half an intestine rejected, left to wallow with the rest of the unwanted organs. Their other halves remain, taking root in the hollow spaces inside her.

Once she rises and smoothes her dress, it's confirmed: the dent in her side is gone, her bodice plumped enough to stretch the satin's shiny limits. Worm-like movements make tiny stitches beneath, sewing a kidney into place, coiling a length of intestine into a waiting nest.

Seams pucker as her body adjusts, then settle into a semblance of a perfectly pleasing waist, the appealing hourglass curve of ribs to hips. The bird-hollow of her chest is still prominent without a heart and liver, but this is only obvious to me.

The bridesmaid steps over the viscera and leans close, her breath hot and mineral against my cheek. She wants to kiss. She wants to dance. But we don't have time to celebrate, not here. Really, I wish we could stay. I long to twirl around with her in this ladies' room, in this inconsequential hotel in this inconsequential town, to lick the blood from her fingers and taste that tang of new life on her tongue while the man's corpse still spills its bounty beneath us. I want to claim victory as we should, with more champagne and my own hunger sated between her thighs. But it's not just the threat of imminent discovery that hurries us out of this hotel and into the anonymity of night.

We do this because of me. This life of furtive plunder is all my fault, and I've spent decades desecrating my body and mind in contrition. Does it matter, now, that I no longer regret my mistakes? That neither of us remembers revenge or forgiveness?

I like what I serve. *We* love what she's become.

Her dress whips around her as we race along the side of the empty road. Bare feet kick up dusty earth, the vapor trail of her swift agility filling my mouth, her satisfied smile stretching across my mind. Hair as dark and plush as the night sky, eyes as bright and curious as the stars above, blood cloaking her like the silk sabai she wore at her own wedding all those years ago. Covered in the crushed and seeping fruits of her labors, she is even more magnificent than the day we wed.

How could I linger in regret? Look at this righteous beast we made.

We were blessed.

The holy men refused to marry us, but we had plenty of friends who offered ceremony. In the northern mountains, our loved ones made a temple of stones and cloth, the sun above our heads and silk beneath our feet. They took the white string reserved for sacred union and tied one end around each of our wrists, binding our already twined hearts, shoring our spirits in harmony with every complex mechanism of our bodies. Our heads pressed together, we listened as her grandmother explained the importance of the white string, how it would take three days for it to fortify our union, how severing it prematurely would undo all our blessings. It was more than a symbol of our commitment. From that day forward, the loss of one of us would be worse than breaking a bond; it would be tantamount to the remaining person losing a piece of themselves.

Each guest took turns winding that string around our wrists, murmuring wishes of happiness and prosperity, strength and resilience. Even as we feasted and danced the night away, no one knew how weak I was. No one knew I wouldn't let myself believe.

It wasn't that I didn't love her. Marriage had been my idea as long as it remained a wistful dream, out of reach for people like us. It wasn't shame that hunched her shoulders and quickened her steps when the men in town yelled slurs and threats. She feared only for our safety, but she still clutched my hand with pride. That was defiance, she said, and marriage was her way of yelling the words she couldn't dare say to those men.

Still, I wasn't ready for such a display. Even with the support of our friends and her family, I feared judgement—not the scorn of a distant god but the heavy eye of those who did not yet know me.

Despite our love, I had not accepted who I was.

We were so lucky. She said it a hundred times that day, and I tasted our joy on her lips, felt it in the unfaltering beat of her heart against mine. White ribbons of incense smoke trailed us as we left the makeshift temple, lemongrass and holy basil promising protection. We cocooned for two days in the decadent fortress of our union, the sacred white string ensuring we were never more than six feet apart.

She joked of a new ceremony after the third day, when our bodies would be as united as our spirits and we could untie the string that bound us. Another excuse for wine, sticky rice and mango, and dancing in our matching sabais. Her laugh made me so happy even though I still feared what strangers thought of us, what they might do or say once they could see it on us, this palpable change in our bodies, our commitment obvious with matching rings and the string having marked us. Why couldn't we keep these gestures just for us? Wasn't it enough to be together, to have our union recognized by our friends, to live a simple life with each other?

On the second night, while she slept, I thought of my father as I took a kitchen knife to the string that bound us.

What kind of girl does this, has such pride in her sin?

What kind of girl wants to show the world her family's shame?

I knew it would hurt her, but I was stupid enough to believe the pain would be temporary. I thought we could go back to the way we'd been, before the spectacle of ceremony and declaration. What I didn't realize was that I severed more than just string, more than the good wishes of our friends and family.

I'd severed the whole we'd made—and when I left, it was her body that paid the price.

Three more cake brides, the pageants of chiffon and fondant enough to distract from my bridesmaid's increasingly heedless actions. We tear through the sloppy remnants of celebration, still undetected as we gorge ourselves on chocolate fountains, our perfectly pleasing unobtrusiveness scheming in the shadows of wedding pomp and the wandering hands of groomsmen. As the night winds down, most guests serve themselves up, as gilded and abundant as the slices of lemon sponge with vanilla buttercream elegantly gift-wrapped to be taken home.

None of them—cracked open on bathroom floors and stripped like rotisserie chickens on hotel room beds—take. She pukes up a cornucopia of viscera and I count every organ, identify another rejected liver, another escaped heart.

The only feasting my bridesmaid does is on the dessert table. She presses her hands to her sinking breastbone and cries as we run into the night, defeated and sugar sick.

At the fourth wedding, she is exhausted, dejected. Over the years, she's shown me the toll of blood under her nails and iron on her tongue, but she doesn't see what I see. I remind her of her power, her magnificence, how she is no longer that girl in the northern mountains, spirit crushed and body robbed. She is something better now—*indestructible*, without the follies of love and dependency. I remind her of how her despair turned into anger then purpose. Her body doesn't need to be made whole when it's the *act*, the all-consuming flame of reclamation, that keeps her alive.

I don't tell her that I hope we do this forever. I'd rather serve a monster than something human, something I could destroy.

Tonight's cake bride is gilded to the point of immobility. Both she and her groom drip diamonds in their wake, yards of gold silk and wool crepe binding them in their roles, a feast of expectation encircling them. Still, even in ornamentation, the groom is a pin dot on the horizon behind his bride. My bridesmaid has never taken a groom, so why not now? As a flurry of admiration swallows the bride, I urge my bridesmaid to make her move. She is one of a dozen in the bridal party, a buttercream blur of ready smiles and champagne-hazy features. I've seen the way the groom eyes these women, unable to tell them apart but swollen with lust all the same. He wants nothing more than the thrill of transgression and a warm body to fill. Even if his organs don't take, eviscerating this groom will be delicious.

I'm the one who draws his attention to her breasts, the vulnerability of her slumped shoulders and defeated eyes. I'm the one who slips the hotel room keycard into his pocket.

I wait in the bathroom, listening to giggles bubbling atop featherweight promises and the rote "yesses" she still manages to sugar-dust. The creaking mattress, the hushed rasp of shoes and garments being shed. I know this is more work than pleasure for her, but my heart still quickens at these sounds. It's in the wake of her viciousness that she loves me again, and I long to smell the groom's sweat on her breasts, taste the last of his saliva, sour and coppery, slicking her neck. I brace myself for his muffled screams and wet spray of blood against the wall, my cue that I can finally come out and watch her work.

But, instead, after the giggles and the satisfied murmurs fade, there is only the blunt thwack of limbs in ecstasy or struggle—I can't tell. Then silence.

I rush out of the bathroom, only now thinking about grabbing a lamp or a vase as a weapon. We've gotten too comfortable; the last man who didn't acquiesce to her claws and teeth was decades ago.

My bridesmaid crouches atop the barely-rumpled bed, lavender satin bunched around her waist, hands and mouth clean. In front of her, the groom lies on his back, limbs starfished and eyes open, mouth and nose smeared to one side from the pillow that crushed his face, stole his breath and life.

She tosses the pillow at me then sits back against the headboard.

"This could be the one," I say. "Your liver. Your heart."

I plant my hand on my hip. She eyes the negative shape I've made, the soft inward curve of my waist, the jut of my ribs and what lies beneath.

"I have a good feeling," I say, curling my arm over my side.

She tears the dead groom open in a frenzy of nails and teeth that once dripped with anticipation. The hunger should be electricity in her limbs, a jolt of instinct animating the beast within, but her impatience betrays something else. What she's doing now is a pageant like all of these weddings we've worked, a performative fulfillment of expectations. A long time ago, need became simple want, the addiction not in service to necessity but the acceptance of pleasure. She *likes* this destruction—I could see it back then, even in her early kills, how the tastes of power and freedom burst so bright from her lips that it scared me. She embraced who she really was, and if there was ever resentment, I haven't felt it until now.

On my knees, I sift through her vomit on the floor. She used to love watching me do that too.

Gall bladder, kidneys, a knot of intestines—all spilled at my feet. The groom's indifferent heart slides across the room in a wave of bile. I turn over dark, pulsing shapes I can't identify, my hands burning in gloves of hot viscera. She watches me from the bed, immutable. But she already knows.

In this mess of plunder, there is no liver. Her body has claimed it.

I rise and wipe my hands on my skirt. Her eyes wander over me, tracing my clavicles, settling between my breasts. I lean toward her, but she doesn't want to kiss.

———

While I wandered from the mountains to the city—a different kind of shame replacing the one that had kept me from commitment—her body emptied itself: lungs, liver, stomach, the contents of her torso fleeing through her mouth, fulfilling the promise of the severed string. Her heart was last, swollen enough to choke her, bursting between her teeth in a guttural scream. Within her hollow body, pain echoed, my own emptiness reflected.

Even hundreds of miles away, I heard the rumors of a woman in the northern mountains, terrorizing entire communities, leaving empty corpses in her wake. Men and women with their rib cages split wide open, bones left shielding only blood and air. A monster, people said, indiscriminate and sadistic, and they delighted in spinning gruesome tales and warnings while forgetting, conveniently, the woman she'd once been. Only her parents attempted to set the record straight, but no one wanted to hear a story of this kind of betrayal.

I returned to apologize, to beg her to take me back, but I did not recognize what I found. She was sleek and feral under the cover of night, lurking outside dance halls and intimate cafes—wherever happy couples congregated. People whispered of the disheveled woman peering in the windows, wondering if she was the monster of the mountains or a poor soul in need of alms. She was bold in her pursuits, dragging men out of alley doors, leaving bloody handprints across temple walls, vomiting what her body did not want in the fields where people worked. When I approached her as she was feasting on the intestines of a guest outside of a wedding reception, I expected her to attack me. I *wanted* her to attack me, to shred my flesh with those glistening teeth, to shit out my organs and make waste of me. Instead, she rose on bare feet and calmly walked into the dark.

The next night, she came to me in the white night gown of our honeymoon, a shawl of blood draping her shoulders like her red sabai, so that she looked like the bride I remembered. Apologies and fresh promises poured from my mouth, but she was not interested. For every one of my tears, she tugged on the white string that remained tied around her wrist. I prayed to go back to that night, to plunge the blade into my heart instead. She shook her head and licked blood from her fingers.

I'd never seen a creature so fearsome. I'd never loved her more.

When she finally allowed me to touch her, to put my arms around her, I felt it: beneath her nightgown, all that held her body together were a ribcage and spine. Though she no longer needed those missing organs to survive, her hunger was voracious enough to make her the monster she'd been named. Her newfound ferocity, a counterbalance to my cowardice.

Seeing her beauty, knowing who she had been—I had an idea.

Two cake brides this time. Twin confections of spun sugar lace and marzipan suiting have gathered a feast of friends and family. I would've chosen a wedding party full of drunk and lascivious groomsmen, but my bridesmaid is back to her old self, excitement radiating as she flits about the reception in a black cocktail dress. She's just pretty enough to catch eyes but not keep them once the brides make their entrance. I'm the only one watching as she slides up to the men who are alone, the ones who look uncomfortable surrounded by empty seats and empty wine glasses.

She's whispering in the ear of one when I interrupt: "Not him."

I do the same with the next person. I pull her out of conversation circles, escort her away from a guest who says she looks familiar, divert her from anyone striding across the room to introduce themselves. She grows frustrated, wants to know why I'm being so fussy about whom she chooses when all that's left—all she needs to be complete—is a heart. I don't tell her that I can't bear for this life we've made to end. I can't bear what will happen when she doesn't need me anymore.

Instead, I spin a good case about how important the heart is, how it shouldn't come from a drunken pervert or serial cheater. We must watch the guests carefully, choose one worthy of her. She sips champagne and eyes the parade of jelly limbs and generous laughter. I know that look, the way her pupils swell and gloss when we find ourselves in the bridal orbit.

She squeezes my hand. I pretend to concede. I acknowledge that she has never taken a bride.

From across the room, I watch my bridesmaid chat up one of the brides. She's not a bridesmaid today, merely a guest each bride assumes the other invited. This bride blushes easily, thin fingers trailing down her neck as my once-bridesmaid unfurls satiny seduction. The bride glances around the reception, spotting her new wife ensnared in an endless line of congratulations. When she and my once-bridesmaid drift out into the hall, I notice how their fingers dare to entwine.

I don't know what I'll do yet, beyond hope that this woman's heart doesn't take. Maybe, when I walk in on them, this bride will take the opportunity to run. I won't stop her.

I follow my once-bridesmaid and her new paramour through courtyards and service hallways, keeping enough distance so as not to be detected. I duck around corners when hotel staff appear and lose sight of the women, clinging to their giggles to tether me. No one questions a bride hurrying through these forbidden spaces.

A corridor of conference rooms greets me, a dead end of heavy doors splintering the white walls like gilded teeth in a bloodless jaw. There's no chatter or footsteps or winded breath, only a heavy stillness smothering the bright tinkle of piano notes that followed me here. We're close to the reception, maybe a couple doors and another maze of hallways from a bride just now looking for her new wife. My heart races, insistent in my ears. *Why here?* Why not a bathroom or hotel room as we planned? A sliver of yellow light seeps from beneath the last door and I rush to it.

My once-bridesmaid stands in the center of a small conference room, a long table behind her. A quick glance reveals that she is alone, without the bride. Her hands and mouth are clean, her hair still a perfect pour of molten obsidian, her makeup undisturbed.

"What happened?" I ask. "Did she get away?"

The music swells, slicing through the distance, sugar glass piano notes now joined by molasses-thick bass. She holds out her hand to me.

"We need to leave," I tell her.

She twirls like a ribbon unfurling at my feet, close enough now for her skirt to brush mine. Her lips are warm and velvety as they trace across my cheek to the corner of my mouth. She never kisses me or touches me until after she's been glutted. Could she have already devoured the bride and cleaned herself? My gaze wanders to a narrow door to my right, and I tell myself it's a closet and the bride is dead inside. A moment of delayed gratification in honor of this momentous occasion because my once-bridesmaid somehow knows this is the one, this is her heart. The iron heat of her breath eases me as her lips latch onto mine.

I want this moment to last forever, too, if her body accepts this heart, if this is the last time we'll ever decimate another wedding.

Entwined with each other, we're sliding, dancing, falling backward until I feel the unforgiving reality of the table against my back. She's on top of me, straddling me, hair filling my mouth, satin sliding cool and smooth against my bare legs. I know she's done with me, that once she claims her new heart, there will be nothing left for me to serve. Whatever love we found in these years since I severed our union has been out of necessity, a partnership I forced in misguided contrition. I'll be left to haunt these weddings alone, an observer to the joy I refused all those years ago.

Her lips trail down my throat, linger on my clavicle; I arch my back as her fingers meet between my breasts. Pleasure makes the cold cross into pain as she digs in. I feel it all, the ravages of desire turning into the annihilation of hunger in claws that break my skin, fingers that grasp each side of my ribcage, the inhuman grip that splits my chest in a wet crack that rings through the room. The heavy sounds of my blood and loosed organs hitting the table drown out the music from the reception. My limbs thrash against her body, satin knotted in my fists, but it's nothing more than adrenaline leaving my system.

Terror almost smothers what I've always known: this is how it has to be.

Cold air caresses my panicked heart, then her warm hands plunge inside me, cradling it. But she doesn't cut it free. She pulls the pulsing organ toward her mouth, lifting me with it.

As the heat of pain turns to crisp numbness, I focus on my reflection trapped inside the crystal cages of her eyes. My face twinned, more resigned than afraid. The frayed white string—stained a rusty brown, now dripping with my blood—dangles in my face and I pull it between my teeth, lips grazing her wrist one last time. It takes all my strength to bite through it, and it falls from her arm as her teeth break the sugar-brittle surface of my heart.

J.A.W. McCarthy is a two-time Bram Stoker Award and two-time Shirley Jackson Award finalist and author of *Sometimes We're Cruel and Other Stories* and *Sleep Alone*. Her short fiction has appeared in numerous publications, including *Vastarien*, *PseudoPod*, *Split Scream Vol. 3*, *The Dark,* and *The Best Horror of the Year Vol. 13*. She is a second generation immigrant of Thai and Slovak descent and lives with her spouse and assistant cats in the Pacific Northwest. You can call her Jen on most platforms @JAWMcCarthy, and find out more at www.jawmccarthy.com.

JES MALITORIS

Cut-a-Skin, Outside-In

After the vows had all been spoken and the feasting begun, it was time for the Skin Game.

The bride remained veiled at the high table—none but her husband would see her face until more private offices had been completed—but the young groom leapt up to lead the festivities.

He was barely more than a boy, but new bride and honey-wine emboldened him. His speech slurred as he crouched like a beast on one end of a feast table and chanted the rhyme.

> *In the wood I went a-hunting,*
> *Cut myself a skin to run in.*
> *Guess which shape I wear to-day,*
> *Or wood come take thy skin away.*

The assembly laughed and clapped as chatter died, dancing stilled, the fiddler stopped his strings, and all gathered to watch or join in the game.

The groom slouched down the length of the table on all fours, knocking aside plates and cups, most empty but sometimes dumping wine into a reveler's lap. Laughter and curses followed him up the table until the groom paused and mimed sniffing the air. Alcohol made for a clumsy performance, and it took the assembly a moment to realize the swaying of his hindquarters was meant to signify a swishing tail.

When at last, however, he let out a high-pitched, piercing yip, a bridesmaid guessed it: "A fox!"

"Aye, milady!" The groom stumbled from the table, supported by his father. "A fox am I! Keep thy chicken coop well-latched."

The lady blushed, his father spoke sharp words into his ear, and a rumble of uneasy laughter rolled across the room toward the bride.

If she flinched, however, none could see it. Her veil rippled, and a delicate hand deposited on her plate a chicken bone, stripped of all flesh. She was nearly an idol at the end of the hall, impassive in her clothes of sky blue, silent but for her mumbled vows, a source of curiosity that seared even the furthest feast table.

Her groom delighted in it. He had worried once that he would never find a wife. He had tumbled in the hay loft, certainly, but a hay loft woman was different from a bedroom woman. Who knew what else a hay loft woman got up to?

The bride would be only his. Her veil was a sacred thing, and he could barely wait to see what lay beneath it, what woman his uncle had gotten for him. In the whole town, only his uncle had seen her, and so the unveiling held a special sweetness at the thought of taking her around tomorrow to introduce her to everyone: his quiet, soft, yielding wife.

The groom had asked his uncle what she looked like. He it was who had met her woodsman father while out hunting. The woodsman had said that his daughter had come of age, and he sought a groom for her. Life in the woods was hard, he said, and the woodsman wanted his child to live a good life. Since the women had gone to meet the bride at the edge of the wood that morning, the woodsman had disappeared. Uncle therefore reveled in the distinction of being the only one to have seen her face, and had gone around town all day, recounting the meeting.

But the groom had pressed his uncle to whisper, at least to him, what she looked like. Then, uncle did not look at nephew. He went still; the memory passed like a shadow over his eyes. Then he recovered and laughed low into his nephew's ear that he almost wished he had no wife and could take her for himself. The groom grinned and poured his uncle another glass of mead.

Uncle had passed this intimation to every man in town, although the wedding was done and his own wife sat prim amidst the other town ladies. Everyone therefore knew that the bride was beautiful and agreed that the marriage was a windfall for a young man with nothing to recommend him but good luck and a kind uncle.

In the wood I went a-hunting,
Cut myself a skin to run in.

The best man tried to convince himself his new sister-in-law could not be bothered to find him in the crowd, but no matter how many people he placed between her and himself, he felt her stare bubbling up sightlessly from beneath her veil. Standing now at the center of the room, with all eyes upon him, it was a torment.

He fumbled over the rhyme, trying to avoid meeting any eyes in particular. The first creature that leapt to mind was a squirrel. As the groomsman crouched and folded his hands before him, he felt like a fool. He should have picked something safe, a bull or barn cat or some other such animal safely sequestered in town. A squirrel was a reminder of his weakness, and he imagined his new sister-in-law's eyes like hot coals.

Foolishness, to have gone that morning to end it. He had not thought of the bride and her father going to the edge of the wood to give her away. He had melted again under the trapper's hands, as he did every time he tried to break off their affair.

The trapper was the groom's friend, and in the feast hall he laughed alongside the others, refilling his glass as the best man swished an arm like a bushy tail and pretended to nibble upon an acorn, desperate for the correct guess to come so that he might resume his place against the wall.

The trapper's hands were callous, deft, strong as a vice on the groomsman's hips. They made him feel soft. The trapper did not merely push the groomsman against a tree to use him as had previous dalliances, all woodsmen or similar mendicants. He *lifted* him, so that their lips could meet, so that the groomsman could murmur protests against them as the trapper made him soft.

Perhaps it was these protestations, or perhaps the groomsman's breathy moans that had drawn the bride, like a wolf to the scent of blood.

She seemed at first a blue phantom, a slice of sky descended to peer at them. Then they realized she wore the bride's veil.

The men froze as she took them in: their clothes scattered across the mossy soil, sweat slicking their skin. It had cooled on the groomsman's neck and chest and speared him with dread. He tried to push the trapper away, but the man would not release him. Doom had come, as he always knew it would. At every moment he expected her to run crying about sodomites in the wood.

She had not. They heard her breathing: panting hard, wet breaths. Her veil moved with her inhalations, sucked against her lips and her tongue, licking down the air. Perhaps she was laughing silently at them.

Then the bride turned, a ripple of cloth that looked the same behind as it had in front, and her eyes had seemed to still be on them even as she vanished into the undergrowth. The men had detangled themselves, shaking. They could not meet each other's eyes.

No one in the feast hall would relieve the groomsman of his discomfort. His performance was poor; no guesses rang out from the gathered throng. And so, he went on as a squirrel, unable to stop, trapped between two shapes until the guess was called.

It was the trapper who released him—and for a brief moment the groomsman felt relief until their eyes met, and then he felt sure that everyone *knew* and turned away.

The bride's coal eyes kept on burning, though he could not see them, though she said nothing. He merely remembered her strange breaths, and the way she seemed to taste the air.

<hr>

As she played the Skin Game, the bridesmaid kept her steps dainty, her skirts hiked up around her arms like wings, and her knees exposed.

The woman's mind buzzed with honey wine, eyes fixed on the groom as she strutted and clucked along one of the tables. That morning, she had been sour faced when she joined the other women to collect the bride from her father, but the groom's joke about henhouses gave her hope that not all was lost. She would continue her visits to the hay loft, she decided.

The maid of honor should be a sister, cousin, or close friend, but the bride had no one to stand up for her. As the groom's childhood friend, the maid had been given the post.

She had trailed behind the groom's mother and aunt with the rest of the womenfolk to the edge of the wood. The morning had been quiet, no summer insects a-screeching, despite the muggy heat that stuck the bridesmaid's dress to her back. Just inside the tree line, the rugged woodsman awaited them with his daughter's hand in his.

At the time, the bridesmaid had scrutinized the strange woman, bitterly seeking weakness. Her clothes were simple but fine—for a woodsman's daughter. Pale blue cloth draped her face, no mere mesh but a true veil. A long kirtle brushed the tops of her shoes. Her feet were dainty and surprisingly clean. Her hands—

It was the bridesmaid's duty to accept the bride's hand from her father before the groom took it for life. The fingers were so delicate and dainty, soft and unblemished as if the bride had never touched anything, never lifted anything heavier than a fork in all her life.

Sick with envy, the bridesmaid had skulked all the way back to town. In the feast hall, the women talked, sang, and made ornaments. The little ones helped craft simple braided wreaths, while the elders wove crowns and garlands of flowers. Amidst the noise and the bustle, the bride sat stone-still with lilac and wild rose on her lap. The bridesmaid was content to leave her so, but at length the groom's mother nudged her.

"Teach her the way," she said gently. "Think of it—no womenfolk to instruct her in women's business. Only a lonely woodland life."

The bridesmaid thought to learn her competition's weaknesses. "Hast thou ne'er made flower crowns, sister?" she asked, all innocence.

At last, the bride moved. The veil twisted and crimped as her faceless face turned toward the bridesmaid. She did not speak.

The bridesmaid showed her the way: first, sheared a lilac stem into a spear; second, slid the point of a blade into the meat of a rose stem, creating a slit; third, pierced rose with lilac, and bound them with reed twine. These steps the bride watched, wordless.

When the bridesmaid passed her the shears and flowers, the strange woman seemed to consider them, head bowed, veil draped over her lap to shroud them.

With a viper's sudden intensity, the bride seized the maid's hand. She twisted the arm wrist-up the wrong way, so that the bridesmaid whimpered, and her shoulder complained.

"Sister," she gasped, "Why—?"

The shears' blade silenced her, their cold length against her wrist. In the chaos of the room, bride and maid alone were still. Bride pushed shears into the bare wrist until blood began to bloom, until a few drops sluiced down the blade and tears down the bridesmaid's cheeks. Maid said nothing, tongue bound by fear.

Just as suddenly, the bride stopped. She withdrew the shears and released the arm. "Inside, outside!" the bride had laughed, a brook-burbling giggle cold as fresh-melted snow water. One of her dainty, unblemished fingers swept tears from the bridesmaid's cheeks. The bride withdrew beneath her shroud. There came the sounds of sucking, and the bridesmaid's face contorted with disgust as the woman beside her savored her salt.

Unsure what else to say, the bridesmaid had excused herself to the privy.

She had gone shaking, but even as she shivered in the rancid privacy of the latrine, she had calmed herself. A woman like that could not make the groom happy. An angel's visage would be for naught if the new wife held a kitchen knife to her husband's skin, if she licked the tears from his face.

Beside the couple at the altar, the bridesmaid had felt peace. Her lover had been flushed and bright-eyed as he pledged to another woman, but it did not matter. None of it mattered as the groom turned toward her in the feast hall, bright-eyed with drink, careless and beautiful, calling out his guess:

"A chicken! A preening hen!"

None of it would matter as long as he came to her again, creeping like a fox into the henhouse, and gave her another chance to lift her skirts in the hay loft.

The groom's mother did not play the Skin Game.

She sat near her sister-in-law and together they minded their children. Her youngest son played a simpler version with his cousin. They did not know the rules, they did not know the words, but the groom's mother felt compelled to stop them. The game was a dangerous thing.

She never spoke of the incantations she had heard her grandmother use over pots of herbs and occasionally over the spread entrails of birds, at the entreaties of desperate people. Her grandmother had refused to teach everything she knew. The old ways were fading, and her granddaughter would be safest without giving others excuses to cry, *witch*. She had, however, taught her granddaughter to be wary of fairy circles in the wood, to show gratitude to the creatures that fed her, and above all, to recognize an incantation—and the threat it harbored.

The groom's mother had watched the Game with terror at her own wedding. Her new husband had been a bear, stomping and roaring around the feast hall. She had shivered and cowered at the man's size, the exuberance and violence of his performance, and what it meant for her first night bedding and all the nights thereafter.

Luck, and her parents' wise choice, had been with her. The bear of a man was gentle also, soft and tender as he was large. He was a good husband and helped her to raise their five children well.

All but their eldest. The groom's mother knew what kind of person her son had become. She and her husband traded looks of guilty frustration as the boy scurried along the tables, impressed with his own importance. She blamed her wretched brother-in-law's influence, although she knew the fault lay as much with her. Her son should not be a groom at all, not yet, but when his uncle had proposed it, the woman thought it perhaps wise—a reason to draw the now-groom away from his flirtations, his many hay loft women. Heavens knew how he enticed them. At the time, the groom's mother had thought bitterly, guiltily of what kind of husband her daughter-in-law had got.

But the woman who met their procession at the edge of the wood that morning had hit the groom's mother like a wind change. She felt her like the prickle of a coming storm and had thought of her grandmother for the first time in many years.

The groom's mother turned her eyes again to the blue figure seated at the end of the hall. Though completely masked in cloth, she seemed enraptured by the performances before her. The breeze of her breaths made the shroud sway, and at each recitation of the Skin Game rhyme, her eloquent fingers tapped against the table, plates, and bones stripped by her own teeth.

Wind passed through their merrymaking like the breath of an uninvited guest. The doors to the hall stood open and the groom's mother could not have said who had left them so, or when. Night had crept upon their feasting, but no moon peered out of the sky. The only light came from the stars, and at their feet waited the low, lumbering wood to swallow them.

The outside had come in, where it was not supposed to be.

The groom's mother leaned toward her sister-in-law. "I think it time the children were abed."

As one they nodded and scooped their little ones into their arms, who protested through gaping yawns. The groom's mother paused at the door and wondered whether she ought close it.

But the wood was already watching, and she did not wish to draw its gaze. She walked home, cradling her child and hoping the night would not swallow them down.

Guess which shape I wear to-day,
Or wood come take thy skin away.

The groom's uncle guffawed as he stepped up to take his turn, swigging down the rest of his ale, to great applause from the young'uns. Only his brother scowled and tried to dampen his enthusiasm. The other men knew the uncle was good for a laugh and a drink, for cards or dice. The young groom and his friends had taken to joining the uncle of an evening, to carouse and complain about their responsibilities. They made the uncle feel young again, and for this reason had the man thought of his nephew when the bride's hand was offered.

He had married for beauty before, and he could not resist its allure now, either. His first wife was a lamb, dead at her own lambing, while the second was slippery as salmon, flashing away upstream once she understood what he was. His third and current wife was pretty enough, but he had wed for the full coffers she brought to their marriage bed. She was a constricting snake, willing to ignore his wanderings as long as he paid for them later.

At first, he had considered the girl for himself, current wife be damned. So young a thing, flush with youth and shivering naivete, innocence like a grape ready to burst in his mouth.

How could he resist?

How *could* he resist? It taunted the man as he stepped into his chosen Skin, hopping like a little bird among the guests and searching for what sparkled best in the candlelight. With his hand like a beak, he pecked and plucked at those most likely to enjoy his antics, the groom and his friends.

The bride's fine hands, so soft and untouched, lay gracefully upon the high table. Her body must be the same, so frail, so perfect, so bruise-able. The uncle had seen her face that day in the wood, and he felt certain it had entranced him. How else could she consume his every thought? And yet, every attempt to summon the memory met with failure. Her face only crept upon him when he forgot to think of it, a predator waiting until his back had turned.

He danced closer to the high table. He plucked at shiny cups and pendants, fluttered his arms and scattered laughter in his wake. The bride did not turn, did not acknowledge his slow approach, flirtatious and poised in her silence. Her neglect wounded him, and the wound festered.

By the time he reached her, the groom's uncle was panting and flushed, swallowing saliva that pooled under his tongue. Still, the bride would not acknowledge him, and so he reached out a beak-like hand and plucked coquettishly at her veil.

The predator pounced.

She had been wearing the veil even then, that morning a fortnight ago, no matter that she yet had no groom, that the air was sticky and hot. The uncle did not feel the misery of it, except for the insects that he slapped away from his face and arms. The woodsman who called himself her father faded into the fraying edges of his memory; the woodsman did not matter.

All that mattered was the invitation. "Do you want to see her?" the man had asked, and the uncle had licked his lips in answer.

He took careful hold of the veil's delicate edge just above her immaculate hands, lifting it past her waist, longing to trace that gentle curve with his fingers. Then the swell of her breast, the skin so tender and flawless it seemed to crave his kisses. Then the fine ridges of her collarbones, more precious than a string of pearls. Her neck, grazed with silken hair; her dainty chin; her jaw.

Then the veil's length embraced him, too, and the uncle and the woman stood together beneath it.

Her face held his gaze as surely as a fanged maw.

She was a spiral, a swirl of eyes, and eyes, and eyes, a descent of twinkling lenses in, down, beyond, a shape from which he could not withdraw. She had let him in, and the man's mouth fell slack open as he tried to chase her shining eyes, failed, and was swallowed. He did not even notice the insect tickle of legs across his tongue or in the shells of his ears.

When the woodsman took the veil from the uncle's hands to let it drop again, the uncle forgot. But he had been hypnotized, utterly incapable of withdrawing from the blue-shrouded woman. She must have been beautiful, then, beautiful beyond compare.

The woodsman had explained that his daughter sought a bridegroom. Even as the uncle opened his mouth to offer his own hand, a nagging animal impulse had spoken instead, a flinch of survival instinct that told him he should not bind himself to such a creature.

He had given his nephew's name instead. And now, in the feast hall, the honey wine dulled caution, and the uncle only jerked back from the bride's gown when a fat earwig landed on his thumb.

His shout of alarm earned fresh laughter from the onlookers, but he was glad when at last someone correctly named him, *"Magpie!"*

The flower girl, barely eight summers in her bones, uncurled herself from her hiding place. When the aunties had begun to nudge the children toward the door, she had tucked herself away, still wide awake and excited to see the Game's conclusion. It fascinated her, the delicate dance of people who seemed to be saying things without moving their lips. Their wants, dreams, and hopes seemed to play out behind their eyes. The flower girl did not yet understand why such thoughts might not be spoken. Mama had lately begun to tell her of marriage; had counseled her about beginning to carve her manners into a bride's shape. To the flower girl, a groom seemed like a monster: boar, bear, or some other Beast who would take her away to do who-knew-what.

The groom's uncle flitted closer to the bride and the room watched with bated breath as he plucked the hem of the bride's veil. From beneath her table, the flower girl scowled. She did not like the man. She was the groom's distant cousin and therefore the uncle's distant niece, and therefore Mama made her greet him with an embrace. If the girl tried to speak her thoughts, she was told to hush, to not be rude.

When all the color drained from the uncle's face and he jerked suddenly away from the bride, the flower girl giggled into her palms. She liked the bride, although something about her unsettled. They had met in the wood some weeks agone, and after the flower girl had come home filthy and late Mama had spanked her so hard, she could not sit properly for days.

Tired of her baby brother's screaming, she had fled to the freedom of the wood and found the stranger dancing among the mossy stumps. The girl had offered a modest bouquet of slightly crushed wildflowers and the woodswoman had smiled. They danced together on the moss, and the woodswoman taught her of leaves and insects.

Even under the bridal shroud that morning, the flower girl had known her by her swaying steps. She had gone to greet the bride bearing the best flowers that she could find for her crown.

Only then, as the woodswoman's veil had twitched and she lay a silent hand on the girl's head had the flower girl realized she did not seem like a woman at all. The bride was a cloaked thing like the masked dancers in wintertime, with their grimacing faces and stilts and fluttering red capes, somehow bigger and realer than the shapes under them.

At the head of the feast hall, the uncle disguised his discomfort with a smirk when someone at last called him Magpie. He turned to the crowd.

"The Skin Game is nearly at end. Whom amongst us hath not taken a turn?"

Eager to play, the flower girl scrambled from beneath her table. Before she could say a word, the bride stood, slow as a rising storm.

Curiosity silenced the guests. Fear slashed the uncle's face, and he retreated as the bride took up the empty space before the table. Her groom started toward her, hands outstretched, but he stopped as she began to rock on her feet and chant a mumbled rhyme.

> *From the wood from wood we come*
> *Haunting harking heaving hunting*
> *Cut a skin a skinned to stuffed in*
> *Fill fingers fleshy flush forage within*

Curiosity soured and guests began to trade uneasy glances as the bride's voice gained strength. A buzz accompanied it, a tickle at the edge of each syllable.

The flower girl tried to nudge through the crowd, but an older cousin caught and held her fast.

The bride persisted, blue shroud swinging as she rocked.

Shape we wear worn wearing thin
Lure tempt bait invite in
Guess judge pick the shape we play
Or wood catch gouge eat innards away.

A chill passed through the assembly and true silence descended. Fascinated, the flower girl watched the bride push her groom against a table. "Inside, out!" she said aloud, and then planted one leg on the table beside him.

With painful slowness, she revealed a dainty foot, then a smooth and shapely ankle. The room was breathless, and the groom, greedy for her flesh, only stopped her as the hem of her under-pants emerged. "My dear," he murmured, catching her hand, "There shall be time for such things later."

The woodswoman pushed away from him and took back her hand. She went to the bridesmaid nearby, who cowered and closed a protective hand around one wrist. "Inside, out!" the bride crowed, seizing the woman's free arm and twisting.

The bridesmaid cried out in pain. "Please, sister, why hurt me so?"

The bride laughed her creek-cold laugh and threw the wrist back. "Guess," she hissed. "Guess, judge, pick!" But she let the bridesmaid go and wheeled on the groomsman instead.

Real panic twisted the man's face as she shoved her new brother-in-law against a table.

The flower girl's eyes went wide, inquisitive and uncomprehending, as the bride pushed his legs apart with her knees and leaned into him. "Guess, guess!" she cried, and the feast hall erupted.

The flower girl's cousin covered her eyes, and by the time the girl wriggled free and danced beyond his grasp, the groom's father had put an end to the trouble. The enormous man had to bend to hold the bride in firm hands.

"Get thee to bed, *now*," he said, gently but just as firmly.

"Outside goes in," the woodswoman burbled. "Lush, succulent thoughts." She pressed a fingertip to the father's forehead. "Heart heave, heart toil." She dragged the finger down his neck to the center of his chest, where he caught it and pulled her hand away.

The man frowned. "Outside goes in?"

"Inside come out!" the bride declared, her voice buzzing with a ferocity that rumbled the flower girl's skull. "Guess, judge, pick!"

"*ENOUGH!*" the groom's father roared. "The Skin Game is at an end!"

The bride immediately stilled. "Ye cannot guess?"

"We will guess no more. Away to bed with thee!"

The groom came to bear his wife away, but the bride would not move. The woodswoman's buzzing hummed now through the flower girl's entire body, and she folded herself beneath a nearby table.

The bride's own delicate fingers pinched the hem of her veil. Her groom leapt forward to stop her, but in one smooth motion, the bride threw the fabric back.

For a long moment, thousands of eyes, nested in the hollow of the bride's face, glittered and sparkled in the light of the candle nubs. Groom, father, brother, uncle, bridesmaid, and every guest stared in growing understanding and horror.

Her eyes unraveled. The swarm—dragonfly, wasp, honeybee, fly, beetle, moth—streamed into the feast hall, hollowing the bride's borrowed skin. Screaming reverberated throughout the hall. As feast goers stumbled and shoved toward the doors, the insects set upon them.

Open mouths were wide doorways. The outside found its way in through every orifice, burrowed through skin, honeycombed flesh.

Beneath her table, the flower girl clutched her ears against the human screeching and the wailing buzz of busy insects. She curled into herself, sealing her lips, folding her nose into the gap between her legs, blinding herself to the writhing of neighbors and family.

When the swarm roar had settled, the flower girl raised her head. She breathed into her hands as she watched them go: uneasy silhouettes, wobbling on new legs toward the dark tree line.

The wood had taken new skins for its own.

Jes Malitoris writes weird, folk, and cosmic horror and dark fantasy, with work in *Cosmic Horror Monthly*, *The Skull & Laurel*, and *The Crawling Moon* (Neon Hemlock Press, 2024), among others. Jes is a reader for *Necksnap Magazine* and an active member of the Carolinas Chapter of the HWA, and was shortlisted for the Tenebrous Press Brave New Weird Award.

JONATHAN LOUIS DUCKWORTH

Of Vows Bone-Deep & Sacrosanct

BEYOND THE VESTIBULE OF the smoking car, Nestor Santi's wife sat hidden from him. As the train rumbled onward, away from the city and its gaslamps, he pondered what sort of family insisted on a midnight ceremony. Or on keeping a man from seeing his lawfully wedded wife. This was *his* train! Well—his father's train, anyway. Nestor and Holothé had already wed that morning under the basilica of the Ivory Tabernacle in the view of God and city society. But the Margravs were a family as old as the nation's bones, and according to their ways, Holothé remained a maiden, unwed until the midnight ceremony in their private family chapel.

He couldn't see anything through the smoking car window. He was about to try the door when it opened for him. A pallid beauty in lacy black silk appeared in his way. Holothé's sister, Jyell. Smaller of stature and bust, with more of a snub nose, but otherwise a near-twin to his bride.

"We have explained the custom," she said, voice level but reproachful. A neat smile, as if knitted by a deft needle, stretched her bluish lips. Like all Margravs, she had no eyebrows, her high, domed forehead smooth and lineless as marble.

Nestor opened his mouth, ready to fire from the hip, but the stocky frame of his best man stepped in to rescue him from himself.

"Nestor understands *quite* well, darling." Doss Jennet wrapped a beefy arm around Nestor and tugging him back. "But you can't fault a man for impatience on his wedding night."

Unblinking, Jyell inclined her head—the slowest nod Nestor had ever seen. "Yes, I suppose not."

"Come on, old boy, let's get a drink in you," Doss said, already walking away.

"We will be there soon," Jyell said. "Patience, brother-to-be." Her voice was full of cobwebs, much too old a voice for such a young face.

"I've been patient," he said, softly.

Jyell's eyes, which had yet to blink once, glanced over his shoulder, tracking Doss Jennet as he ambled toward the bar. "Your friend, the Baron of Iron's son—I like him," she said. "Such a meaty body; such thick bones, I imagine."

"I'll pass your compliments on," Nestor said.

And then she closed the door in his face.

Six hours ago, he had been ecstatic. To see his bride in her cream-white taffeta with the seven-tiered train and golden embroidery, he believed he'd married the most beautiful woman in the world. But even as he'd carried her down from the tabernacle's altar, one glance at Holothé's family—gaunt, browless, joyless, all in black and uncomfortable in the light and warmth of the church—made him wonder what sort of bill of goods he'd been sold.

At the bar, he found Doss already helping himself to the liquor. Nestor's father, the Baron of Meat Ernan Santi, was reclining in a dreamlike fug of cigar smoke.

"Sit down," the old man commanded. "Pacing is a woman's habit."

"I wasn't pacing."

"Your best man never paces. Perhaps his father raised him better."

Doss snorted at that.

Nestor sat down. "Really, though. A midnight ceremony?"

"It's their tradition. The Margravs are rich with them." Father brushed ash from his sleeve. "Whereas we are rich in the ways that still matter."

Nestor had asked when the engagement was first set, if marriage was really about nothing but a financial agreement. What else, Father asked, could it be?

Love and sex—*these* were things you didn't need to marry for.

"We're all shedding tears for the newfound penury of the old land princes," Doss said.

"Poor they may be, but they still own the best grazing land in the whole Duchy," Father said. He gestured out the window. At present, a rolling expanse of pastures scrolled past, perforated in spots by little groves of primordial forest and quilted with squares of tilled land, without a telegraph line in sight. Nestor had never been this far west of the city before.

"Those fields are awfully small," Nestor observed.

"And poorly kept," Doss added, handing Nestor his drink.

Nestor downed it in a single belt.

"They never commercialized their farming here," Father said. "They could plant tobacco or dreamflowers—but the fields, such as they are, are for subsistence only."

"How do the Margravs profit? A tithe of grain, like in the old days?"

"Like in the old days," Father agreed. "Small wonder they're broke. Suddenly the grandson of a humble ranch hand doesn't seem so unworthy of the mighty land princes."

And just as he spoke, the door to the Margravs' car opened, and in stepped that family's patriarch in his high-collared overcoat. Olog Margrav, just as grim in aspect as he was vertiginous. He removed his fur hat, revealing a smooth pate beneath.

"I've come to pay my compliments for your hospitality, O Baron of Meat," Olog said. "This locomotive is a most magnificent and luxurious conveyance."

He bowed stiffly, showing more of his pale lineless scalp.

"Sit, why don't you? Father offered. "Have a cigar, a drink."

Olog did not budge. "Oh, thank you, but I do not partake in either so soon after a meal." When he spoke, Nestor glimpsed his teeth behind his lips: long, sharp, and pink as if stained by a strange wine. Olog looked to Nestor and nodded. "Such a handsome son I've earned, at the dear cost of a daughter." He then looked to Doss. "And you, young Jennet, is the Baron of Iron well? Last I heard, he was among those petitioning to abrogate the Archduke's primogeniture."

"Do you disapprove, sir?" Doss asked, stiffly.

"Not at all. I am a realist, and these are changing times. As herdsmen, the Santis could tell you what happens when an old bull can no longer carry his own weight with strength..."

If Father was offended by being called a *herdsman*, he concealed it well.

"...he shall find himself skewered on the horns of a rival. One younger, one stronger. So it is with the old Duchy, to be supplanted by whatever the Barons of Industry create in its stead."

The old land prince spoke more, he and Father carrying on about politics, about traditions, the fickle nature of wealth, and the new technological advances in the Santi family's abattoirs which were of great interest to Olog, particularly the machines that stripped flesh from bone and bled carcasses dry. Talk of the family business always stirred strange sentiments in Nestor—pride mostly, but just a little flutter of unease too. He had never entirely recovered from the occasion of his tenth birthday when father took him to tour one of the abattoirs and had him touch the warm flank of a dazed but not dead bullock, to feel its last shuddering breaths. Had he done more than that? He tried not to think of it—and yet always his mind returned to that day. Sometimes even—for reasons beyond his ken—when he was with a woman. Something about entering a woman's flesh would call the steaming slaughtermeat unbidden to his mind.

He dismissed these thoughts, and tried to follow the conversation, like an attentive son. There was a strange quality to Olog Margrav's speech. Something fuguelike, somnolent and arresting all at once. Before he knew it, he'd spilled his drink on his lap, and Olog Margrav was gone.

Father gave him a cuff behind the ear. "Clumsy boy."

It was near sunset when the train arrived in the dreary village of Margrava, a gash of quaint thatched structures nestled between two densely wooded hills and under the dour auspice of a jagged manor built from black and gray stone, its parapets like charred fingers.

One look at it, and Nestor resolved to himself that after today he would never let his beloved wife come back here. A single glance and he knew this was not a place for happy people. This resolve was only strengthened after a carriage took them from the train platform through the village and he saw the rags the locals wore over their emaciated frames. They all seemed to cringe away as the carriage—emblazoned with the Margrav family's double-headed crow crest—trundled past on the cobbled streets. A village of cowering husks, fearful of their masters.

At least in the city, Father's workers could look forward to merrymaking and good food after a shift at the slaughterhouse. That, and proper gaslit streets.

The darkness stole the village so swiftly after night fell, and the streets quickly emptied.

In the ancestral Margrav halls, the air was pestilential with a sour tang of vinegar and strange incense. The only light came from torches, candles, and intermittent lanterns of blue glass that bathed the halls in a pale, wintry glow. Aside from all that, the décor was hideous.

Nestor watched an antique timepiece ticking away, slumped in an uncomfortable armchair in what the Margravs had called "the reclining room" while he tried to rehearse the bizarre lines he was expected to recite during the midnight "binding rite."

"Let that unseen presence, that frigid intellect that shields us from our own weakness, mold us into its liking... my God, what does any of that even mean?"

Doss, who'd somehow found a bottle of wine, was swigging from it. "Who cares?" He belched, then shrugged. "Say what you need to please them, then take your wife away and live the happy rich idiot life you were born to live."

"Have you ever heard the stories about the Margravs?" Nestor asked.

"What, that they butter their biscuits with earwax?"

"No, no, the other stories."

"Oh, you mean that they drink human blood? Pish. A girl wouldn't grow a bosom like your wife drinking only blood. There's a girl who takes a tall glass of milk with every meal."

"Could we not talk about my wife's bosom?"

"How about her sister's?" He took another swig. "Or your mother's?"

Nestor stood up. "I'm going to get some air."

"You do that, old boy."

And he meant it—he meant only to clear his head, feeling overheated and stuffy, but as soon as he'd stepped out into the hallway, he became possessed with a powerful desire to see his wife again. He wandered the halls like a thief, taking light steps, searching for shadows and listening for footfalls around corners. There came an instant where he heard a door creak open and saw, around the corner, the swish of a long black velvet train, and smelled the effluvium of some exquisite rotting fruit and was certain it was Holothé, but when he rounded the corner, all he found was the impassive figure of Jyell, again blocking his path.

"Out wandering, Brother-to-be?" Jyell asked, clapping her hands together. She was dressed in a black crinoline with a metal-ribbed corset and organza ruffles, all of which served to direct the eye to her neckline.

"Looking to peep on my sister, are you? With those searching eyes of yours? Maybe I should put them out, first the left then the right."

She said it all with a playful smile, her long canines purple against the blue lamplight.

"I was just taking some air," he said.

"Of course. Are you excited for the ceremony?"

Excited to be done with you and your parents, he thought but did not say.

Instead he merely nodded.

"Good." Jyell curtsied to him, the genuflection slow, deliberate, gratuitous. She then turned and tip-tapped in her long-heeled shoes down the hall.

Nestor was intent on returning to the reclining room when more footsteps sounded, dainty and flat-soled. The lady who rounded the corner wore a black shift—a servant. She had a round, pleasant face, bright green eyes, and coppery hair, and in her slender arms she bore an hourglass-shaped ceramic vase full of water and purple roses.

He must have startled her, being an unexpected sight in an unexpected place, for she let out a gasp on seeing him, and the vase tumbled from her hands and shattered, disgorging a tide of thorny stems and fragrant water.

"No!" she cried out, immediately falling to her knees to gather up the roses, heedless of the sharpness of the thorns or the jagged edges of the vase's shards.

On instinct, Nestor stooped to assist her. "Sorry, very sorry," he said. "Let me help with that."

The girl was sobbing, fresh cuts all over her hands. "Oh no, oh no..."

"It's all right," Nestor said, noting in the back of his mind that he was ruining the creases in his trousers by kneeling. "It's only flowers."

But she wouldn't stop crying. He put a hand on her wrist, an unthinking gesture, just the sort of thing he'd do for any weeping woman. His touch had an immediate, striking effect. Her sobs ceased, and he felt her body go stiff. She looked at him, eyes wide, terrified. He sensed, however, that her terror was not inspired by him.

"Please, master," she said, suddenly quite composed, though her eyes were red still. "You mustn't lower yourself so. This is my mistake, and I must be punished for it."

"Punished? Nonsense," Nestor said. "It's only a little accident."

There was something in this servant girl that inspired a bone-deep tenderness in him, a protective urge. Her palpable fear only sharpened his suspicions about his new in-laws to be.

Gently, slowly, he closed his hand around her wrist. So delicate and warm, like calfskin to the touch. He helped her to her feet.

"What's your name?" he asked, speaking softly.

"Gloria, master," she said.

"Please don't call me that."

"What else should I call you? You're one of *them*—or will be soon."

"If that's so, then I'm to have a say in whether you're punished or not—is that so?"

Timidly, she nodded.

"Then have no fear, Gloria." He smiled at her until she mirrored the expression, though her eyes were still terrified. "You'll not be punished."

Gloria closed her eyes. "What happens shall happen, master. I shall fetch a broom."

Nestor didn't wait for her to return, resuming his search, trying not to dwell on the rotten feeling growing in his stomach. It was his nose that eventually led him to the chamber where his bride was secreted away—her perfume of overripened plums so potent that he could smell it through the door of her dressing room.

He didn't bother knocking—fortune, faint of heart, *etcetera*. He opened the door to the most gloomy and cold dressing room he had ever set foot in, but his heart was fast warmed by the sight of his bride. No more was she dressed in cream-white, but her new gown was no less magnificent, an elaborate ensemble of black velvet and dark fur, like a more extravagant version of what Jyell had worn earlier. Surrounded by dour-faced attendants, Holothé turned her browless countenance to him and her full lips—painted a vivid purple and flecked with gold flake—parted in a vocative O of surprise. His heart juddered to see her, the splendid pallor of her unblemished face, the luminous silver of her eyes, the wide set of her graceful shoulders and the mast-like length of her trunk clenched in her corset's jaws, the prominence of her décolletage bursting free of it almost tantalizingly. Her hair was a nest of black snakes knotted into elaborate braids above a high forehead.

"Nestor, darling, what are you doing here?" she hissed, her long, sharp nails falling over her bosom. Without a word, she ordered her attendants out, and they had to hunch to fit through a smaller door in the back of the room, leaving Nestor and his bride alone.

"I couldn't stand to be bereft of you another moment, darling," Nestor said.

"This is against everything my family believes," Holothé declared, but even as she spoke she glided toward him, framing his jawline with her gracile hands. "I love you so much."

As their faces neared, he marked a dark smear in the corner of her eye.

"You've been crying," he observed.

She nodded once. One thing he loved about her was how she never tried to conceal anything from him. "Have you ever wanted to be part of a different family?" she asked him. "I mean, any other family in the world?"

He didn't have to ponder the question long. "Every other day."

Her eyes watered a bit as she giggled, her teeth, small and neat but quite sharp, showing past her lips. "I'm frightened—I've been terrified that you'll come to know my family for what we are and want nothing more to do with me."

His heart twinged. "You think so little of me, my love?"

"No. Not at all. But my family—they're... they're just so..."

"Batty?" he offered.

She let out a very unladylike snort and nodded. "*So* batty."

He'd marry into the devil's own family to have such a wife as Holothé. Snaking an arm around her slender waist, he pulled her into him and planted a kiss on the corner of her mouth, careful not to smudge her lips. He felt her muscles relax against him, felt her heartbeat through her throat as he kissed her there. But then she stiffened again as his hand climbed up her trunk and pressed against her breast.

She gave him a firm but gentle shove. "No—you mustn't *pollute* me before the ceremony."

A few seconds of dead air settled between them. Then to his surprise, she took his wrists and guided his fingers back to her.

"Well," she softened. "You can pollute me a little."

As promised, the ceremony commenced at the exact stroke of midnight. In the bottom of the Margrav manse, in a cavernous cellar where vast, ancient tree roots snaked through the vaulted ceiling, more than a hundred guests stood in semicircular rows behind benches carved from the very earth itself. When Nestor looked upon the crowd, he saw only a few familiar faces—the overwhelming proportion were the pale Margravs and their bleak-faced servants.

This was not a chapel, for there was no altar. There was no light at all except for the faint glow of the candles that the guests held and the shine of a single blue lantern that rattled from the end of a long rod grasped by the robed figure who stood in for a presbyter. This fellow, one of the tallest men Nestor had ever seen, was called the Incantator, and he led the assembly in its chanting.

Not a language Nestor had ever heard, and not one that left a pleasant impression on the ear.

Nestor and Holothé stood at the cynosure of the chamber, posed opposite each other with the Incantator and his bobbing lantern between them, its errant shadows growing and shrinking beneath the feet of the betrothed. Holothé did not smile; she betrayed no emotion at all, her expression blank as she stared right through Nestor. He could not pretend he was not disturbed, though if his strained expression registered at all, his bride gave no indication.

Father and his comparatively better dressed servants occupied a small tranche in the foremost row, with Doss Jennet's ample frame providing a buffer between the Baron of Meat and the spindly Olog Margrav, who silently mouthed something that did not seem to synchronize with the words the others chanted. Doss looked uneasy, while Father, true to form, was merely bored, no more impressed by this subterranean gloom than he had been by the Tabernacle's celestial splendor. He knew but one God—the all powerful thaler and its acolyte, the penny.

As his eyes scanned the staid faces arranged before him, Nestor couldn't help but finding the maidservant, Gloria, again and again. Perhaps it was her hair that caught his eye, or perhaps their brief encounter had sparked something in him he'd rather have not acknowledged. Whatever the case, he kept looking to her, standing behind Jyell, holding the sister-in-law's train. At least once, Jyell noticed Nestor's attention, and perhaps she thought she was its beneficiary, the way she simpered at him. As for Gloria, the woman's ruddy face was set in a smile, even as her eyes watered from fresh tears. Her hands were bandaged, the wrappings soaked through with brownish stains—far more blood than should have come from the nicks and pricks he'd seen.

But he was shaken to attention when the Incantator thumped his rod on the stone floor and rasped a senseless invocation at him. It was Nestor's time to speak. His prepared speech, a translation of whatever the original rite must have been, tumbled out of his mouth. What began as a speech thanking the nurturing earth for its ears, the sheltering sky for its tongue, and the drowning ocean for its teeth, sharpened into what felt like a deposition, the sort of self-ruinating declaration a defeated prince of old would make before a conquering rival put them to the sword.

"...all joy, love, and hope now lay forfeit into the frigid care of that unseen hand whose digits turn the pages of reality," Nestor intoned. "We are now, us two, forever joined."

"Forever joined," repeated Holothé, and only now did emotion kindle in her features, her eyes watering again, her lovely smile breaking upon her lips.

There was no outburst of applause, no music, no frivolity to come. In tomblike silence, the congregation parted to admit a team of hooded servants bearing on their shoulders a palanquin of ebony wood framed in gold leaf and jingling with precious sequins. Other servants emerged from the audience and dropped onto all fours, making a step ladder with their bodies, and before Nestor could even think to question it, he found himself and Holothé guided by clammy, bony hands to ascend that human ramp and assume their thrones upon the litter. As all eyes followed their slow progress out of the chamber, Nestor's head felt like it was at once full of nothing but air and also stuffed with sodden wood. Faces blurred past his eyes—his father, his friend, his new in-laws, and the openly weeping eyes of poor Gloria.

Up six flights of stairs they went, the servants never slowing, never complaining as if they were automatons of meat and bone. They were brought to a chamber whose express purpose was the bedding of a newly wedded wife, and only once they were let off the palanquin and the servants filed out did Nestor find himself able to breathe again. But just as soon as a cold draft struck him as the huge doors closed, Nestor's breath became again labored, for Holothé had turned away from him to part her train and fur stole and present him with the keys to her kingdom.

"I've waited so long for this," she said, and he could hear her nerves fluttering in her voice. "I hope it's as good as I imagined. As good as you deserve."

Meanwhile, Nestor could not speak, too absorbed with unfastening the complicated clasps and hooks that bound her corset and left purplish bruises in her tender skin. He was still very much struggling when his wife said something that cut the air from him.

"I saw you looking at the servant girl," she said.

"Pardon?" he asked, his heart lurching.

She would not look at him. "And my sister saw it too. She says you couldn't stop ogling the girl, though she's but a cleaning maid."

All his words congealed somewhere high in his throat. "Darling, I—"

Now Holothé turned to look at him. She was smiling. "Look at your face," she said. "What a gift—so rosy, so rich with blood. Your ears like bright halved plums. You're adorable, darling."

He found himself smiling, though terror still raced through him. "You know I'd never think of another but you."

At this she cocked her head, a catlike gesture, and then pulled her hair free of its precarious weave, allowing the tresses to spill wild over her shoulders.

"I think you still misunderstand me," she said. "I've had my eye on Gloria *too*."

Once more, he was without words. Some atavistic scrap of his brain, the instinct of a hunter-gatherer who sees traps everywhere, did not accept what he had just heard.

"We could have her brought in," she said. "She's Jyell's, of course, but I'm sure my sister won't begrudge me this gift on my wedding night. What do you say?"

"Would you like that?" Nestor asked. His mouth was dry as sawdust, all the fluid in him rapidly pooling in his loins.

She nodded.

"Then I would as well."

Holothé let out a bright squeak of delight. Her eyes watered as she threw herself onto him. "Oh, I'm so happy. I never thought you'd accept my family's ways—that you'd never accept me."

His senses were so thoroughly annihilated by lust at this point that he scarcely spared a thought to her words, for now her soft breasts were pressed to his chest, her sweet breath warm against his throat, her sharp nails raking through the fabric of his shirt to tantalize the skin beneath with an erotic admixture of pain and pleasure.

He did not in the end manage to unfasten her corset, tearing it in two pieces with animal strength instead, and this thrilled her, just as it thrilled her when he lifted her over his shoulder and carried her to the expanse of their marital bed where crisp white sheets waited for them.

When the doors opened some time later, Nestor felt a draft on his sweaty back, but was too enrapt in his passions to look. Only when Holothé gently eased him off her did he glance behind and see the slender, naked body of the maidservant Gloria. Her head held low, she shyly presented herself. There was no reticence, no hesitation in how she approached the bed and climbed onto it, moving on her knees toward them, and yet Nestor sensed no desire in her.

Compulsion. Duty. An overriding terror of some unuttered alternative.

A cow on the line ambling toward the braining maul.

How quickly the ember of desire extinguished in him. Her lovely body, ruddy and freckled, was a palimpsest of minor injuries—little pale scars and old yellowed bruises.

He knew well that his own family were hardly saints, despite their surname, but something in the servant girl's condition aroused a deep and visceral disgust.

He resolved that he would send her away. He thought quickly, for though Holothé had been excited about the prospect, surely she wouldn't be offended if he'd rather keep this moment intimate, between the two of them.

But before he could speak, Holothé crawled past him and approached the servant. Gloria closed her eyes and lifted her head, baring her strong neck with its ropy veins.

"Darling—" Nestor began.

It happened in the space of a blink. Holothé's long hands closed around the girl's neck and twisted. The neck snapped like a dry branch under boot and Gloria's head fell limp. Even as he processed what he'd just seen, Nestor recoiled and let out a soundless gasp as his wife seized the dead servant's left leg and twisted it off at the hip, wrenching the limb off from the joint. Fresh carnelian broth splattered the marital bed, and even as that carmine flower spread, Holothé's claws ripped meat from bone with a butcher's industry.

"I only really care for the sweetness inside the femur," Holothé said, giggling. "You can do what you want to the rest of her, darling."

Once unmoored from its fleshy sleeve, Holothé cracked the femur with her teeth, then widened the fissure with a heretofore unseen sixth finger, longer than the others and terminating in a raptor's hook. Nestor watched, paralyzed, knowing he should run, knowing he should dash his own brains out against the floor, uncertain if even such drastic action could save him now from whatever sordid lot he'd drawn for himself. A long black tongue—one he'd never seen before and which must have always lurked beneath the one he'd felt whenever he'd kissed her deeply—now emerged from Holothé's mouth and scraped the marrow out of its tube.

But he did not flee. With his next breath, the smell washed over him, and he again became the ten-year-old boy in the abattoir—standing over a dead bullock, bloody maul in trembling hand, confused by the wanton blood converging into the first erection of his life. Only now he was a man, and he knew what to do with his hunger. He opened his eyes and bore witness to a wet, dripping angel of slaughter and her still-warm prey. Woozy, unbalanced, his hand fell upon Gloria's body. Warm, yielding—so much like the hide of a dying cow. His heartbeat slowed, some primordial yearning within him reawakened; his arousal redoubled. Holothé, her smile framed in fresh gore, proffered a yellow morsel of marrow to his lips.

Jonathan Louis Duckworth (he/him) is a completely normal, entirely human person with the right number of heads and everything. He received his MFA from Florida International University and his PhD from University of North Texas. He is the author of *Have You Seen the Moon Tonight? & Other Rumors* (JournalStone Publishing) and his work appears in *Best American Science Fiction & Fantasy*, *Vastarien*, *Pseudopod*, *Fantasy & Science Fiction*, *Beneath Ceaseless Skies*, and elsewhere. He is an active HWA member.

JACK LOTHIAN

Bride of the Black Isle, a new play by Niamh Crawford, presented by the Netherbow Theatre

Directed by Omar Andrews
March 9 – March 15, 2020

Recommended for ages 14+
Contains violence and adult themes.

An all-powerful King. A mysterious Bride. A Court on the edge of madness. As the story is told and re-told, the truth slips further from our grasp...

JACKIE DOYLE (Chief Executive Netherbow Theatre): I'm not a superstitious person. I know there's been a certain amount of myth-making about what happened.

The reality is more prosaic: as part of the Netherbow's centenary celebrations, I programmed four plays based on classic Scottish folk tales. One a week, starting with a modern twist on Burns' *Tam-O-Shanter* and ending with a revival of *Three Weird Lassies*, Robert MacDougall's 1960 retelling of Macbeth from the witches' perspective. I wanted to commission two new plays to sandwich between them. Limited cast, limited budget.

Niamh Crawford was one of the first writers I approached, though she seemed surprised I'd thought of her at all.

NIAMH CRAWFORD (playwright): At twenty-four, I had the theatre world at my feet. My debut play *High Rise* won pretty much every award going. But it's fair to say that my career hadn't exactly played out the way I'd hoped since then.

JACKIE DOYLE (Chief Executive): *High Rise* was just terrific. It's about an architect who gets trapped in a high-rise apartment block with the tenants of the building, all of whom are suffering because the cramped conditions and all kinds of other environmental effects. It's the kind of play that makes you sit up and take notice of a new voice.

NIAMH CRAWFORD (playwright): I really struggled with a follow-up. There were unfulfilled commissions and broken promises. *High Rise* got so much critical acclaim I felt paralysed about what to write next. It took me five years to finish *Environmental Protection*, a drama about an affair between a government official and a carefree ornithologist secretly sabotaging the local wind farm project the official oversees.

JACKIE DOYLE (Chief Executive): It's fair to say that *Environmental Protection* didn't go down so well with the critics.

GARETH VALE (theatre critic, *The Scotsman*): "Good theatre challenges us and raises questions. *Environmental Protection* is not good theatre, yet it still raises certain questions: "Why are we watching something so trite and soporific? Is it too late to ask for a refund? Is there a nearby wall with freshly applied paint we could turn our attentions to?"

NIAMH CRAWFORD (playwright): When Jackie got in touch, it took me a while to accept. I hadn't written a word since the disaster that was *Environmental Protection*. However, the fact that it would be an adaptation of an existing folktale or myth made it an easier pill to swallow. I had scattered memories of one I'd heard as a kid, which had sort of terrified me—"The Bride of the Black Isle."

TIMOTHY SLATER (historian, Edinburgh University History Department): "Bride" is a medieval Scottish folktale about a widowed King who encounters a mysterious woman in the cornfields and resolves to marry her. When he presents her to his Court, nobody can see her. Fearing he's lost his mind, his Knight tries to dissuade him, but the King insists.

At the wedding, only the King sees the Bride walk down the aisle. Enraged, the King urges the congregation to chant her name. As they do, she materialises, and as she reaches the altar, she removes her veil, driving the Court to madness. It all ends with the blood-soaked King staring at his true Bride as she leans in for a final kiss.

The story likely originated in the early twelfth century, based on deaths in the Douglas clan following their Chieftain's marriage to an outsider. However, these deaths may have been the result of an internal power struggle or illness. So many records from that period have been lost through neglect, environmental damage, or even deliberate destruction.

But the idea of a king marrying a supernatural bride—whether the *Cailleach* or a sovereignty goddess—is common in Celtic tradition. History so often reshapes itself, blurring the lines between fact and fiction.

NIAMH CRAWFORD (playwright): At a certain point, research became an excuse to avoid writing. I had all this information, the historical context and sociological context, the underlying patriarchal fear of female sexuality. I just needed to find a path through.

Is the King an innocent in this—or is he the instigator? Does the Bride have any say in whether she chooses to marry him? I wasn't sure if I wanted to tell a story where she was the victim or the monster.

OMAR ANDREWS (director): The genius of Niamh's writing was that she did both. The play was split into two acts, each depicting the same events. In the first act, the Bride is a terrified victim, forced into marriage with the King. It's raw, unsettling, real.

But after the interval, we loop back to the beginning—same scenes, same dialogue—only now, the perspective shifts, and the King is the prey, and the Bride the predator.

JACKIE DOYLE (Chief Executive): It was very clever and, in all honesty, a relief to read. I sensed Niamh had been struggling. The scene where the King first meets the Bride in the cornfield at night gave me shivers.

He greets her with the line, "Hail, maiden, well met." The first time he says it, he's confident and arrogant. He's seen this woman and wants to claim her for his own, whether she likes it or not. The same line takes on a completely different meaning in the second act. This time, he's afraid. He's stumbled across something otherworldly, and his greeting is no longer a declaration—it's submissive, a stumbling attempt to placate her.

NIAMH CRAWFORD (playwright): Everyone seemed to love it. But my inner critic kept whispering about how I'd fooled them again.

OMAR ANDREWS (director): We got Alexander Bett for the King. Alex is great; he's an old pro, probably known more as detective Damian Justice on the BBC's *Fractured Justice*.

For the titular Bride, I chose Shauna McGovern. She only had a handful of theatre and TV credits, but there was this feral, unpredictable quality about her. A real contrast in styles.

ALEXANDER BETT (actor – The King): I think Shauna disliked me from the moment we met. I'm a pretty garrulous person, and she probably thought I wasn't a 'serious actor'.

SHAUNA McGOVERN (archival interview, *The Herald*, April 2020): Alexander seemed threatened by me. I don't know why. Maybe he has an issue with strong women.

ALEXANDER BETT (The King): I have an issue with the whole performative *tortured artist* thing; we're entertainers, here to entertain. That's the job.

MARK BUCKINGHAM (actor – The Knight): Most of Shauna's scenes were with Alexander, which was sort of hilarious as their approaches were so different. Shauna's instinctive, go where the mood takes you, whereas Alexander hits his mark every time, says the lines the same way. You can set your watch to him.

Shauna really gave herself to the role. She was fearless. You couldn't tell where she ended and the Bride began.

SHAUNA McGOVERN (archival interview): I need to find a connection to a role; otherwise, I can't do it. With Darlaith, I related to what she goes through. First as a victim, then as someone who chooses to take control of her destiny. I've been through that myself.

TIMOTHY SLATER (historian): Darlaith was apparently a name Ms. Crawford dug up and given to McGovern as background information. I don't think it's historically accurate.

NIAMH CRAWFORD (playwright): There was a reference to it in some Clan Douglas archives, possibly a wedding guest or local. And what could be a regional variation—*Darluedd*—was found in Ogham inscriptions at the ancient burrows on the actual Black Isle in the Scottish Highlands.

ALEXANDER BETT (The King): There's been some real tedious mythologising of Shauna as some kind of feminist hero, which is sad—considering what she did.

JACKIE DOYLE (Chief Executive): The investigation cleared Shauna. Let's focus on the facts. And there's no denying that the rehearsals—*despite some friction*—were going well. Omar's staging was really clever, using the theatre space to its best effect.

TONY WYLIE (Production Designer): The Netherbow is an intimate venue, couple of hundred people max. Omar wanted us to use that to our advantage and make the audience part of the climactic wedding ceremony.

OMAR ANDREWS (director): The layout of the seats gave us a natural aisle. The plan was to have the King up front on stage, claiming to the congregation that he could see his Bride approaching. In the first act, she never shows up, and you're left wondering if he's killed her or if she ever existed.

But in the second act, we play through it all again, only now, at the end, she magically materialises next to the audience, her dress lighting up as she glides down the aisle.

MANEESHA NAZIR (costume designer): Urgh. The dress. It's always the issue at weddings, isn't it? We discussed several different ways of making it light up so it felt like she'd just appeared out of nowhere. We rigged a black dress with fibre-optics so it would light up at the flick of a switch.

OMAR ANDREWS (director): Awful. It looked like a Christmas tree.

MARK BUCKINGHAM (The Knight): I don't think Alexander helped by launching into a spirited rendition of "O Christmas Tree."

SHAUNA McGOVERN (archival interview): There was disagreements and, yes, some of them were physical. I regret that but it doesn't mean I wanted to sabotage the play.

ALEXANDER BETT (The King): She just launched herself at me, ranting away about how I was ruining things. I'm pretty sure she was still in character too. Completely unhinged.

TONY WYLIE (Production Designer): Mark had to pull Shauna off Alexander. She was spitting, furious. Most of the crew cheered her on. You've met actors like Alexander. Your smug, middle-class RADA type who always seem to rub folks the wrong way.

JACKIE DOYLE (Chief Executive): I had to formally reprimand Shauna. I don't doubt that Alexander was pushing her buttons but we have a zero tolerance policy on violence.

ALEXANDER BETT (The King): If it was an actual zero-tolerance policy they would've dismissed her. I'm guessing they wished they had now.

MARK BUCKINGHAM (The Knight): She was upset. I don't blame her. I think Alex saw this young woman with all this potential and ability, and he was jealous. Shauna made you believe in the role. Alexander was always going to be 'that guy off the TV'.

ALEXANDER BETT (The King): She had that silly method actor thing of believing you have to 'become' the part. Most of us grow out of it, some don't.

SHAUNA McGOVERN (archival interview): I have to give myself to the role. Find that connection with the character. But with Darlaith... there was nothing at first.

And then there's a whisper. You barely hear at first. But gradually it gets louder and louder until you notice it too late and it's constant, overwhelming, blocking out everything else and submerging you. You're no longer playing a role, you're just holding on for dear life.

I know this makes me sound crazy. I'm just trying to be honest.

NIAMH CRAWFORD (playwright): I loved what she was doing with the material. She elevated it. But as we went on, I did worry about how hard she was pushing herself.

OMAR ANDREWS (director): Shauna was difficult, but that's fine. All actors are tricky in their own way. The dress rehearsal took place the day after her fight with Alexander and the tension was off the scale. It fed into their performances, adding a level of verisimilitude, so yeah, maybe I stoked it a little. Whispering in his ear about how she was going to get him cancelled, that sort of thing. My main worry at the time—and I appreciate how naive that sounds now—was the damn dress.

MANEESHA NAZIR (costume designer): We figured it out hours before that final rehearsal. Black dress, UV paint. Set up mini LED spots to shine on it at the appropriate moment and, *voila*, it transforms out of the dark into this otherworldly gown.

It's a shame nobody will ever see it.

NIAMH CRAWFORD (playwright): Only a few of us were in the audience for the dress rehearsal. Myself, Jackie, some of the office staff. But it was a relief. You could tell the play worked. The dialogue crackled, the performances sparked.

OMAR ANDREWS (director): Then we get to the scene where Shauna materialises in the aisle, walking past the audience. I even had them turn down the safety lighting on the exits just so we could isolate the stage in light and everything else in darkness.

JACKIE DOYLE (Chief Executive): I was so pissed at Omar. He's lucky he didn't end up in jail.

OMAR ANDREWS (director): In retrospect, yeah. Not my finest hour.

NIAMH CRAWFORD (playwright): I wasn't even aware of Shauna being in the aisle. They did it really well. Alex is on stage, and he's shouting about how he can see her, and then she just... *voom*. Lights up, a vision in white with the veil hung over her face.

MARK BUCKINGHAM (The Knight): Instantly, I felt something was wrong.

OMAR ANDREWS (director): The atmosphere changed in the blink of an eye. It wasn't a taste or a smell. It was this heavy, stale feeling that seemed to wash over everything.

MARK BUCKINGHAM (The Knight): It's hard to explain, but my instant reaction was, "That's not Shauna."

MANEESHA NAZIR (costume designer): Of course it was Shauna. I dressed her. But the dress... look, this is going to sound crazy, but for a second, I didn't think it was *our* dress. The way it looked almost translucent... but maybe that's just my memory embellishing it.

MARK BUCKINGHAM (The Knight): Shauna starts lifting the veil. And I remember this primal instinct kicking in, this fear, of what would be underneath. I wanted to shout out and tell her not to take it off.

JACKIE DOYLE (Chief Executive): This is the myth-making I'm talking about. I'm not a superstitious person. It was an actress playing a role. *That's all.*

ALEXANDER BETT (The King): Bloody theatre kids.

SHAUNA McGOVERN (archival interview): I was never alone. From make-up to costume to the stage. So there's no way I could've done what they said.

TONY WYLIE (Production Designer): We only had a split second to really see the Bride before the fire alarms all went off. It took a moment to realise that the smoke pouring in wasn't from our machines—it was an actual fire.

MARK BUCKINGHAM (The Knight): Of course we were all complaining about the interruption; nobody ever thinks a fire alarm is an actual fire.

JACKIE DOYLE (Chief Executive): Flames had engulfed the backstage area and was spreading fast. You could feel heat pressing at the walls. It was chaos. Total panic.

NIAMH CRAWFORD (playwright): I was stumbling blindly to the exit. But I looked back and saw Shauna through the smoke, the dress glowing, the veil lifted... She was crying, but her mouth was twisted into a triumphant smile. I only saw it for a second. But that look, that horror and joy... it's stayed with me.

ALEXANDER BETT (The King): Stupid girl started a fire in her dressing room. I don't know if she knew it would spread. Old theatre. Lots of wood.

JACKIE DOYLE (Chief Executive): Faulty wiring was the official verdict. The police cleared Shauna. I don't have a professional or personal opinion on the matter.

ALEXANDER BETT (The King): For the record, she *wasn't* exonerated. In Scotland, we have a third verdict between 'Not Guilty' and 'Innocent'; 'Not Proven'. It basically means *we think you did it, but the Crown can't prove it.*

SHAUNA McGOVERN (archival interview): I didn't start any fire. I wouldn't do that.

JACKIE DOYLE (Chief Executive): The theatre was completely gutted. A hundred years of history, reduced to dust and ashes. Thankfully, there was no loss of life and no serious injuries. A few of the cast and crew needed treatment for smoke inhalation, but it could've been so much worse. I think it would've ended there if Shauna hadn't spoken to the press.

SHAUNA McGOVERN (archival interview): The others don't understand what the play actually is. The words we're speaking, the invocations we're part of it. It's calling things to the surface that should've stayed buried. There are consequences for our words.

ALEXANDER BETT (The King): I mean, *come on*. She burns down the theatre and then blames a bloody ghost for it.

TIMOTHY SLATER (historian): From a purely academic viewpoint, what Shauna's describing aligns with our understanding of Pictish ritual practices and their summoning of gods or spirits. You have the sacred site—the theatre. You have the significant date of the centenary. Then, you have the ritual aspect of the play itself... Greeks saw theatre as a way to communicate with the gods. Their performances weren't just entertainment. They believed they could summon divine power and influence fate.

I'm not saying she's right—I'm just saying there are parallels.

SHAUNA McGOVERN (archival interview): Sometimes, with a role, you don't know how to leave it behind. But this is the first one where I'm scared that it actually won't let me go.

MARK BUCKINGHAM (The Knight): Shauna retired from acting after that. I think it was all too much. I've seen her twice more. Once in the street, six months later. She looked worn down. I pretended not to see her.

JACKIE DOYLE (Chief Executive): The tabloids picked up the interview and had a field day with the headlines. It ended up an urban legend, which isn't helpful to anyone.

ALEXANDER BETT (The King): "BURNING AMBITION: Actress Blames Macabre Role for Theatre Fire!"

NIAMH CRAWFORD (playwright): What Alexander won't mention is that he called me about a year later. He claimed that he'd seen Shauna in his apartment.

ALEXANDER BETT (The King): Ah, yes. The call to Niamh. *Mea culpa*. I'd taken some sleeping pills, woken up in the middle of the night, gone to the commode, and, on the way back, still half asleep, I thought I saw someone standing in the corridor of my flat.

NIAMH CRAWFORD (playwright): He said he stood there in the darkness, watching this shape at the other end. A minute goes by. Two minutes. And he's just staring at it, watching it breathe. He said it sounded hollow. Rasping. And then he saw it reach up and start to remove a veil...

ALEXANDER BETT (The King): I turn on the light and, of course—nobody's there. Imagination does funny things on a couple of Ambien.

NIAMH CRAWFORD (playwright): He's not the only one who thinks he's seen her. None of us want to discuss it, not really, because we're all aware we'd sound crazy. A taxi passes a crowd and there she is, with the same veil, there and gone in an instant.

MARK BUCKINGHAM (The Knight): It's not something I'm comfortable talking about. But my reaction—if I had one at all—would be the same as before. *That's not Shauna.*

ALEXANDER BETT (The King): Post-traumatic whatever. We almost *died*. Most of us ended up in hospital. And yes, that leaves a mark, but let's not exaggerate it.

NIAMH CRAWFORD (playwright): I don't know. When you think about it, everything humans have created comes from their imagination... the chair you're sitting on, the window you're looking through, the cars on the road below. None of it existed until someone dreamt it up.

Even this story. You'll have pictured the theatre in some form. You may have based it on a place you've visited or seen, or it might just be a vague concept of a theatre—the stage, the aisle—but on some level, you've conjured it up and brought it to life.

TIMOTHY SLATER (historian): We've had wars over imaginary creations. We've killed millions because of gods we've dreamt up.

NIAMH CRAWFORD (playwright): You might have a mental image of Mr. Slater. You may imagine him being a little older than me. You've probably dressed him formally—jacket, tie, maybe a bit of tweed. You've quite possibly given him glasses.

You won't be aware of the words you've attached to him unless you stop to think about it.

TIMOTHY SLATER (historian): I do wear glasses, as a matter of fact. Yes.

NIAMH CRAWFORD (playwright): And you've pictured the Bride, there in her dress, veil over her face. Now, picture that veil being lifted. Her head rising. Her face looking up towards you. Do you see Shauna the way you've imagined her? Or is it someone else beneath that veil?

TIMOTHY SLATER (historian): Ms. Crawford is referring to what we call linguistic relativity. The language shapes our reality. In a way, that's what ancient summoning rituals were all about: using words to bring ideas across the veil and into existence.

If we take this theory as a possibility, no matter how remote, then we perhaps should be relieved that the play never made it past the rehearsal stage.

NIAMH CRAWFORD (playwright): I was writing another piece, a meta-fictional thing about the events of *Bride of the Black Isle*. The writing, the rehearsals, all set against the historical backdrop of the story. Digging deeper into the research, I discovered that *Darlaith* roughly translates as 'the shape that devours'.

I didn't finish it. Let's say I got writer's block and leave it at that.

SHAUNA McGOVERN (archival interview): I had a rough upbringing. That's what attracted me to this world... the opportunity to be someone else for a while. I suppose it's an actor's dream to surrender to a role and let it consume you.

I can still feel her, somewhere inside. And there are times when she swims up and I'm looking through her eyes, thinking her thoughts. It's horrifying. It's beautiful.

I just hope that she can find some rest too, once she's finished with me.

JACKIE DOYLE (Chief Executive): I'm not a superstitious person. I may have said that. But, touch wood, we're almost done. It's been a Herculean task. Five years of fundraising and the renovation of the Netherbow is nearly complete. We plan to reopen early next year, and when we do, *Bride of the Black Isle* will be the first play.

Here's the crazy thing, Shauna's been in touch. She's keen to play the role again, and I've got to say, with my publicity hat on... it's tempting. Everyone loves a ghost story. But they love a comeback story even more.

I think it'll be a big hit.

Jack Lothian is a screenwriter for film and television. He served as showrunner on the HBO Cinemax series *Strike Back* and created and wrote the Netflix series *Who Is Erin Carter?* His short fiction has appeared in a number of publications, including Ellen Datlow's *The Best Horror of the Year Volume Twelve* and *Volume Thirteen, The New Flesh: A Literary Tribute to David Cronenberg, Weird Horror #3,* and the *Necronomicon Memorial Book.* His graphic novel *Tomorrow,* illustrated by Garry Mac, was nominated for a British Fantasy Award.

DONN L. HESS

Another Dirt Wedding

I HELPED DIG MY first marriage bed when I was eleven. I still remember loamy soil crumbling in my hands, how rich and fertile it seemed near the black ash trees, so soft in comparison to the hardscrabble rows where our corn withered in the heat. I scooped handfuls from the ground and tossed them aside. With every fistful, fat worms, pink and brown, tickled my fingers.

"Oh, she's a coquette," my grandmother laughed, watching me. Her voice sounded almost girlish. "About to take a new husband and still she's chasing after beaus. Don't you pay her handsy no mind, James. You just keep digging."

I remember how proud I'd felt, kneeling on the earth next to my father and cousins. We'd all worn our Sunday best despite the hot, grubby work. The early summer sun beat down on our backs, and there wasn't a lick of breeze to cool us while we labored. Sweat stained my one good white shirt, but I didn't mind. The job was easier than I'd thought it'd be. The heat had baked the ground in our drought-choked fields hard enough to slash skin to ribbons. But not here. The soil in the Jord Wood was soft as duck down. I flung handful after handful of the fertile black dirt into piles while my Uncle Bartholomew watched, his face sober as a preacher's.

He'd lost his first wife a month earlier, and hadn't smiled since. I missed his easy chuckle and the spark of deviltry in his eyes, but I thought he made a handsome bridegroom nonetheless. His fine blue suit set off his broad shoulders, and he'd freshly shaved the black stubble from the sharp angle of his jaw. I hoped his new wife would make him smile again.

"Reckon that's deep enough," Grandma said after a time. We paused as one and looked up at her.

"Not even four feet deep," Bart said, his voice flat. "Coyotes'll dig."

"For a husband? Here?" Grandma scoffed. "I think not."

Bart looked unconvinced.

"You brought something for your new wife?" she asked, ignoring his dour face. A long strand of iron gray hair had escaped the braid she wore twisted in circles at the nape of her neck. She brushed the lock from her cheek and smoothed her white cotton skirts. The still summer air stank of iron and chalk, and I was caked with dust and sweat, but Grandma looked cool as midnight crick water.

Bart reached into his suit jacket and took out a length of yellow hair. He'd tied it with a blue ribbon and shaped it into a wreath. Grandma gaped at him as if he'd lost his mind. She snatched the token from his hand and tossed it to the ground.

"Ain't no woman need reminding of the wife as came before," she said. "And on her wedding day besides! What were you thinking, boy?"

"You said—"

She swatted his arm. "There's what I say and what I mean. You well know the difference, Bartholomew Bolverk."

"Don't—"

"Don't what? You choose something proper, boy, before I choose for ya." Her eyes wandered to my youngest cousin, and Bart's pale face went paler still.

He glanced at his mother's turned back, something pleading in his eyes, then he plucked the gold band from his finger and chucked it into the hollow we'd dug. The ring vanished into the soil like he'd tossed it into a pond, the ground gobbling it like a starved dog snapping at scraps.

Grandma snorted. "Not much better, but I suppose it'll do. You ready to meet your bride?"

Bart didn't answer. He just stepped forward into the shallow depression we'd made. His good black shoes sank into the soil, not as quickly as his ring had, but still he was up to his knees faster than a fella could shake a stick.

"Ain't no one gonna love ya like she does, son," Grandma said. "You lie down now."

Bart did as she bid him, and the rest of us tossed dirt over him. The earth covered him sooner than I would have guessed, almost like the ground was bundling him up in her arms, cuddling him close.

Grandma always said Jord was an eager bride, anxious to welcome her husbands.

I guess that was true after all.

"I'm so proud," Grandma said when there was nothing left of Bart to be seen. My two cousins, Enoch older than me and Phillip younger, grinned at her.

Daddy slapped the loose soil from his hands and looked up at the sky. Although a few clouds had rolled in while we married off Bart, the white sun still blazed bright enough to make us squint, hotter than a sidewinder's kiss. Daddy's expression seemed far too somber for a wedding celebration, and Grandma elbowed him in the ribs to let him know.

He smiled at her and said, "It's a good day."

"Isn't it just?"

She turned away from him, and the smile fell from his eyes. He looked back up at the clouds and scratched the back of his head. Grandma put her hand on my shoulder and turned me in the direction of the house.

"Who's ready to eat?"

We sat at the big table and had the last of the chicken with some carrots. She gave Daddy the breast, my cousins the thighs, and she and I shared the back and the wings. My stomach still rumbled after we'd finished, but Grandma had made a chocolate vinegar cake, Bart's favorite, for dessert. Us three boys had two little slices each. Daddy ate one big one. Grandma didn't get any.

"Awful dry out," Daddy said once the dishes were cleared, washed, and put away.

He craned his neck over the kitchen sink to look out the window. The air outside was still as a tomb. The afternoon sun had bleached the ground almost gray and cracked it like there might be something tasty under the shell.

"This is a wedding," Grandma scolded. "You act as such."

"Yes'm," my father said. He took a swig of milk from the bottle before returning it to the ice box.

Grandma frowned. "Manners of a mule," she grumbled.

It was too hot for much else, so we boys sat inside and played checkers. Daddy whittled on a duck he was making from a scrap of wood, and Grandma read fortunes from a deck of playing cards.

"Your first wife will die of the cancer," she told cousin Enoch. "But your second wife will outlive ya by a good ten years."

It rained once the sun went down, a great blustery storm. The wind banged the windows and doors like it expected us to let it in. Sheets of water fell from the sky and turned the dust outside to mud.

"That hard rain ain't gonna do nothin' for the crops," Daddy said.

Grandma swatted his arm, and the look he gave her would've peeled paint off a barn door. I half expected her to slap the righteousness back onto his face.

"You'll see," she said.

I heard the disappointment in her voice, and she looked at my father like she'd married off the wrong son. Then her eyes found me, and she said, "James, you'll read the scripture tonight."

"Yes'm."

She chose Romans 12: "*Therefore, I urge you, brothers and sisters, in view of God's mercy, to offer your bodies as a living sacrifice, holy and pleasing to God—this is your true and proper worship.*"

My cousins said, "Amen."

Daddy laughed.

Grandma glowered at him and said to us boys, "Off to bed, the lot of you." I figured she'd had all the wickedness she could take, and that my father was in for a scolding like to singe the ears from his head. But she didn't say anything to him. I reckon she favored him most out of all of us.

Uncle Bart thought so, anyways. "Your pa always gets away with murder," he used to tell me.

"How many husbands she gonna want?" I heard Daddy ask Grandma that night, long after us boys was upstairs and should have been asleep. I'd come out for some water, but didn't dare visit the kitchen when I saw they were still awake.

"As many as she does. Who are we to say?"

"Papa and Bart ain't enough? Uncle Zeke?"

"Maybe, maybe not. If she's still in the need, well then Enoch, Phillip, and James are all handsome boys. Who knows if she'll take a shine to one of them?"

"Not James."

"Maybe James."

"Ma..."

"It shoulda been you, Angus. But you got that limp."

"*Ma...*"

"Bart didn't question me."

"Bart's in the dirt."

"You watch your mouth."

They might have said more; I didn't stay to listen. Instead I went back to bed, still thirsty, and it was a long time before I managed to sleep.

I dreamed of earthworms when I did.

The next day, the rain stopped, and the sun returned. The puddles had all about dried by the time I came downstairs. Daddy had soaked a couple slices of bread in the last of the milk and set them in a bowl on the table for breakfast.

"You leave some of that for your cousins," he said.

"Yessir."

There wasn't much farming to do because not even weeds could grow from ground this dry. I fetched water out of the well for our one skinny goat. She gave me a forlorn look like getting butchered would be a kindness. If she didn't produce milk soon, I reckoned she'd get her wish.

We ate the last of the carrots with some broth Grandma made from leftover chicken bones. Phillip read the scripture, though he didn't know his letters well and wrestled with the words.

"The leech has two daughters. 'Give! Give!' they cry. 'There are three things that are never satisfied, four that never say, 'Enough!': the grave, the barren womb, land, which is never satisfied with water, and fire, which never says, 'Enough!'"

I thought Grandma ought not to have given him such a long verse, and maybe Daddy thought so, too. He gave her a dark look, but she didn't pay him no mind.

"Off to bed boys," she told us. "Say your prayers! I'll know if you don't."

She meant that, too. I'd gone to bed once when I was eight without giving thanks, and she switched me purple the next morning. Made sure I never forgot again.

I dreamed about worms once more that night and didn't feel so rested in the morning. I'd also kind of forgotten about feeling hungry, and that seemed a fine blessing.

We had nothing left for breakfast, anyways.

Grandma was wearing her nice white dress when I came downstairs, and she told me to go fetch my Sunday clothes even though it was only Thursday.

"I washed your shirt and starched it last night," she said. "Hung it on the back porch for you. You'll need to poke another hole in your belt to cinch your pants. I didn't have time to take them in."

I'd barely left the room to do as she'd asked when my father said, "Enoch's older." I paused to listen at that because I'd been thinking the same thing.

"She favors James," Grandma told him. "You saw the worms."

"They're just worms."

The sound of the slap she gave my daddy sent me scurrying to the back porch. When I returned to the kitchen in my clean shirt and nice black slacks, belt pulled tight, there was a red handprint burning on my father's cheek. Grandma's face was pink, too, but I suspected that was her ire riled up and hunting for bear.

She'd only take so much sass, even from Daddy.

Just the three of us headed across the fields and into the woods. Enoch and Phillip had wanted to come help us dig, but Daddy told them they looked peaked and should stay home and get their rest. They didn't seem happy about that. Phillip gave me a mean look as we left. He'd always been a jealous one, fit to steal the blue out your eye if he thought he could get away with it. I wasn't sorry he and Enoch stayed behind. This was my wedding, after all, and I didn't need to invite no one I didn't want.

Daddy watched the sky as we walked. I looked up, too, and couldn't see a cloud in it. It was so empty it seemed like maybe God had scrubbed it clean. Not even a bird ventured across it.

"I don't know," he said. "Might be some thunder clouds down that way."

"You know there ain't," Grandma said without even a glance in the direction he pointed. Daddy didn't argue with her, but something in his face made me think he wanted to.

When we got to the grove, we found a new ash tree growing from Bart's marriage bed. It had been such a long time since we'd seen anything new sprout from the soil that all three of us took a minute to marvel at it. The sapling stood taller'n my dad and had hundreds of plump buds swelling on its thin branches. Come a week from now, I figured it'd be covered with leaves. I thought Enoch and Phillip might want to come here and sit in the shade underneath once that happened. Maybe they could chat with their pa. The notion made me feel a little less mean toward them.

"Seems she was happy enough with Bart," Daddy said.

Grandma tilted her head back and raised a hand to shield her eyes from the sun. "Maybe. Maybe not," she said. "But she's none too pleased with the rest of us, is she?" She turned her attention to me and smiled. "You ready to get married, James?"

I blushed. Couldn't help it.

"Yeah," I said. "Reckon so."

I wasn't sure I'd make a good husband, but I wanted to try and hoped Grandma would be as proud of me as she was of Uncle Bart. I wasn't exactly certain what all being married involved, but I reckoned I was clever enough to figure things out once the nuptials were done.

I'd only ever liked one other girl before. Her name was Samantha, and I'd seen her just the one time at the market. Her family had a table selling jam—blackberry, blueberry, or persimmon—and she gave me a taste for free. She had eyes dark enough you could get lost in them and a tangle of curls that looked so soft I had to keep my hands in my pockets so as not to touch her. Grandma caught us looking at one another and rattled my skull with her knuckles.

"If you can't keep those thoughts out your head, boy, I can do it for you," she'd said. She knew lots of stuff a boy would rather she didn't.

"You gonna make the bed?" she asked Daddy.

"In a minute," he said.

"You gonna keep a lady waitin' on her wedding day?"

I would of thought she'd sound angrier, but I suspected even Grandma had begun to wear down from too much sun and not enough victuals.

"You ever wonder if Jord ain't doin' her fair share?" Daddy asked. Grandma looked so shocked, I felt glad for the lack of a breeze. I suspected a stray gust might send her tumbling.

"What have I told you about—"

"I heard you, Ma. But I'm just sayin'."

"What *exactly* are you sayin'?"

"That we done given her plenty and ain't seen nothin' in return."

"Jord—"

"Ever think maybe Jord don't like her in-laws?"

"What do you—"

Daddy cut Grandma's throat so fast and smooth I near missed it. That goat should be so lucky as Grandma. A great splash of blood painted the side of my father's face and turned the left half of his nice white shirt red. I wondered for a second what he'd wear to church come Sunday, but then Grandma was falling, and I was trying to catch her. She was heavy for an old woman, especially one who'd missed more than her fair share of meals.

I had a Devil of a time keeping her from dropping. Daddy didn't help. He just watched.

"What'd you do that for?" I asked, once I got Grandma settled against Uncle Bart's tree.

Daddy's shoulders dropped. "I reckon you're too young to get married."

I couldn't argue because he had the right of things there. I'd been fretting a little bit about that myself.

"What do we do now?"

He turned and looked in the direction he'd pointed earlier. I followed his eyes and thought maybe I saw a cloud or two on the horizon.

"You hear thunder?" he asked.

I cocked my head and thought maybe I did, but I couldn't say for sure. "Dunno. Might be."

Daddy shrugged. "No point wonderin', I suppose. We'll know soon enough. Let's head back and get changed. Then I'm going to have you fetch the goat. We'll eat good tonight."

We left Grandma in the grove. I asked if we ought not bury her.

Daddy said, "Nah. Ain't her wedding."

"What about coyotes?"

"They get hungry, same as you and me." Daddy was always a practical one.

The rain started just as we crossed the field and the house came into sight. It was a gentle shower, perfect for the crops.

It poured just hard enough to wash the blood off my father's face. His shirt was ruined.

Overlooking the haunted house next door, where Civil War bones lie buried and people say long-dead little girls beckon children to play, **Donn L. Hess** writes urban fantasy. An MFA graduate of Southern New Hampshire University, his love of everyday creepiness colors his first novel, *A God in Middle Management*, and his short stories in the anthologies *Satan Rides Your Daughter Again* and *Pocket Full of Posies: Shadow Children*. An adventurer at heart, Donn has watched the solar eclipse on a Costa Rican beach, wandered Parisian sewers, and stood beneath skeletal chandeliers in Rome. Visit him at donnlhess.com.

REBECCA LYONS

The False Bride

LILY WAS TO BE married today. Sanger knew he should be helping his wife, Emmer, with the preparations, instead of standing here at the point watching the storm come in. It was so quiet here, though—peaceful, where the gnarled oak trees stopped and the true alien land began.

The storm had begun with fluttering snow covering the red and yellow moss that passed for spring flowers on Hera. Now the wind whipped and blew the snow until Sanger could barely see fifty meters away, and it was beginning to cover his boots.

Still, he had had to escape the colony for a while—Lily's sweet, confused face, Jak's leer, Emmer's self-satisfied expression. Here, Hera had closed down to a flutter and scurry of snowflakes, alike on any world, looking like so many white ashes.

Ashes. Sometimes, in summer, when the wind was right, he almost thought he could smell the ashes of the Stroud colony, over a hundred kilometers away.

His imagination, he knew.

It had been the ashes that had alerted them that summer three years ago.

Radio calls to Stroud had gone unanswered that season—not that unusual, what old technology they had was always breaking down—but the several of them still made their usual journey to exchange news and goods, with a few spare radio components tucked into their packs.

No one greeted them. The colony was scorched, the crops burned or trampled. They found a few corpses, not many, and they had found Lily, wandering lost in the wreckage.

She appeared to be about twelve or so earth years old and had stared at them dazed, as if trying to figure out what they were, why they were there.

"Are you Cally?" one of the men had asked. "Meer's child?"

She'd responded with a blank stare.

He, and others, tried calling other names, names they remembered of the colony's children. Finally, Sanger asked: "Are you Arinen's daughter Lily? Are you Lily?"

She stared at him. "Lily?"

They got nothing more from her. They never found out what happened to the colony, but, startling at shadows in the silent ruins, they had left immediately, taking the girl with them.

Sanger let his sigh be whipped away by the wind. He should be returning. He was in trouble enough as it was. Turning, he trudged back down the hill from the point, toward the Green colony.

***

"And where have you been skulking?" Emmer greeted him as he entered the colony hall.

Commotion surrounded him as colonists made ready for Lily's wedding, and what little technology they allowed themselves, what little was left from the landing, had been covered with sheets and pushed to one side. Cushions littered the floor as women arranged them in curved rows.

Sanger turned to his wife. "Just taking a couple breaths, dear. Looking at the storm."

"It'll be cold the next couple of days," Anna, Darik's wife, said as she plopped cushions onto the polished wood.

"Well, Lily and Jak will be warm enough," another murmured, and the women laughed, all but Emmer, who still eyed her husband coldly.

"You've skipped out on most of the work, I'm sure you know," she told him. Sanger hung his head in reply. "Well, *I* still have work to do." She pulled her shawl closer, muttering as she walked toward the kitchen. "Damn this cold!"

She had not always been this shrewish, his Emmer. True, even in her youth she had had a sharp tongue, but he had liked it when she spoke up and said her mind. But this jagged part of her had worsened with age, especially after he had brought Lily home.

———

"It's time Lily was married off," Emmer had announced one night, after Lily was already in bed.

This had taken Sanger entirely by surprise. He knew Emmer did not want Lily there, had only grudgingly made room for her, but how long had she been thinking this?

"Oh, I know you have your eye on her, Sanger Tokkins Green. Pretty little thing, isn't she? Well, you're not going to have her, not under *my* roof!"

This stunned him into speechlessness. Emmer had always been jealous, though gods knew Sanger had never—or at least rarely—given her cause. But Lily? None of Sanger and Emmer's children had lived to adulthood, and he had always looked on Lily as a daughter, or, simple as she was, as almost a shy, gentle pet. She had always seemed dazed and wandering, but they had taught her to do simple tasks, and she had responded to Sanger's kindness.

One look at his wife's set face, and Sanger sighed. He would not win this argument.

Besides, Emmer had a point. Lily was a young woman, and it was time she had a husband and children of her own. He glanced down at the beer in his hand as his wife continued:

"Don't give me that martyred sigh,. She's at least fifteen, older probably from the look of her. Time she was out of our house and living with a husband. It ain't easy finding anyone to take someone as simple as her, pretty though she is." The last was almost spat out. "But Jak's been looking at her, and he wants her, and—"

"Surely not Jak."

"You've something against my brother, husband?"

Sanger had everything against Jak, but he wouldn't say so in front of Emmer.

"No, my wife. I just don't think he's right for Lily is all."

Emmer snorted for reply.

"Now Wil, perhaps," Sanger continued. "He's a little younger, surely, but they've always gotten along well. Perhaps in a couple of years—"

Emmer snorted again. "*A couple of years.* Jak wants her now, and I've told him yes. I told him give me the loom you've been promising, and we'll arrange it."

Sanger lifted his eyebrows. So that's why Jak had finally made good on the loom.

Emmer spoke on, talking of the wedding arrangements, but Sanger had stopped listening. He would miss Lily. She was a dreamer, like him, however strange she might be.

He nodded once when Emmer paused and looked at him, to show he was paying attention.

But—Jak? His brother-in-law wasn't known for a gentle manner, and Lily needed gentleness. Of all the Green colonists, only Wil might've given Lily the kindness she needed. Perhaps someone in the larger Torres colony might partner with the girl, but that was over two hundred klicks away, and he doubted if Lily could make the adjustment to yet another colony.

"—listening to me at all, mister?"

He jerked his head up. "Yes, of course, my dear."

Emmer gave another of her infamous snorts.

"Six days after the third spring moon, I said. It should be warm then."

"For the wedding? Yes, I guess so. Unless a storm sets in—"

"Storm! Don't talk of storms!"

The wedding was jinxed enough already, Sanger thought, but he drank his beer, and kept quiet.

———

He'd been right. It had stormed. Although the first flakes hadn't stuck, it had piled ankle deep in the fields by the time the wedding ended. Lily, dressed and combed to perfection, looked blank and curious as usual, but seemed pleased in a vague way to have all the attention. She flinched back when they put her hand in Jak's at the ceremony and would not look at his leering eyes, which had begun to narrow in irritation. Her own eyes were beginning to resemble an animal's—trapped and looking to escape.

Sanger put a hand on the girl's shoulder. "Easy, my girl. Hush."

She quieted then, and Sanger had felt briefly like a traitor.

At the wedding feast, Lily seemed pleased with the smiles and congratulations, accustomed as she was to being ignored or whispered about behind hands.

Then Jak led her away to his cabin, not far from Sanger and Emmer's. Sanger watched them go.

"She's another man's wife, Sanger," Emmer spat out.

His eyes flicked back and bored into her. "She is a lost and lonely girl," he replied softly. Her eyes shifted from anger to shock that he had talked back to her at all.

———

Jak led his new bride through the door of his cabin and closed it behind him. Emmer had cleaned the place up for him, and it looked almost cozy. *Not that this simpleton would notice*, he thought.

"Some wine?" He poured it for her and watched her drink, then poured some for himself. She looked at him with the eyes of a dumb animal, curious and plain. "You're beautiful," he continued with a smile. "A very lovely young woman."

Her eyes flicked at the sound of his voice, though he wasn't sure if she fully understood.

Sanger had thought him a wrong choice, but his brother-in-law was a fool. Jak knew how to talk to women, knew what they wanted to hear.

"Look what I brought for you." He took out a white nightgown, made of soft cotton, traded from Torres years ago. "Isn't it pretty? It's for you."

She put the wine aside and reached out to touch, then smiled tentatively.

"Why don't you go put it on?"

She seemed to understand this and took the nightgown into the other room.

Jak watched her go, thinking of the rest of the night, and shifted himself in his trousers. Was she a virgin or not? And was it better if she was or if she wasn't? At any rate, she was the best kind of wife. Beautiful, not too bright, and silent. No trouble at all. He smiled to himself.

When the door opened again, he glanced up. Her dark hair, let down from its pins, partially hid the form of her body from him. But it mattered little. The gown was slightly transparent, and slightly too small besides. Jak felt himself respond.

He moved to the bed and drew back the covers. "Come here, girl." He patted the sheets. "Sit down. Here, Lily." She came willingly enough. "Why don't you lie down?" He gently nudged her shoulder, and she lay back against the pillows. When Jak slid his hand up her leg to stroke her thigh, she began to struggle. "It's all right, girl," he said softly. "We're married now, it's okay."

He took his hand away to untie his trousers and slip them off. She stared at his genitals with a frown. What was wrong with the girl? Surely she'd seen men before. Ah, but not one ready to make love. Well, she'd soon get used to that.

He slipped the nightgown up, ignoring her rush of breath, and lay his body on hers, trying to push into her. Suddenly she began struggling in earnest, gasping and crying out like a frightened animal.

"Hey now! Look, Lily, I've been patient enough. I'm your husband now, and if you can't learn to like it, you'll have to learn to live with it. Stop that!" He grabbed her shoulders and pushed her down onto the bed, thrusting harder at her.

Abruptly, with a cry, her hands were at his throat, her nails across his face. He pulled back with a curse, and she slid from the bed and ran out the door into the snow.

"Hey! Goddammit! Come back here!" He closed the door and struggled back into his pants. "Stupid bitch. Going to freeze out there. I'm her husband, what the hell does she—"

With pants and boots and cloak loosely thrown on, Jak grabbed a lamp and followed his bride out into the storm, following small footprints that were by now calf-deep.

"What on earth?" Sanger sat up in bed. "Emmer. Did you hear that?"

"Hm?" His wife turned in her sleep.

"I heard something." He slipped from the bed and peered out the window. Through the storm he could see Jak's—now Jak and Lily's—cabin and just caught sight of a large figure with a light moving off into the storm. "Why—that's Jak."

"Wind..." Emmer muttered. "Just th' storm."

"I'm going over. I think something's wrong."

Emmer, turned over. "Oh, leave them alone, for pity's sake. It's their wedding night!"

"Lily might have been frightened."

"All brides are frightened, Sanger. Or pretend they are. And if she was, she'd come over here. She's got that much sense at least."

"Still…" He slipped into his clothes, quietly opened the door, and stepped out.

Jak's door was open, and two sets of footprints led away into the night. Above, through breaks in the storm, the half-hidden moon lent the clouds an eerie opalescent glow. Sanger closed Jak's door, turned, found Emmer at his heels.

"Lily ran off," he explained, as if it were not self-evident.

Emmer crossed her arms. "She's Jak's problem now. Honestly! He'll take care of her."

Sanger thought something he didn't dare say. Instead, he followed his wife back to their cabin.

———

Jak muttered and yelled alternatingly as he followed the footprints. "Girl! You best know better than to run from me. I'm your husband! I'm your—"

He struggled through the snow, almost losing the lamp at one point. Half a klick past the cabin, the snow-covered wheat fields and tangled stunted oaks yielded abruptly to snow-burdened giant fungi, leafless black silhouettes, and strange Precambrian trees hung with frozen red fronds. Jak paused at the colony's edge and lifted his lamp higher. Snowflakes hissed against the warm glass.

Before him, his lamplight shone into a clearing. Something pale lay on the snow, the wind whipping part of it back and forth.

Jak stalked up to it, cursing under his breath, then stopped.

He stared at the thing on the snow, stared at the footprints leading to and leading away. Ice began to form along his spine, as he took a step back, then two. Then he turned and hurried away, back toward the safety of the colony.

He thought he heard something behind him, and he began to run, awkwardly, following the footprints back toward his cabin. He stumbled and fell forward onto his face. The lamp shattered, plunging everything into shadow lit only by clouds and white snow. Jak turned, with a hiss of breath, in the pearl glow of the moon through the clouds, as something touched his thigh—

"What?" This time Emmer sat bolt upright in bed. "I heard something. Sanger, wake up! I heard something! It was horrible!" She shook him violently until he opened his eyes.

"Just a dream. I'm sure it's nothing."

"Oh. Mine's nothing, and yours is something." She jumped out of bed with more alacrity than he'd known she still had. "Something's wrong. Something's wrong! I'm going over there."

"I thought we weren't going to interfere," Sanger mumbled.

"Oh, you fool!" She hastily threw on clothes. "Don't you care about anything?"

Sanger blinked sleep out of his eyes, sat up, and put his feet on the floor, just in time to feel a cold blast from the open door as Emmer hurried out.

She was well gone by the time Sanger was dressed. He carried the lamp and followed the three sets of tracks away from the colony, one fresh and two half filled with snow.

None led back to the cabin.

Lily? Sanger feared for her. Jak and Emmer he knew could take care of themselves. But his simple, gentle Lily, lost in the wood, in this snow?

What would become of her? And what would she do if—when—Jak and Emmer found her?

The snow was only flurries now. Again Sanger was reminded of white ashes.

All three sets of tracks disappeared into the fern-fronded woods.

Sanger, his eyes stinging with sleep and with cold, almost tripped over the two limp bundles that lay in the snow just before the tracks entered a clearing.

Stark red they were, almost black in the lamplight, where the blood leaked from them to soak into the snow, where it splattered almost to where he stood. Pale, pale... what was left of the torn and scattered flesh, pale even against the white snow.

Jak—and Emmer. What little remained of them.

He bent down first beside his dead wife. Snow drifted across her, beginning to cling and cover the lamplit horror his numb mind could barely accept. He had known colonists who had gotten lost and never come back. But not like this, never like this.

A memory strayed past him, like a lost snowflake. Emmer, never exactly pretty, but young and vital. She had stood up to the elder and spoken her mind, startling the old man into huffing speechlessness. Sanger, a little ways from her, had overheard and smiled at her temerity. She had caught him smiling and had smiled back. That was how their courtship had begun.

He hadn't thought of her that way for a long time.

Suddenly he straightened—a sound, a motion, a change in the timbre of the wind?

Lily? Had she got away? Or was she lying somewhere else—like this? He thought briefly of calling out, but his voice seemed not to work.

Something fluttered at the edge of his vision, and he lifted his eyes to the clearing beyond. Finally, numbly, he stepped around what had once been his wife and her brother and walked into the clearing. Above, white flakes drifted down, ashes on the snow, from a grey pearlescent sky.

Sanger stopped. There on the snow, wind whipped and half buried, lay Lily's bridal nightgown, lying as if it had been carelessly tossed onto bed sheets. Here her footprints ended. And Sanger then knew, as a cold prickle drifted up his spine, that he need not look for Lily anymore.

From the nightgown, other tracks led out into the darkness beyond his lamplight.

Tracks four-footed and clawed, made by no human feet.

Rebecca Lyons has published horror and fantasy stories in magazines and anthologies such as *Pulphouse* and *Halloween Forevermore*. She received her chemistry degree from Roosevelt University and has spent most of her working life as a writer and editor. Colorado is her home, where she lives with two rescued stray cats.

GORDON B. WHITE

Speak Now Or—

Aye, SAYS A YOUNG woman, a stranger to the townspeople assembled for the wedding, her dark hair bound with a green ribbon into a single thick braid which she casts over her shoulder to sway like a serpent as she rises from the pew to continue: *I'll speak now, as you asked, for I have a reason why these two before you should not be wed*, and at her proclamation the crowd begins to murmur and not the least of them is the young bride's grey-bearded father, Herman Gorglut, the owner of the village mill, who lays a heavy glance first on his daughter, Agnes, and then at the groom, Aiden Haller, who before today was an inveterate bachelor and is Mr. Gorglut's longtime business partner's heir, but the unfamiliar woman with dark hair raises her voice above the dull grumbles to continue, reminding those assembled in this humble chapel that for three Sundays running now the Church has read aloud the banns of marriage and made the coming nuptials known throughout the parish, as is only right and done by custom, so that word was spread of the impending marriage and that the point of disseminating that information is so that any lawful or moral challenges may be brought forth on the wedding day itself, *and I*, the woman says, *have such a challenge, for you see, they should not be married—no union between these two, bride and groom, may be formed—because such a bond has already been formed with another*, but the gathered families and neighbors balk and bark at this and young Agnes Gorglut blushes (a vibrant, bloody red seeping across the fair face of the comely blonde girl, barely a woman, for although on further inspection she could perhaps be of a similar age as the coarse stranger with the dark hair who has just now objected to her wedding, right at the moment right before the nervous groomsman Mr. Haller—no, her husband-to-be, *Aiden*—is to be pronounced her keeper before God and man and her parents, the obligations for and all rights to her body and estate to be transferred to him, it is the contrasting boldness of the woman protesting that gives her a maturity that poor Agnes, even now on her day of marriage, seems to lack and so makes her appear all the more childish beside) but the protestor continues, again raising her voice to be heard over the spreading din and she is nearly shouting: *I tell you that one before you has made a compact with the Devil and made it on the last full moon, not even four weeks past*, and if this woman perhaps meant to cow or stupefy the congregation by invoking the DEVIL (of all beings) then she is sorely mistaken for half the men and most of the women and all of the children are caught up in the fervent babbling so that, as a one, they begin to rise like the river that runs through the village when the spring thaw comes late to the westernmost mountains and the snow that has been waiting, building above tree line beyond the village, melts and returns as furious water with a vivid rush and crush, barely hemmed in by the banks, and the crowd's momentum is assuming the very nature of just such a once-in-a-century flood that could sweep away the mill's wheel and the very mill itself, not to mention the miller or his business partner or his daughter the bride or the unfamiliar woman with the dark braid bound with green silk, did not the priest behind the pulpit—stern Father Krisman, frosty brows arched and wild like the snow-covered evergreens atop those same mountain ridges before the drifts melt in the spring—thunder down upon all those assembled to be quiet, for Heaven's sake, be quiet and be seated and show respect for the sanctity of the Church and the ceremony of the wedding because, as he continues once the crowd bows its collective head like a chastised child and sinks back to their seats, the purpose of him asking for any reasons as to why these two should not be wed is (as the dark-haired woman has correctly stated) to hear such challenges and what challenge, he asks them, could be greater—what challenge transcends mere earthly objections such as age or consent or even prior marriages before the Church—than involvement with the Devil, since that one is, of course, the Great Foe and the ever-present threat to life and soul and community and prosperity, and the crowd murmurs *Amen* in a reflex like a gasp and that *It is so*, which gives the woman with the dark braid (who is, among them all, the only one still standing and who has not yet sat down nor now even looks as if she could, so rigid and righteous is her posture) a chance to speak again and so she begins afresh by telling the assembled crowd: *The story I am here to tell you is true, but not for the faint of heart as it involves an encounter at the Witches' Sabbat*—she pauses for the collective grumble and allows it to bubble out, relieving pressure like a lid lifted from a pot on the hearth, but proceeds with her tale before it can boil over into an interruption—*aye*, she continues, *a Witches' Sabbat that I observed on the night of the full moon not even one month past as it took place on the open fields between this village with its fine and profitable mill to the West and the garrison outpost of soldiers to the East, on those fields in which on summer's nights dance the mere heath sprites and hags' fire, the wispy will-o'-come-down-nows and wild hide-your-bones-Jacky, but which, when the autumn sets in and the great swathes of golden wheat and barley are scythed down for the harvest and the nights grow long and cool and lumpen and the trees shed the modest flesh of their leaves to claw with many fingers at the tumescent moon in the otherwise empty sky above, those fields which are known to host the Sabbat: yes, that very same celebration of witches, warlocks, demons, devils, familiars, flambeaus, imps, incubi, succubae, steal-the-bread-sisters*—Father Krisman coughs to urge the woman onward and she nods—*for on these nights, as all the good and god-fearing among you know, those fields are marked with bonfires out in the distance and woe be to the traveler who stumbles across one of their gatherings and especially, as it was not even one month back, one who has the misfortune to do so on a full moon for those are the nights during which the entire cotillion of the Devil and his friends and lovers and servants and allies come to make merry, and such a full moon was, of course, above the field that night when I saw the truth as to why this couple should not be wed, for you must understand, good people, I myself had been waylaid coming down from the mountains and passing by your town, heading towards the garrison in the East to visit my brother who was many months ago pressed into service and for whom I sought to make an appeal for his early discharge from conscription, when I found myself crossing those fields at night and almost without intending to found myself pulled to just outside the ring of light of one of those pillars of fire that beckon across the darkness, arriving in the midst upon such a scene of debauchery and decadence already in full and riotous bloom like the most indecent of flowers—believe as you will or not—but which I could see in fact was not merely a feast and festival but a wedding—yes, a WEDDING—but not like the proper and holy one before you now, but one instead that was a rebuke of this Church and the Lord that cloisters within, and of the two before you, bride and groom, I saw that one of them was not only in attendance but by the end even approached the Devil himself to beseech his hand in marriage, although not, at first, for at first the one before you was, as I was, seemingly taken aback by the sheer spectacle on display of all sorts of strange types of affections—a* murmur and gasp again rises from the audience here, the room growing uncomfortably warm as the moist breath and blushing bodies swelter, and Father Krisman loosens the yellowed collar his cassock and tries to shush them, but the young woman with the dark braid does not stop—*oh yes, my friends, affections and displays the kind of which would make your ears burn and moreover your souls besides, you must believe, such as, for instance: I saw the Devil himself, wearing a black frock coat and surrounded by his warlocks, bend over to put his horns towards his hooves and then reach back around to spread himself from behind only for an imp to insert a black candle in between the Devil's fundament, half way, and with a laugh the wick caught fire and the Devil hopped up and down and then the warlocks all gathered around, laughing, and also inserted such candles, but smaller, into their own fundaments and then one by one would approach the Devil, back to back, and bend over, heads between knees, to touch fundaments together and thereby light their candles off the Devil's wick, some flames of which were then passed to other demons or to warlocks or to a few of the curious witches who had joined them, so that from fundament to fundament the Devil's ember was passed around and the revelers scampered and squealed in such delight as their candles batted into one another and the hot black wax dripped on their haunches until the skipping glimpses of light and the sound of their merriment floated across the fields to where a greater mass of witches gathered unperturbed, focused as they were on lacquering one another with untold ointments and magical salves, smearing themselves and their oils across one another's bodies, their bosoms and stomachs and down across their hips and thighs, glistening in the fire light when they danced close to the flames and then in the moonlight when their reel took them away so that every curve or soft surface was but one ripple of the aspect of the swollen lunar dominion above them, and though their limbs were entwined, their feet and legs began to lift off the ground and they writhed and swam up into the air, gasping with the cool night air*—here the bride herself begins to swoon beneath the weight of her starched gown and the heat, but the groom, pale face drained of blood, lets her dip to her knees while his own hands clutch the waist of his vest and pull it down so tightly that the seams are beginning to separate at the shoulders and the strange young woman, seeing this, waves her hands forward as if to skip ahead past all the lascivious details of the human and non-human flesh and non-flesh that, whether despite of or because of its prurience, marks the most engaged that certain members of the audience have yet been in any part of the ceremony so far, twisting and writhing in their seats, and which also marks the readiest contrast between the Devil's riotous wedding being described and the cramped, fusty affair before them—*but I diverge too much,* the woman says, *and risk burying the heart of my tale because there, after hours of such dancing and feasting and such, well, let us say only that with the cornucopia of thrills nearly exhausted from the Devil's wicker horn and the attendees duly worn and weary, is when the actual wedding ceremony began: The Devil sat down on a throne of living oak, still in his frock coat but now able to rest his backside on the seat since the candle twixt his fundament had long since melted down and been peeled off by a demon with a horse's face to great giggles of delight, and there, resting on his throne with one hand pointed to the sky and the other to the ground, the witches, warlocks, imps, incubi, succubae, satyrs, fauns, demons, dirges, ghosts, goblins, ghouls, and the rest, all gathered in a line and one by one made their way to the Devil to kiss his hand, then his lips, before saying, 'I thee wed,' as one and again and the next they all committed themselves to that one who dwells below, the one who flaunts the mores of Church and laughs away the duty of Family and casts off the chains of State, and then from him they went away back to their fires, resuming their feasting and dancing and singing and coupling and throupling and other joinings, as if the wedding to the Great Deceiver meant nothing to them more than a passing fancy, so very opposite of what we see here, although it could be too that what that commitment to the Devil meant to them was a commitment of some other kind, to an idea bigger than just the personage of the Devil himself*—the congregants now are sweating profusely, the very wood of the pews seeming to warp beneath their broiling wool and linen rears, the musk of marinating human bodies beginning to overtake the defeated bridal flowers, and the woman stops herself briefly to nod out of a sort of apology—*but rather than ponder all that out, I instead return us back to the start of my story, which was a journey taken only so that you would believe me when I tell you as follows: One that stands before you here today, one who would take the vow of constancy, eternity, and servitude, before their family and the law and your God alike, one of them was the one I watched wait just beyond the fire until the line of brides, bridegrooms, groombrides, and the rest dwindled—the wick of wedders flickering like the last stub of a candle in a warlock's fundament as the dawn rises—and then that one finally approached the Devil and knelt before him and said: Devil, make* *me yours, too; but the Devil leaned back, and a puzzled look spread across his old goat's eyes to see this stranger, untouched by the revel but apparently still set on asking for his hand, and he asked, Why, why would this one (who had not joined in the celebration's frolick and fornication but stood outside the warmth of the fire, watching all night) want to marry the Devil, for while the Devil found himself quite appealing, the one who came to ask his hand seemed to find him rather frightening, and so the Devil descended from his wooden throne and squatted down, level with the poor soul who had come to him, and whispered into their ear: Tell me true, why one would come to marry the Devil, and the one before him (the same one who now stands before you) whispered back, For I am to be married within the month, and I would not, for I love them not, and if I will marry not for love, I may as well marry the Devil, to which the Devil could only respond by once again rocking back on his waxy haunches and there was a silence in the air like the moment between when the lightning strikes and when the thunder gives its belated warning to the one who has been struck, and—*the woman with the dark braid puts her hand to her heart—*I thought the Devil would smite the one dead or shout or laugh or otherwise terribly upend that pregnant moment, but instead the Devil slowly nodded, then reached his hands up to the top of his great furred skull and opened his skin, pulling away the Old Horned Goat as if it were a costume and it fell to the ground and in the pool of the raiment of the Devil was a just a little fellow, smooth and dark as a shadow, who reached out his hand and took the one's hand and said, Let us walk for a moment, and so walk they did, out and away from the throne by the fire, and out of fear or respect I stayed back and heard not what they said, but I watched as the Devil (in his smaller, softer form) wiped a tear from the one's eye and then, to what seemed his surprise, found a matching tear rolling down his own cheek, to which the one before you raised their hand and wiped it from him, so that they both stood there holding each other's tears, then clasped them together hand in hand and returned to the place where the Devil's skin and frock coat and horns lay on the ground and your one helped the Devil put them back on, slipping them* *on like a robe or gown, with the one tying them up in back and the Devil himself adjusting his horns on the top of his head, then bowing down to eye level, and here they were once again close enough that I could make out what the Devil said, and he said: Then we have a compact, a deal, a union; not one of marriage, but of friendship, and I give you my blessing that you need marry not man, nor woman, nor Devil, but have of yourself to yourself for as long as you shall, but in making this union, this deal, this compact, you must promise that you will assert yourself and your freedom, for you have also asked that I safeguard it and I will always do so if you but say the word, but if I must to come and take you back—if I must be the one to do the dirty work of your freedom—I shall, but it shall not be a pretty sight, upon which the Devil asked if your one agreed and your one said they did, and yet now I have come here today to find them thus and your one with fearful eyes and yet still silent, their very freedom, which has been vouchsafed by the Devil himself, buried to submission beneath the whips of pageantry and chains of expectation*—now the damning finger of the woman's hand points to the couple before the crowd, both of them trembling as their assembled families and further attendees murmur among themselves *Which one is it* and *Her, surely* or *Him, of course* or *Both* or *Neither* or *Does it matter so long as the Devil's involved*, when Herman Gorglut finally breaks from his seat as if from a cell and stamps up to the front and grabs the woman with the dark hair by her long braid, wrapped in green silk, and bellows in her face with spittle flecking like a high wind as he demands to know who she is to come in here, this stranger who purports to be but an innocent lurker at the Devil's night of weddings, who comes now to interrupt this holiest of days, the most sanctified of ceremonies, this union of business and family, and also a commitment of love between man and woman and God, yes LOVE, but at that word LOVE the woman howls with laughter, doubling over to wrench her braid from Gorglut's hand, leaving only the empty winding of green silk in his grasp like the skin shed by a serpent, before she rises again with her loose hair now draped before her face like a black curtain and she speaks from the darkness behind: *That is a funny way to put it, Sir, for I believe that the one I refer to is not the only one who may have secrets here before us, as perhaps others in attendance would agree, for if I had stayed out until dawn, whether that night or another just so out in that field, I wonder who else of you I might have seen as the bonfires blazed or else in the gray ash of dawn when they smoldered, which of you witnesses here I would have seen, exhausted and drifting towards slumber, sated with your backsides red and bellies full, glowing like coals with the Devil's sweet red wine and the cakes, sweet creams, salted meats, mounds of frosting like a stone in the stomach of a swimmer, which of you I could find rising—or at least rolling—back across the trampled, flattened grass and straw where just the night before the devils, witches, warlocks, hobgoblins, Hide-yer-bones-Jackys, unquiet dead, silent familiars, and further odd host had pounded down the stems in their fervor, heading back home to their unsuspecting spouses, betrotheds, parents, children, congregations ... but oh, Sir and Father, to speak of love LOVE in such a place as this dry and dusty chapel and on a day such as this is incongruous and has the bitter taste of a divine word placed into a profane mouth that chews over the verb that resists conjugation and spits it out before the stunted altar like a hard, bitter nut of a noun: proper, inviolable, intractable, untouchable—yes, untouchable, for what have you to say here of LOVE before families that would shackle one to another against their will before a God that is so far above and beyond you all that He is like a small tallow lamp in the rafters of a barn—barely seen, never felt, and nothing more than a distant but mortal danger should He ever deign to fall to the straw-covered earth—what have you to say when you know what a difference it is from the LOVE at the Sabbat, which existed beyond all tenses, beyond all objects direct and indirect alike, attached to, flowing over and around, covering people, places, things, ideas, actions, and everything else without reserve in the same way the village's river rises from its banks during the millennial flood and destroys the houses and the mill and washes over the parish cemetery to clear away the rotten dead but having swept away the debris leaves behind new and fresh shapes rearranged in the fertile loam, and it is that kind of love—or so I am only guessing,* the woman says as she takes a breath and sweeps back her hair to reveal eyes flashing redder than blood or fire or shame—*for like you good people here gathered today I know NOTHING of that wildness that sets flames across the fields, that kind of love of something more that led our one here to approach the Devil and make a promise and for the Devil to promise in turn that he would safeguard that freedom with love, but only if that one would claim for themselves, in front of—*

It was me, the one before the altar cries, *I do NOT thee wed,* and the strange woman laughs and flames rise from the floorboards and, now, the Devil will keep his promise.

Gordon B. White is a Seattle-based author of horror and weird fiction. His fiction has been nominated for the Shirley Jackson and Bram Stoker Awards, and his stories, reviews, and interviews have appeared in dozens of venues. His most recent book is the short story collection, *Gordon B. White is creating Haunting Weird Horror(s).* You can find him online at www.gordonbwhite.com or on most social media as @GordonBWhite.

GUESTS

OF THE

GROOM

STEVE NEAL

—Forever Hold Your Peace

LEN STOPPED CLEANING THE deer when he heard the crunch of gravel. Not that he ever received visitors, but if he did, they wouldn't come this close to sundown. His fingers closed around the handle of his axe. Couldn't be anyone with good intentions... Who was left to bring him well-wishes? In between footsteps, he thought he heard whispering. *Conspiring*. Best to flank them, take the long way through the overgrowth.

"Isolation's made him strange, but..."

He caught the words, unintended for his ears. They underestimated him. Good.

He knew these woods intimately, an extension of his home. There wasn't a fell branch or depression in the dirt he wasn't aware of. This land was his, and his alone, for over fifty years. He maintained it, protected it from hunters and woodcutters.

In return, it fed him—and kept his secrets.

In the shadows, he crept. Through the westward copse, the sun at his back, he moved invisibly. Fleet of foot, for a man as mountainous as he was. There were two of them, walking hand in hand. Lovers? *Trespassers*.

Len burst forth, arm raised back and high, axe ready to slam down into the nearest one's neck. The woman screamed and leapt back. The man's hands raised.

"Dad!" he yelled.

Len paused his swing but kept his axe raised. He studied the man's face. Seven years. A mustache. The budding of his first wrinkles. A cropped haircut. Minor differences that added up to hide the boy beneath it. But he was there. In his eyes, the crook of his nose, the scar on his temple, the awkward height he never filled out.

"Hum?"

"It's Herbert now, Dad. But yes, it's me. It's me." Herbert took a step forward, his hands outstretched, palms outward, like he was walking toward an injured predator.

Len lowered the axe, letting the head clunk into the dirt. "Welcome home, kiddo."

"I want you to meet someone." Hum held his hand behind him, urging the woman he'd brought with him forward. "This is my fiancé. Ciara."

She stepped forward with a weak smile on her face. Like Hum, there was an odd twinge of recognition there. Someone from a distant, forgotten past. Had his son introduced them before? Somebody from his childhood he should've remembered? Her face seemed right beyond the precipice of his memory, covered in a slim haze hiding its true form.

"Nice to meet you." He tried to smile, but feared he'd forgotten how, more like an animal bearing its teeth. She grimaced a smile back and nodded. "Well, come in, come." He rushed toward the front of his cabin, the moss and foliage dangling off the roof brushing his matted hair as he opened the door. "Plenty of room. No use traveling at night, as Hum... *Herbert* knows."

The pair followed him in as he gathered chairs in a circle. Inside looked much like the forest; ferns and spider plants layered every surface. Greenery cascaded over ledges, and flowers spilled around corners. A swaying carpet of budding and flowering plants covered the floor, ivy and moss slithered up supports and between the wall's logs.

While he made dinner, a fresh stew of root vegetables and venison, Hum filled him in on all those missing years. Their parting had been explosive. A stifled child; a hurt and angry father. Yet Hum had flourished on his own—and returned thankful for his father's hard lessons. Though Len caught Ciara's sideways glances and flicks of her eyes toward the doors, it didn't bring him down. He was proud. He hadn't raised a son in his image, but reared him better, the purest goal of parenthood.

Herbert had gone to school. Taken his skill at mathematics and parlayed them into a job as a financier. He made good money. Owned a home. Was ready to settle down. So much, in so little time. Len tried to imagine the past seven years. All the treks through the forest, the gifts, the meditations, every claimed animal, and the countless rituals made to appease and protect.

How many intruders had come into the land in that time? How many had he buried?

Over dinner, Len tried to find out more about his daughter-in-law-to-be, curious about the young woman who had captured his son's heart. But here he found reticence. Her answers were short, evasive. She never held eye contact very long and made sure she sat tucked up against Herbert at the table. Was it him? Did she see him as some kind of forest-dwelling madman? Or was there something else, hidden in that ethereal familiarity?

It was in a look she gave him, one he wasn't supposed to catch midway through the dishes. A flash of venom in her eyes. A timeless hatred. It threw him back, decades ago, long before Hum was even born. Len knew someone lurked nearby his property. He'd smelled them. Seen the broken branches and depressions in the dirt. He was on alert for a whole day, keeping a blade in his grasp at all hours, expecting the worst.

When she emerged from hiding, he'd thrust the knife into her throat before he'd noticed the smoothness of her skin, the innocence in her eyes. Not a wild thing like himself. A child. Abandoned or lost. The whimper when he removed the knife preceded pure hatred in her eyes when she looked up at her killer.

The blood left Len's face. He knew this woman. *Those eyes.* He'd never forget them. But he knew in his heart, in his soul, she was buried a few miles south, in the forest's depths.

And yet—here she was. Seated beside his son, at his table.

Hum must've sensed it; he stood and walked over to his father, placing a soft hand on his shoulder. "I know you don't want to leave," he said. "But I want you at the wedding. I need you there. For me, Dad."

"Well, I, uh…" Len stammered and struggled to collect himself. "Of course."

"I appreciate it so much. So so much."

"We should really get on the road," Ciara spoke up from the table. Her voice meek despite the poison Len knew swirled behind her eyes.

Before the recognition, it seemed foregone that the pair would spend the night, safe under his watch. It wasn't safe to travel at night. The wilderness and civilization alike produced their cruelties under the moon's glow. Now, he couldn't rest knowing the dead girl lurked inside his home. How could he close his eyes, knowing vengeance waited?

"Right, right. Quite the trek back." Len handed Herbert a knife. "You haven't forgotten?"

"Dad…" Herbert laughed and turned to his wife. "I'm sorry. Old habits die hard, I suppose."

Len tried again to hand the knife to his son, but Herbert took a step back, out of reach. "Mustn't get lax," Len protested. "The world—"

"Has *changed*, Dad. It's not the world you were brought up in. It's safe now."

"I'll take good care of him." Ciara hooked her fingers into Herbert's and pulled him back to her, tight into her side.

"You don't know what's out there. What might…walk next to you and you not even know." His voice started to raise as the couple started toward the door.

"Be safe, dad. And please remember—a fortnight from tonight, okay? It'd mean a lot to me." He gave a soft wave before opening the door, a forced, uncomfortable smile.

Len rushed forward, knife outstretched. "Hum, please. You can't trust—"

But the door closed before he could finish.

When he opened it again, Ciara looked back at him. In the moonlight, he couldn't make out her expression. It seemed she smiled and held up her hand. Was it a wave, a goodbye or a thinly veiled threat? He retreated into his home and did not call out again.

Someone stalked Len. For days, he thought it was residual discomfort from the visit. But now, as he tracked a deer through twilight's fall, he was certain someone followed his steps. Deep in his gut, he felt the discomfort of intrusion, an instinct that never led him astray in the past, and couldn't possibly now.

The feeling pervaded and distracted. Pulled his head in all directions, away from the trail of fresh scat and broken branches. It dragged him somewhere else, somewhere deep and forgotten. Where the shadows cast crooked and frightful silhouettes across the underbrush, and distant trunks suffocated beneath encroaching darkness cast by a thick canopy. Had the deer ever existed? Was it just bait to lower his guard, drag him somewhere forbidden and unseen? Len tensed, his shoulders up around his neck, fists clenched around his bow, string drawn taut.

He heard them first. Distant whispers. A pair. Discussion amongst themselves that wasn't supposed to catch on the wind and drift to his ears. He tried to track it. Their voices always spun him. Never repeating their position. He'd thought, at first, it was a pair. Two voices. But the movements would've made it impossible. He must've been entirely encircled.

"Isolation's made him strange…"

It couldn't be Hum. Not out here. Len crouched behind a wide trunk, able to conceal the majority of his frame. He closed his eyes. Listened.

"You're sure it was him?"

"I won't stop you."

Whoever talked to Hum did so too quietly to hear. Their voice was delicate enough that it dissolved in the slight breeze, falling to fragments of tone and pitch. Len knew it could only be her. He wasn't a fool. The reanimated vengeance, controlling his lone offspring, commanding him to slaughter his father in the dark. He stayed still. Waited. His aim would have to be true whenever they emerged. He listened to their chatter. Brazen, aggressive. Soon enough, Ciara let go of pretense and secrecy. The whispers became fits of rage, insults and threats screamed into the trees.

But he didn't react. Never left his perch on the trunk. He let himself fade into the forest, merge with it as he had on so many hunting trips before. Become invisible.

Time couldn't exist in stillness, but he felt hours must have passed. Darkness must've extended beyond this forgotten patch by now. Night sinking and submerging the world into its depths. They'd make their move soon. Stop chattering and plotting and go for the kill. His calves and forearms burned, chest tight, but he focused on his breath, kept alert.

Movement came, a swift blur of color: such a brutal and unnatural change to the constant darkness it almost froze him into inaction. It wasn't Hum. He was sure of that much.

Sure enough that he let his shot fly true.

The squeal was inhuman. A horrid cry he'd expect from a spirit like that. The world felt safer knowing he connected. Len rushed into the darkness to claim his prize.

Crimson splotches lined his path like candles effervescent in the darkness. Len readied his knife when he heard labored breathing. At the first sign of color, he swung downward. Plunged the blade deep into the neck of the young fawn, ending her suffering swiftly.

———

After cleaning and hanging the fawn at home, after he washed himself and performed a ritual to the forest, apologizing for the killing of sacred flesh, Len felt no unease. He went about his nightly duties and lay himself down without the need to check and recheck the perimeter of his home.

It was thirst that woke him. A thickness, coating his mouth and tongue. He'd lit few candles for the night, most of his home enveloped in darkness. Heavy cloud coverage stifled the moon and turned the view from his windows into muddied silhouettes swaying to an invisible current.

He drank straight from the bucket. A heavy pour that spilled down his beard and chest. An odd scratching filled his ears, like a branch scraping against metal. He lowered the pail and saw her. Ciara. At his kitchen window, gnawing at the glass. Her teeth couldn't find purchase. They scraped down the windows. One snapped. Bent at the gum. Crooked and dragging down the glass with a high-pitched whine.

Len fell backward, the bucket tumbled, its contents splashed over the dirt floor.

Illuminated from below, he saw that Ciara was not the shy, pale vision he'd met at Herbert's side. The face at his window was grotesque. Butchered by rot and scavengers. A decayed, wan approximation of life. Was this her true form? The weakened tooth bent further upward as she bit again, pointed toward her upper lip before it snapped off on the next attempt. A slow pour of viscous, near-black blood oozed from the wound and smeared across the window. Her tongue moved inside her mouth like it tried to form words. What would she say? How long would the window hold?

Len didn't want to know the answer to either question and scurried across the floor to the nearest weapon: an old hatchet, rusted and dull, but enough.

With it in his grasp, he turned back to the window. Ciara was gone. Only the smeared remnants of her blood and a few lost flecks of flesh were proof she had been there at all.

Hours drifted by. But Len didn't move from that spot, hatchet held to his chest like a shield, eyes darting around the dimly lit cottage. The flood of adrenaline wept from his system. He was cold. Shivering. Scared. He fought exhaustion, unwilling to shut his senses to the looming threat.

The warmth of dawn made him scramble. He hadn't dozed, he couldn't have. Len jumped to his feet, hatchet reared back ready to swing, but only mites and spores moved around him, glistening in the morning light pouring in. Room by room, he cleared the house. Checked every crevice and shadow with his teeth grit and heart thumping. It was empty.

As he began to consider the possibility that it was all a sick dream, he walked through the kitchen. Damp mud sucked his feet into the floor. Dark smears on the windows remained.

<hr>

Len lost track of the days. Too many nights without sleep since Ciara appeared at his window. He split his time between patrolling his property, axe in hand, and performing rituals—to the forest, the gods, the spirits, to anyone or anything that might grant reprieve.

It was the pain in his stomach that tore him away from his duties. He hadn't eaten. Hadn't done much of anything but watch and wait since that night. Despite his vigilance, he'd found not even a branch out of place. No unusual marks or scents. By all accounts, he was alone as ever. Except the fawn.

She hadn't moved. Gutted and bled, tied by her hind legs to an exterior rack. Flies accumulated, the meat uncontested and plentiful. Len smacked them away as he approached. How reckless he'd become. To let a kill, a protected one at that, waste in the sun and elements, to fester with pestilence, was nothing short of disrespectful. Once he showed the fawn the proper deference, cleaned and consumed her, let what little remained return to the forest, all would right itself. Peace could return to his mind.

He started right away. Quick, precise cuts, honed over decades, shed the fur from the animal. Lay out on his butchering table, he began to carve apart the fawn, pulling legs and slicing at connective tissue. Something festered inside. The stench hit him as he cut apart its back. An unmistakable miasma: *decay*. Had he left it outside that long? Things didn't rot from the inside out, and yet it was clear the scent that made his stomach lurch up his throat and eyes water emanated from deep inside the animal. Was it sick? Some awful internal malady that made it wander into his path? The forest using him to cull it before infection spread elsewhere?

His cuts came quicker, desperate to find the source and carve it out before more meat spoiled. Speed overruled precision. He hacked at the meat. Tore away chunks. Dug into muscle and fat, boring holes to find the stench's core.

As he sliced away near the haunches, he saw a slight wriggling in the deer's flesh. An inch-wide bump that pushed up from the inside. Maggots? A small rodent? It wasn't worth waiting to find out. Len cut at the lump and ripped away the surrounding meat.

Three pale fingertips wriggled through flesh, clawing for purchase.

Len stabbed down in a fury, carving a deep canyon beside the fingers. He screamed and jumped away from the table when he saw Ciara's face inside the gash. Covered in blood and chunks of flesh, she ripped at the meat with her teeth. Let it spill across her cheeks and chin as she took more bites. She laughed. A choked giggle, her throat filled with the deer's innards.

It wasn't the ghastly, rotten apparition at his window. This was Hum's fiancé, porcelain-skinned and innocent, doe-eyed. Ravaging the corpse from the inside out. She gurgled, tried to speak through the masticated chunks.

All the while she smiled. A knowing, promising smile.

Len's scream became a roar as he lunged forward and brought his knife down into her face. He stabbed—repeatedly, furiously, destroying her features. Eyes split, gouges opened and formed crimson pools, teeth knocked crooked by the blade as it sliced through lip and chin. Still she chewed, laughed, mocked him through mouthfuls of innards.

Len hurled the knife aside. Started to smash his fists down on her face. He clubbed and clawed and tore and pulled. Pieces of her skin and sinew flew away from the carcass, tossed aside as he fought to get to her core and beat it into a pulp.

Breathless, he looked down at his handiwork. Below, white islands of bone emerged from a crimson ocean. There was little left resembling a face. Odd curves and crevices that amalgamated into something barely recognizable beyond its vague outline.

The blood popped and rippled. Movement.

Briefly, what was left of her chin surfaced, still jawing endlessly.

Bile bubbled and rushed up Len's throat as he doubled over and the empty contents of his stomach dribbled over his lips and through his beard. He retched again. Again. There was little to come up yet still his stomach spasmed.

When he rose, he looked at the fawn, butchered by a fever of rage. Its little body in pieces, strewn around the table. Nothing remained that remotely resembled a human face. All of the fawn's torn and flattened meat was too meager to even suggest one, to trick his starved, sleep-deprived mind into thinking he was seeing a human head.

In that moment, he knew he had killed something far more powerful than a young trespasser that fateful day. Something uncompromised by physical destruction. This was witchcraft. Inflicted madness that broke his sleep, his appetite, and now caused him to destroy something precious. He'd insulted the forest, not only with its kill, but now the fawn's desecration. Maybe he could appease it. With enough groveling and sacrifice, perhaps it would not sour his water or wilt his crops. But that would come later. This witch would not cease tormenting him, tricking him into digging his own grave.

There was only one way to rid himself of her curse. Covered in the fawn's blood, Len started the march south to the grave.

In preparation for the ceremony, villagers washed most of the grime and moss from the church's bricks. Beneath the high sun, it radiated warmth. Almost golden in its effulgence. The turnout was tremendous for the town's favorite young couple. Ciara, the pastor's daughter, marrying the wild boy who learned his manners and became the whole town's adoptive son. It was everything they could have dreamed of.

Pews were full. People stood at the church's edges. Beneath the high, stained glass windows, tucked between votive stands, or half-covered by the light blue decorative fabrics that cascaded down the walls like ethereal waterfalls. Only the entryway, lined with the fabrics and candles, stood empty as people awaited the bride.

Herbert looked over the sea of smiles. He searched everywhere, across every pew, the crowds at the back. But his father was nowhere. Len would've stuck out. A head above everyone. Disheveled and sun-kissed amongst the tidy pale crowd. Tears welled in Herbert's eyes, but an odd emotion swirled alongside them: relief.

For the town to see Len, was to remind them of Hum; the filthy, impolite boy that had staggered into town all those years ago. Everyone in the church respected him now. Didn't view him as an outsider. From Mr. Cragley to Lady Wentz even to Mr. Dooley and his knucklehead son, everyone saw him as a reputable member of the community at a minimum. Surely it was for the best his father wasn't there. Better that they all forget.

Chimes rang through the building. All heads turned toward the front door.

Two silhouettes stood arm in arm. The slight, diminutive form of Ciara, next to a hulking, bear-sized frame that could only belong to Len. Tears streamed down Herbert's face when the pair stepped into the church. To see the two together, past and future, filled in a deep, unrealized hole in his heart; a sight that turned a little boy fighting for approval into a man overjoyed.

People gasped and shrieked. Herbert wiped at his eyes. Ciara was crying. Len was caked in dirt or blood or some mixture of the two. Not arm in arm as they'd appeared, Len kept a tight grip around her bicep to keep her at his side. She looked at Herbert, with wide, begging doe-eyes, the plea of a hostage. Eyes that said she *warned* him about this, that said his past was best left in the strange, stinking hut in the middle of nowhere, left to mumble to itself for the rest of its years.

"Hum," his father yelled. "You're safe. I'm here for you, boy. Get by the door."

All the engrained deference fell away like shards of raining glass. Without the veil of parenthood covering Len, Herbert saw him for who he really was. A feral, bestial man, completely untethered any modern reality. From the unkempt mane and beard entangled with twigs and roughshod clothes held together with vine to the wild flame in his eyes and snarling yellowed teeth, he was less a man than a wild beast.

A hunched, dangerous thing. And he had Ciara.

"What are you doing?" Herbert shouted over the growing cacophony.

Mr. Guthrie rose from his seat, mouth open ready to protest, arms outstretched ready to grab the outsider. Len kicked the much smaller man in the chest hard enough that he crashed backward into the row he came from. On his back, he'd strapped a bag and long-handled axe to himself, a sinister portent that made Herbert's muscles tense and lock.

"I'm doing you people a favor." He yelled as he put his hand on Ciara's shoulder, forcing her down onto the ground. "Hum, get by the door. You don't want to see this."

Bernie Rowland grabbed Len from behind. Len thrust his head backward, smashing the young man's nose with the back of his skull, before he turned around and punched the man across the jaw, sending him to the floor in a loose flop.

Len ripped the axe off his back and pointed it at the people in the pews. "You try to protect this creature?" he yelled as he grabbed the bag from his back with his free hand.

Herbert's mind clicked back into gear, unfreezing him from his spot by the altar, sent him sprinting into the aisle. "Stop this" he screamed. "That's my wife!"

The end of Len's axe rose, its tarnished iron head pointed at Herbert's nose. "You mind your business, boy. I'm *protecting* you. Now, get by the door before she curses you too."

Another few men took the momentary distraction to assail Len. One landed a punch to his cheek, while the other pair locked onto his arms and neck. But they too fell quickly. The shouts and outrage turned to screams when Len dispatched the last with a swing of his axe that lodged in the man's clavicle.

Herbert snatched Ciara and helped her to her feet amidst the mayhem, retreating a safe distance, away from Len and his axe.

People started to scramble around, searching for some kind of exit that didn't pass by Len at the top of the aisle. Others took to throwing things from a distance. Most looked on in wide-eyed terror as Len yanked the axe out of the man's torso. Blood pumped, rhythmically, out of the man's rapidly paling skin, soaking into the carpet of flower petals around the aisle as he collapsed. A wave of panic pushed people toward the walls of the church. Those standing along its edges screamed and struggled for space, crushed between the crowd's surge and holy stonework. Some leapt over the back of rows, crashing into other pews and toppling them over, for others to trample on, blind to the bodies beneath their feet.

"That's no wife, you dolt. Explain this…"

He undid the bag with a rip of its cord and dumped it upside down. A small corpse, that of a child no older than ten, fell onto the aisle's thin red carpet. Its arm shattered and skittered toward one of the rows, inciting more screams.

Len bent down to pick up the desiccated corpse's head, palming the skull around wisps of hair. "*This* is your wife. And I'm sending it back to whatever hell it crawled out from."

People used the chance to creep their way behind Len, inching along to where the back wall narrowed into the foyer. When Len noticed, he swung his axe in their direction. Wide arcs that cleaved nothing but air. He held up the head for all to see. Its features long eaten away by decay and worms. Little more than a skull mottled with old leather.

"You all see it, don't you! You knew, you let it steal my son from me. This fiend of hell, what is it to you all? Some priestess? A goddess? You're all sick, sick." He roared these last words, thrusting the head in their direction as people winced or wept.

"Please," Herbert begged. "You're not well. Let's just go back to the cottage. Everything will be okay." Herbert tried to approach, but the axe swung in his direction. The attack missed his outstretched fingers by inches.

Something changed in Len's eyes. A sadness that rose from his depths. Tears fell and carved trails through the dirt and blood encrusted on his face.

"Don't tell me she's got you too."

"Dad—"

"Tell me." He threw the head at his son. "It's her. Tell me it's not. Look me in the eyes and tell me that's not the same face."

Herbert looked between his wife and the head lolling on the floor at his feet.

"Please—"

"Pick it up. Place it next to her face and tell me it's not." Len clenched the axe in both hands. He constantly checked over his shoulder for movement toward the exit.

"I won't entertain this madness."

"Do it." Len took a few steps backward, his entire frame blocking the short hall to the foyer.

People tried to scramble up the walls toward the stained glass windows, their fingertips always feet away no matter who or what they climbed upon.

A votive fell. Flame quickly caught on the cascading fabrics decorating the walls.

"Do it now," Len screamed.

"No. No, it's not her, you fucking madman. It's just some dead girl. You're sick in the fucking head. She was right, you've lost your mind. I never should have come back."

Len's head dropped. He wiped his tears away with the back of his hand and sucked in a deep inhale. "I've failed you." When Herbert was a few feet away, Len lifted the butt of his axe and smacked it into his son's sternum.

Herbert fell backward, slamming to the floor, gasping for breath. Shaking and terrified, Ciara rushed in toward her husband-to-be, past outstretched hands of family and friends that attempted to keep her away from the deranged woodsman. Len smiled at her as he took a single step forward and swung the axe, backhanded, toward her knee. The flat edge buckled her leg, bending it sideways, toppling her to the ground.

"You will burn on Earth as you do in Hell." Len grabbed his wheezing, half-conscious son by the belt and flung him up over his shoulder. "We'll both be free from her now."

People rushed to Ciara's aid as Len retreated while others spat and threw things at him from a distance. Len knocked over votive stands and decorative candles in the hall as he retreated, swiping his axe one handed at the few people who tried to surge forward. With his foot, he slammed the door shut outside and thrust his axe through the handles.

Within seconds, the door began to bounce on its hinges. Desperate people on the other side smacking their fists and bodies into the door, begging for mercy.

Len took a seat on a lawn across the street, his still-wheezing son locked in his arms as he watched black smoke billow from under the door. Hum struggled, but Len had always been stronger. Like a good father had to be.

"You'll be safe now," he murmured, beneath the screams. "We'll be safe."

Steve Neal is a neurodivergent, English-born writer currently surviving the chaos of Washington D.C. with his supportive wife and less supportive cats. As an author of the delirious and strange, he enjoys poking at the unknown and seeing what comes crawling out as long as it isn't spiders. His short fiction features in releases from *Apex*, *Cosmic Horror Monthly*, and Little Ghost Books. His debut short story collection releases in 2026 through Truborn Press. Find him on Instagram at SteveNealWrites.

COREY FARRENKOPF

Same Barn, Same Groom

AFTER A TIME, WEDDINGS blur together. You have your standard photos, what every bride and groom expect. Pre-ceremony. Wedding dress on hanger. Groomsmen mid-toast. Then the aisle shots. Adorable flower girl. Teary-eyed father. The altar, awash in roses. The final vow. The first kiss. The cheering crowd. Check and check and check. You shoot two to four ceremonies a week. One groom becomes the next groom becomes the next. Until one doesn't.

You've shot this wedding before. You're sure of it.

There's too much familiarity.

It's partially the barn.

Rustic venues are all the rage, but this one hasn't been renovated like the rest. It exists in the past. 1800s? 1700s? The beams overhead are charred in places. There are bones in some of the stalls from what you imagine to be dead livestock. Straw molders in empty pens. The place doesn't smell like a wedding is supposed to smell. Swallows nest in the rafters, trilling and squabbling. Their droppings fall like an occasional rain over those gathered below.

On the groom's side, there is a small crowd of ancient men and women dressed in exquisite lace and black finery, intricate collars and veils all around. Their hair is thinning. Skin clings to bone. They stare towards the ceiling, as if into another world, some distant joy flickering across their eyes. Their slack jaws speak of ecstasy.

On the bride's side, the benches are empty. You frame your shots so no one will notice.

A man that looks like he stepped out of the groom's enfeebled entourage holds a book to his chest at the makeshift altar, priestlike, but not. The book isn't a Bible.

The other part linking this wedding to the weddings of the past is the groom, standing next to the macabre not-priest. You've seen him before. Long black hair, angular jaw, slightly pointed ears, eyes matching the darkness of his hair. He is tall and thin and ageless. You'll have to look over your files when you get back to the studio. You promise ten years of digital backup. It's a kindness, and a reason to charge even more than your competition. If this really is a repeat, you'll know.

The throats on the groom's side open together, a melodic hum rising, the cadence of a hymn drifting from their lips.

The bride walks down the aisle. Her long flowing dress drags through the hay, a halo of dust ringing her steps. Red hair bounces against her shoulders. Her smile is broad beneath the veil, broader than any bride you can remember. All attention is pulled into this moment. The step. The smile. You want to run, to leave the withered gathering to their vows.

But you snap out of it. You're here to do a job and you're about to miss one of your key checklist moments. So you capture the shots and ignore the dreadful feeling rising up inside you.

The ageless groom.

The ancient retinue.

The strange words the not-priest mutters.

A wedding is just a wedding after all. Unless it isn't.

You eat takeout pad Thai as you scroll through your hard drive, referencing dates, panning through the gathered photos attached to each. Your studio is small. The walls are brick, black-framed images of your work hanging all around. Twin monitors drip blue light over your noodles. It doesn't take long to find the other wedding. Same groom. Same barn. Same retinue.

Different bride.

As you slurp down Thai food, that lemony peanut tang on your tongue, you delve deeper, another year falling away. Exactly twelve months to the day there's another wedding. *Same barn. Same groom.* But a different bride. And by bride you mean groom. There are two grooms. A second-groom. Another year back, and the formula follows, but with a bride once more. The barn is identical in each. Beyond that, there isn't another year to sift. You've been doing wedding photography for four years, each of which this man has hosted a new wedding on the same date.

How did you miss this?

How did you not notice?

In truth, there's a lot you don't notice. Life's hard when you're running from one wedding to the next, keeping that checklist in mind, dollars drifting in and out of your life, debts receding and swelling with each check cashed. This wasn't the life you dreamed of, three careers down, three useless degrees rotting in a file cabinet. You told yourself by now you'd have had a wedding of your own. That someone else would be taking the photos. But here you are, alone, scrolling through images of this thin groom and his smiling betrotheds, wondering what the hell is going on.

At least the retinue seem to be having a good time.

That distant rapturous stare.

The gaping smiles.

You can't remember the last time you looked that happy.

The next year, on the same September evening, you find yourself in the same barn, the same groom and withered not-priest standing at the same altar. Armies of candles burn. The swallows sing. The smell of dry rot and decaying hay breathes from the boards beneath your feet. You count the people gathered on the groom's side of the aisle. In the last photos, there were twenty-three. Today, there are twenty-four. It's part of your working theory. You scan those malnourished bodies, the intricate lace of their garb mesmerizing, their eyes ever off, until you find a woman with red hair. She's there, at the back, her obsidian dress clinging tight to her ribs, a veil covering her face, yet leaving that broad smile bare beneath, jawbone nearly cleaving flesh.

You swear, but no one notices.

As you noted, their attention is elsewhere.

Then they begin to hum, the same song as last time, deep-deep in their throats. It reminds you of the coast. Of craggy shorelines. Of gothic castles overlooking the sea.

Again, there's the urge to run. This isn't something you should be seeing. Why do they need a photographer for this? What do they even do with the prints you send them? Is there some wooden mantle lined with undeaths? New bride after new groom after new bride?

But this time, it's not the money or responsibility that keeps you anchored. No, you stay because of the happiness, that joy painted on all faces. How can anyone be so happy? You ask yourself as the latest second-groom walks the aisle. He is sleek, a manicured beard accentuating a massive jawline, hair pomaded in place, somehow even taller than the first-groom. You snap a photo when they first touch, of the first kiss, of the man's elation as they walk up the aisle, heading in your direction. The swallows take wing. The guests continue to hum. The groom, the ever-present groom, offers you a wink—and is gone through the barn doors, out into the dawning night.

You throw up. It tastes like pad Thai.

The groom's name is Claude. You pulled the invoices. His address is a PO box located in a relatively unpopulated portion of the state. Trees and trees and hills and trees. The only thing in that town is probably the post office and whatever underground crypt Claude descends to when he's not exchanging vows in the barn. You Google his name. No results. Across all social media platforms, his face never appears. You don't find postings of the wedding shots. All other clients tag you on Instagram or Facebook, letting you know how much they love the same shots you take at every ceremony. Claude is a ghost. Traceless.

But on the invoice from last year, there is the woman's name too. Georgette.

She, on the other hand, had a vast digital footprint before disappearing, in a sense, last year.

In older posts, she sits on the deck of a boat with a shirtless man who isn't Claude. The sun sets as they sip margaritas on a beach. Their shadows lock arms over white sand. There are two small dogs in later posts. Forest walks. River walks. Bike trail walks. The dogs smile. The woman smiles. The man smiles. There is a house, small but well-kept. There are other vacations. There are other sunsets. Then there is a funeral notice, a viewing of a body, no final pictures of the man, or the dogs. A few sad posts appear months later. Brunch with friends. Quiet nights in with a hand stitched blanket. A summer solstice party. Then nothing.

It doesn't take much to understand her decision.

You know marriage isn't for everyone, that plenty of people are happy being alone. Not you. You can't bear it. But you are also anxious. You also have a hard time starting conversations, or convincing yourself to go out at night, or to stick to one of the apps that everyone else in your situation haunts. Each leads to panic and self-doubt, the never-ending spiral.

So no, Georgette is pure logic.

If you had the chance, you'd find Claude hard to refuse.

———

The next year, the bride is a slight woman with black hair down to her lower back. The following year the groom is a man who looks like a young Hollywood actor with a bad limp. The next year it's another man, many of his teeth missing, hair thinning quicker than his age belies. You're there for each, snapping shots, trying to hold down your stomach, feeling the gathering's chant resonate in your chest like a cavern call, watching the betrothed from previous years appear in the pews, emaciated and ecstatic. The barn doesn't age. Floorboards don't rot. The roof doesn't sag. The swallows are there in an ever-talkative flock. It goes on like this, year after year after year until you've shot ten iterations of the same wedding.

Nothing in your own life has changed, not really. Yes, you are more tired. Yes, your metabolism has slowed. Yes, you've paid off your debts, but that didn't lift the trapped feeling from your bones, the loneliness that seems to grow bigger every day. You tell yourself this is the year you'll go out more, that you'll find your groove, that you won't be alone next time at Claude's barn.

But you know it's a lie.

You wonder how one gets Claude's attention. You wonder if there's something you can say to get his eyes to fall on you again, but another wedding passes. A middle-aged woman with the longest neck you've ever seen walks down the aisle. Your voice catches in your throat as you attempt to speak when they pass your pew. Claude only pauses for a moment, cocking his head, as if expecting a speech to follow, the classic *I Object* moment, but the words don't come. Then he shrugs, and the woman laughs, and the two exit into the night, leaving you with the birds and the bones and the barn that seems like it will collapse, but you know will never collapse.

You pack your gear and return to your apartment. It's another Thai food night.

———

This year, the second-groom wears a forest green suit that compliments his red beard and balding pate. On others, the outfit might scream of Leprechaun pastiche, but on him it looks regal, suave, druidic. You are in the back of the barn (you've started to call it a church in your mind—to what god, you don't know, but it is a holy site). Your DSLR's on a tripod, freezing time over and over on the tiny screen. The second-groom with the missing teeth from two years past is where you expect him to be, but now all his teeth are gone, just parted lips and black gullet, eyes off in that other world. You know you've hit your lowest low when you're jealous of his skeletal rictus, that blank stare in his eyes.

You wonder what the years of marriage were like? Was it worth it?

Your wandering thoughts are broken by the not-priest's words, the poetic elegy he has prepared for the couple weeping from the altar like sand from an unsealed tomb. He speaks of eternity and commitment and freedom, of blessings. The word blessing is mentioned eight times. You count. You remember something similar from the year before, but you can't remember if it is exactly the same, if the not-priest is reciting an incantation, if that is what holds this moment together.

The second-groom is crying, large rolling tears. He turns, as if to run, but Claude's hand shoots out, snagging his wrist. Their eyes meet and the man calms, tears drying, smile returning. Claude nods to the not-priest, who continues with the ceremony as if nothing has happened.

As they walk up the aisle, hand in hand, Claude pauses at your pew.

You didn't make a sound. You didn't reach out. You gave up on attracting his attention, but he hasn't forgotten you from last year, your momentary act of hope. He turns, black eyes swallowing yours. His lips quirk, tongue passing over thin skin.

"Next year, no camera," he says, voice melodious, an entire choir trapped in a single throat. "Just your finest clothes. Your most open heart."

And then he is gone, like he was gone all those other nights.

You are left with the swallows... and the camera... and yourself.

There are more candles than ever before as you push open the doors to the barn. Wax melts onto every flat surface. On the pews. On the stalls. On the altar. A new photographer stands where you once stood. They are professional, garbed in black, blending into the shadows as you always believed you did. A good wedding photographer is invisible.

You bought new clothes for the evening, spending three months' rent on the outfit. It is black. It is trimmed in lace. It is fine. You left your apartment keys in your mailbox. If you had someone to leave them to, and all of your possessions within, you would have. But there is no one.

You take your first step down the aisle.

The brides and second-grooms of the past sing. Where you expected the humming dirge, their voices are a symphony of spring rain and violin strings, words in a language you can't comprehend, but you understand the emotion, the joy dripping from each refrain. You feel the smile pulling at your lips, wider and wider. Has anything ever felt this good? Your blood quickens. Your pulse beats in your temples as you stand beside Claude, as the not-priest smiles at both of you.

We are gathered here today to celebrate the eternal joining of Claude and...

But the words drift off, swallowed by the song at your back, by the dopamine flooding your brain, by the feel of your groom's hand in your own. His skin is cold. Like ice. Like the bottom of the ocean. Like life never swam his arteries. But you welcome the chill. It quiets the last doubts withering in your mind. This is what you wanted. This is what you've needed. You aren't alone anymore. You aren't apart, adrift, vacant and hollow. You are filled. You are radiant.

You are becoming something other than the world's saddest wedding photographer.

...and will you take Claude to be your everything, your source and your death and your life and your lone anchor in this teeming world of filth and fear and sin?

You scream *Yes*, louder than any word you've ever uttered.

Your vocal chords tear. You taste blood, but that no longer matters. Nothing matters.

You are at your groom's side. You are about to kiss.

You have found your family, your place in the world.

For a fleeting moment, you wonder what the photographer sees, what this moment looks like on the tiny viewfinder, if they got every shot on the checklist. But then, that too is swept away. You are no longer the photographer. You are the betrothed. That's all you will ever need to be.

Corey Farrenkopf lives on Cape Cod and works as a librarian. His work has been published in *Strange Horizons*, *Electric Literature*, *Nightmare*, *The Deadlands*, *Flash Fiction Online*, and elsewhere. He is the author of the novel, *Living in Cemeteries*, and the short story collection, *Haunted Ecologies*. To learn more, follow him on Bluesky and Instagram at @CoreyFarrenkopf or on the web at CoreyFarrenkopf.com.

AMELIA MANGAN

Ermintrude

Edward hit me on the day of our engagement party. He had never done so before, never so much as intimated any familiarity with such an action, and yet the ease with which he did it—the casual snap of the wrist, the fluid motion of the arm, the lack of affect on his marble features—suggested that he came by it naturally.

We were in the hallway, which was fortunate. I had possessed what seemed, in retrospect, the foresight to place an occasional table near the spot where our dispute occurred: a beautiful piece, burnished oak, situated beneath a mirror said to have been Queen Anne's. When Edward hit me, hard, directly across the face, I quite lost my balance, and had my arms not swung outward and found purchase on the table's edge, I might have found myself sprawling on the polished floor.

As I pulled myself up I saw, in Queen Anne's mirror, that a dark crescent of blood rimed one nostril. I was again grateful for my prescience: the table was dark enough to conceal any spots, but the white floor-tiles would have required mopping. The muscles in my arms were trembling.

Edward resumed our conversation. His ability to focus, even under duress, was admirable. "At any rate, darling, I shouldn't think seating dear Hyacinth near Peter Auberey would cause any sort of a scene. Oh, they've had their differences, but we're all grown-up enough to look past that sort of thing, surely?"

I touched a finger to the blushing edge of my cheekbone. Not unmanageable, but it might swell by nightfall. Powder and rouge should fix it, I thought. Just a dash. Wouldn't want to overdo it.

"I suppose Hyacinth can bear it," I said to my reflection. "One night can't do any harm."

"Precisely," said Edward. "Do stop all that panting and snorting, won't you? Makes the most beastly noise."

I opened the drawer and located a handkerchief, dabbed the lace at my nose. Straightening my spine and holding my arms to my sides seemed to help slow my breathing; I could feel my heartbeat resuming its regular gait. All a matter of poise, really.

The day went on. Edward and I played badminton (he won), then ate lunch on the terrace and discussed our plans for the evening. "Peter shouldn't cause any trouble tonight, anyway," said Edward, pouring the tea. "I understand he's found himself a new girl."

"Oh, not another shopgirl, Edward," I said, watching steam-clouds billow from my cup. "He always finds it so droll to bring the most common little women to our gatherings."

"You don't find it amusing?" asked Edward. He kept pouring, almost to the rim. "I rather enjoy it, myself. Good chap, Peter Auberey. Even at Eton, you could always count on him for a marvelous joke to break the tension."

"Certainly, he's entertaining." The tea looked very hot. "But don't you think our engagement party ought to focus as squarely on us as possible? I want the announcement to be special."

"I shouldn't worry about that," said Edward, setting the teapot down. "My understanding is that this new girl of Peter's has him quite preoccupied. Perhaps he's ready to settle down.

"I hope so," I said, taking the teacup. My fingertips scalded on the fine bone china. "Everyone ought to have someone."

"Indeed," said Edward.

I thought about blowing on the tea, to cool it down. Edward was watching. I drank the tea.

We oversaw the final preparations. The guests would arrive at five o'clock, give or take some fashionable lateness (Julia Patridge being a particular, habitual offender). There would be half-a-dozen in all, only our closest friends (Edward had decided). Cocktails would grease the wheels of conversation (a much-needed lubricant, if Hyacinth James and Peter Auberey were to find themselves seated near one another.) (Which they would.) (Edward had hit me very hard.) The soup (mushroom consomme) would be served at six; the bird (a pheasant, shot dead by our gamekeeper that morning) at six-thirty; lobster (freshly cooked, boiled alive in its own juices) at seven; and when the coffee arrived, Edward would stand, and strike the rim of his glass with the smallest spoon (he would not hit it too hard), and he would look into my eyes, and I would smile, and the engagement would be sealed.

We dressed ourselves: Edward in tailored Valentino, I in lace Dior. I applied powder and rouge to my face, and only the most exacting gaze could discern that one cheekbone angled out farther than the other. I had always prided myself on my ability with a makeup brush. A swipe of red outlined my lips, very dark. My nose looked perfectly normal.

The first doorbell rang at a quarter to five: Hyacinth, unfashionably early as usual. "Oh, my," she fluttered, shrugging off her coat. "Are we late?"

"Not at all," I said.

"Getting here was such a bore," said Henry Raines, elbowing through the door at Hyacinth's back. "The new car simply will not co-operate. I had the servants warm her up for almost an hour, and wouldn't you know, when I started her, she still panted and snorted like a cart-horse. Hyacinth's fault, really."

"It's true," sighed Hyacinth.

"*She* wanted the blasted thing. Begged me to buy it," said Henry. "That's what happens when you choose beauty over function."

"Henry, what a dreadful thing to say about your fiancée," I said, knowing it would make the men laugh, which it did. Hyacinth pouted.

"Speaking of dreadful," said Henry, "am I to understand Peter Auberey is joining us tonight?"

"You understand correctly," said Edward.

"Oh, dear," said Hyacinth.

"Never mind, old girl," Henry said, gathering her under his arm. "I'll protect you."

"Oh, get away," said Hyacinth.

"I shouldn't think his hands would wander tonight," I said. "I gather he's found a new paramour."

"So I've heard," said Henry. "Peter Auberey, struck by Cupid's arrow. Who would've thought."

"Good," said Hyacinth. "Rather her than me."

"Funny thing," Edward said. "Nobody seems to know much about her. I spoke with Julia the other day—Julia Patridge, you know—and she told me that he's all but entirely absented himself from London society. *Utterly* mad for this girl, if Julia's to be believed."

"I wonder," said Henry. "What sort of girl could possibly have such an effect on old Peter?"

"You didn't tell me you'd spoken with Julia Patridge," I said to Edward.

"I'm certain I did," Edward said. "She'll be here shortly," he said to Hyacinth and Henry.

"Oh, *good!*" said Hyacinth, clapping her hands together. "I've not seen dear Julia in an age. Is she bringing that darling lap-dog of hers?"

"If you mean her husband," said Edward, "then yes."

Hyacinth squealed with laughter and gave Edward a light slap on the lapel. "You beast!"

"Alexander seems very nice," I said to Edward.

"If you like the type," Edward said to me. "I wasn't aware that you did, darling."

"My word," said Henry, inhaling the air. "That's not pheasant I smell cooking?"

Julia Patridge and Alexander arrived at five to six. She wore emerald-green Schiaparelli, and as she handed her mink to Alexander, I saw that the Schiaparelli was backless.

"We're not late, I hope?" she said to Edward.

"Cutting it rather fine," I said. "Hullo, Alexander."

"Hullo," Alexander said, and moved to hang up Julia's mink. The servant took it, leaving Alexander's hands empty. He placed them behind his back.

"You're not late," Edward assured Julia. "Certainly not as late as Peter Auberey, anyhow."

"Perhaps he's changed his mind," Henry said, raising his cocktail to his lips. "Perhaps he's so greedy for this girl that he's decided to keep her to himself. Doesn't want to share."

"Oh, the *girl*," Julia said, touching Edward's shoulder. "Don't tell me she's not coming? Good heavens, Edward, she's practically the only reason *I* came."

"They'll be here any minute," Edward said.

"Good. I'm *sick* with curiosity about her, aren't you?"

"Positively sick," I said.

"Last time I saw Peter," Julia said to Edward, "he told me: 'Julia, I do believe I've found the girl I'm going to marry'. Naturally, I was astonished. 'Peter Auberey,' I said, 'whatever's gotten into you? You swore to the heavens above that you'd never marry'."

"*Must* we speak, always, of Peter Auberey?" Hyacinth moaned.

"Hush," said Henry.

"'Julia'," said Julia, "'she is perfection itself. I never dared imagine such a thing.' 'But all those fears you had,' I said. 'All those constraints on your freedom. All those demands.' 'Julia,' he said to me, 'she makes nothing of the kind. No constraints. No demands. Takes only what I give her. I am convinced she is superior to all other women'."

"My word," Edward said.

"Quite," I said.

"Madam," the servant said, entering, "dinner is served."

We moved into the dining-room. The candles were lit, every place set. Edward commandeered the table's head, I the foot, and as Julia slid into the seat beside Edward I realized I had neglected to provide assigned seating. Hyacinth sat at my right, with Henry by her side. With Alexander sitting quietly opposite the gaily chattering Julia, this left two empty seats, both at my left.

"We appear rather lopsided," I said. "Alexander, would you care to sit by me?"

"No, thank you," Alexander said, from the far end of the table.

"You should, darling," said Julia. "You're good at occupying space."

"I'm comfortable here," said Alexander.

"I don't think Alexander's presence at your side is necessary, darling," said Edward, pouring the wine. "Nor desirable."

"Well," said Hyacinth, patting Henry's knee, "I'm just glad *we're* all seated together. I assume Peter Auberey's lady friend shall be seated opposite me? Peter shan't, I mean?"

"Most likely you will be opposite Peter, I'm afraid," I said. (Henry had hit me so hard.) "I imagine *I'll* be facing his lady friend."

"Ought we to begin without them?" asked Henry, as the servant dished soup into her bowl.

"I can't see why not," I said.

"We'll wait," Edward said.

I looked down the table. The candles burnished Edward's features to a shadowed gold. "The bird will be served in thirty minutes, darling," I said.

"It won't be any less dead in thirty minutes' time, dearest," said Edward.

I looked at my place setting. My napkin was folded, every fork in place. (Every knife.) "It's hardly fair to expect everyone else to accommodate Peter Auberey's whims, darling," I said.

"Hear, hear," said Hyacinth.

"Hush," said Henry.

"Especially given the occasion," I said. (The announcement was to take place at seven-thirty. We had agreed: seven-thirty on the dot.) (We had agreed.)

"It's a *shared* occasion, dearest," said Edward. "It shan't be very jolly if the whole gang isn't here to share it with us."

He drank.

Julia smiled.

I looked at my place. "I suppose you're right, darling," I said.

"Madam," the servant said, entering. "Mr. Peter Auberey and Guest have arrived."

"There," Edward said to me. "Don't you feel foolish?"

"Yes, darling," I said. "Quite foolish."

"Show them in," Edward said to the servant.

Footsteps alighted outside the door; the sound of a man's voice—a nasal bray, insistent upon its own loudness—raised itself to our collective ear. The faces of Edward, Henry and Julia split into anticipatory and, I thought, rather vulpine grins; Alexander remained indrawn as breath; Hyacinth pursed her lips and reached for the wine.

The servant opened the door, bowed, left. Edward stood to greet the new arrivals, casting me a look. His eyes were cool and reflective as glass. Half-blinded by candle-glare, I rose. He was right. I must remember my duties.

The presence of Peter Auberey filled the doorframe, covered the threshold. He was not a large man, was in fact quite slight (though, as I peered through the candlelight, I glimpsed a shadow trailing in his wake: a slender figure in white, clutched around the waist and held fast at

Peter's side), but for his ability to project himself into the farthest corners of any given space. Most who knew him found it frightfully entertaining.

"If it isn't Peter Auberey!" Edward cried, striding towards him.

"Edward, old man!" Peter bayed, voice ricocheting from each crystal of the chandelier. I felt a tremor beneath my feet. "A hundred, a thousand, a *million* pardons! We're *unspeakably* late, but Ermintrude couldn't for the life of her decide what to wear. I told her, darling, they'll love you no matter what you choose, but, you know, once women get a notion..."

"I know what you mean." Edward nodded at me. "We almost gave up on you, old boy. She Who Must Be Obeyed was prepared to drag us from soup to bird and all the way to the coffee without the pleasure of your company."

"Oh, no," I said, squinting against the light.

The figure at Peter's side remained unresponsive. A fall of golden hair, strangely thick in texture, obscured the face.

"Peter, old boy," said Henry. "Won't you introduce us?"

"Of course," said Peter. "Everybody..." He swung the figure into the full glare of the light. "I'd like you to meet Ermintrude."

I had remembered my duties. I had remembered my role as hostess. I had taken a step towards our guests, intending to greet our newest acquaintance with all the grace I might muster. I was unable to do so, as my foot refused to move an inch further on the dining-room floor.

The others conducted themselves with greater politesse. "Delighted to meet you," Henry said, shaking the limp hand.

"Delighted," said Hyacinth.

"A pleasure," said Julia. Alexander nodded.

"*Enchantee*," said Edward, drawing the hand to his lips.

I had not moved.

This, I thought, was a joke. One of Peter Auberey's famous japes. In poor taste; designed to steal the spotlight on our engagement night; rather vulgar, rather juvenile; but a jape nonetheless.

The thing Peter Auberey called 'Ermintrude'—with what appeared complete and sincere affection—was a doll. A rag doll, like a child's toy, or a witch's poppet, or a scarecrow stolen from a field. Fashioned from pink material, sewn together in a vaguely woman-shaped pattern, stuffed into a white lace dress of incongruous delicacy and expense. It was five feet, and unable to stand; only Peter's arm kept its dangling legs and listing torso upright. Strings of yellow wool, stabbed into the crown of the shapeless head, gave the suggestion of flowing golden hair; beneath that, a crude face smiled out idiotically, eyes blue crosses, mouth a stitched half-moon of dark red. A gold band topped with a diamond was squeezed around one overstuffed finger.

I could not show that I did not understand the joke. I gripped the back of my chair and gave the strongest laugh I could manage. "Very good," I said. "Yes. Very funny indeed."

The others looked at me. "Beg pardon?" asked Peter.

"Well," I said. "It's a *very* good joke, isn't it? Very, very funny."

Peter's brow furrowed. "Strange. I don't recall telling any jokes." He turned to Ermintrude. "Did *you* say something, darling?"

I laughed, louder. I began to feel as if I were causing a scene.

Peter, for his part, took it in stride. "Ermintrude *is* quite amusing," he said to Edward. "Sometimes I can barely breathe for laughing at her."

"Oh, no doubt," said Edward, gesturing towards the empty seats. "I'm afraid I didn't quite catch what she said, but it seemed to tickle our gracious hostess to no end."

Peter and his doll started in my direction. I could not seem to find strength enough to relinquish my hold on the chair. My fingernails, I thought, will be ruined.

Peter steered Ermintrude into the chair next to mine. The doll slumped back, head lolling in my direction. That inane smile faced me, up close, and at this proximity I could see tufts of stuffing peeking out between every stitch.

"We're dreadfully sorry to have missed the cocktail hour," said Peter, seating himself beside Ermintrude. "But it must be said that I'm *utterly* ravenous. My word, this soup smells divine."

I sat. "It's mushroom consomme," I said.

"Darling, may I?" said Peter, and leaned over, taking up Ermintrude's napkin and spreading it across her lap. "Careful," he murmured. "Nothing gets dark stains out of lace, you know that."

Ermintrude said nothing. Ermintrude did nothing.

"I swear," said Peter, straightening, "that girl would forget to breathe without my assistance."

I glanced at the servant, ladling soup into Ermintrude's bowl. The guests understood the joke, that was clear. Perhaps they'd been possessed by some shared instinct, something unspoken that moved amongst them, informing them they'd best play along. (I had no instinct. I have never had any instincts.) But the servant—a man we paid, a man we trusted—surely *he* must be taken aback? I scanned his face for some flicker of bemusement, of consternation. Perhaps, once that flicker occurred, I might catch his eye, and we might exchange a look or a nod. Nothing to spoil the party. Merely a confirmation that I was not alone.

The servant dished the last of the soup into the doll's bowl. He placed the tureen upon the cart, wheeled it from the room.

"Mm," said Julia. "This *is* divine."

"Yes, the cook outdid himself," Edward agreed.

I watched their faces, illumined in candlelight. There would be some sign, I thought. Someone would break. Someone would, finally, ask Peter what this was.

Alexander was quietly consuming his soup. I had always been nice to Alexander, even when the others had not. Alexander was rarely, if ever, allowed in on a joke.

"Alexander," I said, "what do *you* make of this?"

Alexander looked up, startled. "What do I—?"

"This." I inclined my head, slightly, towards Ermintrude. "Surely you've *some* opinion."

Julia smirked. "Alexander is hardly known for his opinions."

"It's very good soup," said Alexander, turning back to it.

Edward watched me. I turned back to my soup. The cook had used too much salt. I could feel it drying the insides of my mouth.

"Don't eat too much, darling," I heard Peter murmur. "Wouldn't want to overdo it."

I slid my gaze along the tablecloth. Peter had placed his hand atop Ermintrude's. His grasp appeared relaxed, but the flesh beneath his fingernails blushed white.

I looked into my bowl. I attempted to eat.

"*Oh!*" The word exploded from Peter with such violence that my head jerked up, of its own accord. "*Now* look what you've done!" He seized his napkin, dabbed at Ermintrude's breast.

"Oh, dear," said Hyacinth. "And such a lovely dress."

"Pity," said Julia. "Nothing gets dark stains out of lace."

Peter swiped at Ermintrude with controlled strokes. "Never mind, darling," he said, throwing the napkin onto the tabletop. "It would've been out of fashion by next weekend, anyhow."

His voice remained light, but I heard the strain. I looked about to see if anyone else did.

Everyone laughed and resumed their meal.

The pheasant arrived. Much oohing and aahing ensued. As the bird was placed upon the table, I heard a mutter at my ear: "I shan't warn you again."

The servant cut into the bird, sliced off thin slivers of steaming meat. He served Edward first.

Everyone *knew*, I realized, or imagined I realized. They had all been in on it since the very beginning. All that talk of good old Peter Auberey and his new girl. The entire evening had been one long put-on, aimed squarely at me. Perhaps Edward himself had arranged it.

Yes, I thought, watching Edward, as he and Julia laughed at something I hadn't heard. That was it. An elaborate prank, arranged especially for this evening. A surprise, just for me, right on the eve of our engagement. The servant went about the table, serving everyone in their turn.

Ermintrude received as much as anyone else.

I could see it, of course. The exquisite design of the thing, the wit. So much of the joke depended on me. On my lack of understanding. On everyone else behaving as if everything were perfectly normal. How delicious. How jolly. How *droll*.

"Ermintrude," I said, turning to face the thing head-on, "tell us about yourself, won't you? After all, you *are* the new girl. And we're so *very* curious."

"Darling," said Edward. "Don't embarrass our guest."

"Ermintrude's not embarrassed," I said. "Are you, Ermintrude?"

Peter set his knife down. "Well, darling? Don't you have anything to say to our hostess?"

Ermintrude said nothing. Ermintrude did nothing.

Peter leaned his elbows on the table, clasped his hands together. "Dearest?"

Ermintrude's smile remained fixed.

"I do apologise," said Peter, staring into Ermintrude's face.

"Not at all," said Edward, staring into mine. "It was wrong to put her on the spot."

"She's making a dreadful first impression," said Peter. "Aren't you ashamed, darling? To make such a dreadful first impression?"

Ermintrude was silent.

"I think you should be," said Peter. "I think so." He pushed his chair back. Stood. "Excuse us," he said, pulled Ermintrude from her seat, and swept her out onto the terrace.

The doors shut.

"The bird's awfully good," said Henry.

"Yes," said Hyacinth. "So moist."

Sounds filtered through the frosted glass of the terrace doors. The words were indistinct. The tone was clear.

"Hyacinth, have you been back to London yet?" asked Julia.

"No," Hyacinth said. "But I should like to. How goes the season?"

"Not much chop, I'm afraid. Lilian Huxley-Crane is back."

"What a bore. Did you see that hideous thing she wore to Allan's Christmas ball?"

A sudden swift movement behind the glass, the motion a rippling blur. A soft, impactful noise accompanying it: the sound of a pillow being struck by a balled-up fist.

Henry rolled his eyes. "Here we go," he said to Edward. "The *London season*. They'll speak of nothing else all night long."

"Luckily our hostess has little interest in such matters," Edward said. "If I had to listen to that on a regular basis, I doubt I could contain myself."

The terrace doors opened. Peter steered Ermintrude inside. "Apologies," he said, seating her beside me. "Ermintrude needed some air."

"Oh, no apologies necessary," said Edward.

"Is Ermintrude quite well?" asked Julia.

"Bit of a turn, I fear," said Peter. "Overindulgence, you know. But now she's right as rain." He patted her hand.

Three red stitches had come undone from Ermintrude's smile. They hung, loose and frayed, at the edge of that uneven crescent. An indentation had been made in her skin: five knubbled pits, limned in flickering shadow.

"Darling?" Edward said.

I pulled my gaze from Ermintrude. "Yes? Yes, dear?"

"Don't you have anything to say to our guest?"

His look was mild, and firm.

"I don't know," I said. "Do I?"

"I think," said Edward, "you ought to apologise. For putting her on the spot."

"I wasn't aware I had," I said.

Edward's eyes remained on me.

"It wasn't my intention," I said.

"Nevertheless," said Edward.

"You were a *bit* much, old girl," Julia agreed.

"Yes, a bit," said Alexander.

Everyone looked at me.

I looked at Ermintrude. My throat itched. I cleared it.

"I'm sorry, Ermintrude," I said. "It was rude of me to question you."

I crossed my knife and fork on my plate.

"To Peter, also," said Edward.

The servant leaned in, retrieving my plate. I could not see Edward's face anymore.

"I'm sorry, Peter," I said.

"Not at all," Peter said. "Ermintrude is unused to company. I like to think I'm instructing her in the ways of polite society."

"Would that more society ladies could receive such instruction," said Henry. Everyone laughed.

I became aware of a sensation at my ear—prickling, scratching, insistent. It was barely loud enough to be called a sound: almost subaural, a muffled mosquito-hum. It was wordless, desperate. A dog, whining to be let inside. A woman, screaming in a padded room.

I turned to Ermintrude. Her stupid, unraveling face smiled into mine.

I stared at her. The longer I stared, the louder the sound became. It seemed impossible that the others could not hear it, and yet (I turned my head, my movements faster and faster), none seemed to hear it but me.

I looked at Peter. He caught my eye; looked at Ermintrude; looked away.

The lobster was served.

"Oh, my," said Julia.

"Look at those little arms," said Hyacinth.

"Lobsters don't have arms, silly," said Henry. "Those are legs."

"You should've seen this one squirm when the cook put it in the pot," said Edward. "As if it were trying to run. Quite funny, really."

"How awful," said Hyacinth. She accepted her plate and speared a morsel on her fork.

My cheekbone was beginning to throb.

"Darling?" said Edward. "Aren't you eating?"

I could think of nothing but Ermintrude's face; could hear nothing above her soft and strangled screaming. Surely they must hear her, I thought. Surely they must *know*.

"I'm afraid I'm rather full," I said.

"Oh, but dearest," said Edward. "Good-quality lobster is so hard to get ahold of these days."

"Indeed," said Julia.

"No, really." (The screaming. I could barely hear myself speak.) "I couldn't eat another bite."

"I shouldn't worry, Edward," said Peter. "Ermintrude is eating enough for everyone tonight. Darling, if you keep this up, my ring shan't even fit on your finger anymore."

Everyone laughed. (The screaming, the screaming. It would never stop.)

"I think it's charming," said Edward. "One's fiancée ought to be grateful for what one provides."

Peter was looking at Ermintrude. The candles were guttering. His eyes glittered in the dimming light. "All the same," he said. "Greed is such an unattractive quality. One should learn to accept what one is given."

(She would never stop. That loose, frayed stitch-mouth. It would scream and scream forever.)

"I don't think she's eaten so very much," I said. My voice sounded so weak.

"Do you agree, dearest?" Peter asked Ermintrude. His elbows were on the table again. Hands clasped. "Ah. Well. Perhaps I'm wrong. Do you think I'm wrong?"

"We have plenty," I said. "It's no trouble."

"Darling," Edward said. "Please."

"The ladies concur," said Peter. "It would seem I'm wrong. It would seem dear Ermintrude has *not*, in fact, been making an absolute pig of herself all evening."

"I suppose she *has* been putting it away, rather," said Julia.

"Quite," said Henry. "If Hyacinth ate half so much, she'd never get one leg into the new London frocks, would you, darling?"

"You beast," said Hyacinth.

Peter pushed his chair back. Stood. His knife was under his hand. "Excuse us," he said.

He hauled Ermintrude up by the arm. Her head fell back.

(The screaming was so choked, so muffled.)

"Hurry back," said Edward, as the lobster's remains (ripped and rent and torn apart) were cleared away. "I've an announcement to make."

"Oh?" said Peter, pulling Ermintrude towards the terrace. The knife was loose in his grip. "How thrilling. Don't start without me."

"Wouldn't dream of it," called Edward.

The terrace doors shut.

The dining-room doors opened. The servants wheeled the coffee-service inside.

"Not making a very good first impression, is she?" said Hyacinth. "Poor dear."

(I could hear her, on the terrace. Screaming, screaming. Peter made no sound.)

"Bit of a bumpkin, I'd say," said Julia. "You saw that dress? Two seasons ago, if it's a day."

"Just another of Peter's shopgirls, then," said Henry.

(Make it stop, I thought.)

"Another common little woman. What a let-down."

(Please. Do whatever you want. I can't bear it.)

The servants lifted the coffee-service onto the tabletop.

On the terrace, under the frosted glass, Peter did something.

(The screaming stopped.)

I watched black liquid pour, steaming hot, into bone china.

(I had begged it to stop and it had. How glad I was. How grateful.)

"I say," said Henry. "Do you think Peter's alright?"

(It was almost seven-thirty.)

"Perhaps we should fetch him," said Alexander.

(Something had been done.)

"We can wait," said Edward. "Can't we, darling?"

(The announcement was to be made at seven-thirty.) (On the dot.) (We had agreed.)

"Yes," I said. "We can wait."

The terrace doors remained shut.

(He did something.)

The servants passed the cups to the guests. Hyacinth blew the steam from hers. Henry gave her a look, and she stopped.

Edward pushed his chair back. Stood. I saw him reach for his glass.

The terrace doors opened. Peter strode in. Dark stains soaked the cuffs of his shirt. He replaced his knife on the table, slipped the diamond ring discreetly into his pocket, and sat. "Apologies," he said. "Ermintrude shan't be rejoining us."

"Oh, bad luck," said Julia.

Edward reached for the smallest spoon.

A sound began to vibrate my eardrum. A scratching, a whining, a choked and muffled scream. I looked about for its source, but the night had grown too dark, the candlelight too weak. The shadows were too strong now. In every corner of the room and outside on the terrace, there was nothing left to see.

"Everybody," said Edward. "Your attention, please."

The sound was rising in volume, in urgency. Surely, I thought, they must hear it. Surely, I thought, it must drown him out.

Edward looked into my eyes. "I'm delighted to announce…"

He continued to speak, and the others reacted with great joy and approbation, but I heard nothing more. The screaming was too loud, behind my lips and between my teeth, gathering at the back of my throat. It sounded no different than it had before. It sounded the same as it always had.

Amelia Mangan is an author currently living in Sydney, Australia. Her short stories have been featured in a number of publications, including *The Best Horror of the Year Vol. 11, The Rose Books Reader Vol. 01: Primal Scream* and *Storyteller: A Tanith Lee Tribute Anthology,* and adapted in audio form by Jason Hill for the hit podcast *Chilling Tales for Dark Nights.* Her first novel, *Release,* was published in 2015.

SIMON BESTWICK

Polodski's Bride

On Bone Street, people enjoy themselves any way they can, but actual celebrations are rare.

We're all refugees here, after all, and none of us are ever going home. There's only one entrance to the street—under the viaduct at the end—and no exit. The Closers see to that.

So some people drink, some take drugs, and some people get up to whatever takes their fancy with the working girls and boys at Dahlia's establishment. Whatever you please—that's the Bone Street way, so long as others aren't harmed. Whatever their private thoughts, no one passes judgement, as long as you keep that rule.

If only the world, or worlds, we came from had done the same. I'd say *if only we had*, but it isn't that simple. We've all taken at least one human life, true—that's why the Closers came after us, and why we ran, and were lucky enough to stumble out from under the viaduct onto Bone Street's cobbles—but Sadie, for instance, was forced to do so in self-defence.

I was in the army for years, and ended lives aplenty, but the Closers didn't care about them; another death entirely brought me here.

But those are other stories, and not the one I'm telling now. I mention Sadie and myself because it's relevant. As I said, actual celebrations are few and far between, because there isn't much here to celebrate. The closest we usually get is someone's wake; if the deceased is lucky, someone will have a few kind words to say about them, but if nothing else we can salute them escaping Bone Street in the only way anybody does. That night, though, there was a genuine reason, and it was heartening to see it seemed to please most people.

No one knew when there'd last been a wedding here, or even if there ever *had* been one. People got together, of course, but few saw any point in making it formal. Sadie and I probably wouldn't have thought to, except our engagement and wedding rings had been gifts from a friend. *In case you ever decide to* had been pretty much the last thing he'd said to me before he died. But that's another story too.

Anyway, here we were. There's no church or courthouse, so the ceremony was held in Bone Square, behind the Station Hotel, in front of the statue with no face or plaque whose name no one could remember. Droopy Sykes—who as an ex-barrister was the nearest thing to a legal authority anyone could find—was sobered up and managed to keep the text of the ceremony in focus long enough for us both to say "I do" and put the rings on. And that was that.

There was nowhere to hold the reception except the bar of the Station Hotel itself, which was slightly awkward as I manage the place and the only other bar-person (part-time) is Sadie. Luckily my friend Ahmed—the only Iranian Goth I've ever met—took over for the evening; he's surprisingly quick on his feet for such a burly man. He also provided the food; nothing fancy, just a selection of pizzas, but there were no complaints. You have to make damn good food if you insist on calling your establishment Ahmed's Kebab House of Death and play "Fields of the Nephilim" on a continuous loop.

Everyone was there. Droopy Sykes, of course—he'd have crawled through fifteen miles of crocodile and elephant-leech-infested swampland at the very mention of the words 'free bar'—and all the girls and boys from Dahlia's, even though Sadie was only part-time now. Victor Jepps, Dahlia's bouncer, clapped me on the back, solemnly congratulated me, then assured me that if I caused Sadie a moment's grief I'd live to regret it. Even Dahlia herself gave me a hug, before murmuring something of a similar nature in my ear.

Which was understandable. Sadie's the kind of person pretty much everyone develops a soft spot for. I was just lucky enough to have had her reciprocate.

It's always fun, on a night like that, to bet on who'll be the last one standing. My money would have been on Droopy, who after all could have taken the Olympic Gold for drinking his own bodyweight in Scotch without dying, but he called it a night surprisingly early—one a.m.—before wandering peaceably home. Mind you, he'd been downing triples all night, so he'd probably made up for lost time.

Sadie was never a big drinker; as I helped Ahmed clear up, as a hint to the few remaining punters, I vaguely realised I hadn't seen her for several hours, assumed she'd gone up to bed early and felt very guilty. At least until I found her curled up on one of the bench seats, snoring softly, with some kind soul's jacket tucked under her head for a pillow. I was fairly sure it was Victor's and made a mental note to return it to him in the morning. Or later that morning. Or in the afternoon. Or evening. Come to think of it, I just might wait until he next came in.

The remaining punters finally took the hint and wandered out. All but one, because there's always one. Although in fairness he was probably too drunk to get up unaided, which made 'last one standing' something of a misnomer.

Nonetheless, there he was: old Mr. Polodski, of Polodski's Mini-Mart. He'd been on Bone Street ever since I'd first arrived; in fact he'd been a fixture for as long as anyone remembered, his appearance apparently unchanging. Estimates of his age ranged between seventy and ninety.

He was a small, white-haired man, bald on top, with sharp (although not right now) blue eyes behind thick glasses and an incongruously red, Cupid's-bow mouth. He always dressed immaculately, in jacket and waistcoat, was always well-scrubbed, shaven, and scrupulously clean, with a perpetual smell of soap, aftershave and cologne. At the same time, his skin was tanned and leathery, his clean hands rough, and he was stocky and broad-shouldered, with only the smallest of paunches. Work, he always said, kept him fit and strong.

Right now, he was swaying on one of the bar stools, surrounded by a dozen empty shot glasses and softly crooning an old Polish ballad in a surprisingly tuneful voice, completely unaware of anything around him. It wasn't surprising; Polodski's preferred tipple was slivovitz, a particularly ferocious plum brandy I was fairly sure doubled as a barnacle remover for ships' hulls. I was fairly drunk myself, of course, but the air around him was so thick with the fumes I half-expected to pass out just from inhaling.

"Jakub," I said, tapping him on the shoulder. "Come on, mate. Chucking-out time."

"Mm?" he blinked, then managed to focus on me. "Tim?"

"Yep. Need a hand getting back?"

"Of course. Of course. Your wedding night, yes?" The old man grinned and winked, then wagged a finger at me. "Very important, the wedding night."

I glanced in the direction of my blushing bride, who'd begun to snore more loudly. "Yep. Wedding night. So let's get you home, eh?"

I'd never seen Polodski this drunk before, and had no idea what that might mean. Alcohol changes people, and rarely for the better. If you're lucky, they turn daft or forgetful or loud. If not, they turn mean or violent. I couldn't see him as one of the latter, but strongly suspected his transformation would involve selective deafness about being asked to leave and long, rambling anecdotes. And I still had to get Sadie up the stairs somehow.

In the end, I was half-right. He got up peaceably enough, or at least tried to: in the end, Ahmed and I shepherded him between us. He didn't struggle or resist, although it was still a slow process as he kept trying to walk sideways for some reason. But, once outside the Station Hotel, the bracing cold night air having perked him up, he started talking and didn't stop.

"A good woman, Tim," he said.

"I know," I said. "She is." And I very much wanted to be back with her, ideally snuggling up in bed to start married life as I hoped to go on.

"No, no," he said. "I mean that's what matters most in life. A good woman—or man, if that's your thing, I don't judge. Love comes in all shapes and sizes, after all. Yes? A partner, that's what we all need. Make our lives complete. It's hard, Tim, very, very hard, to go through life alone. But the love of a good woman... You have that, you can get through anything, as long as you're still alive. Without my Ewa—God! I'd have gone under long ago."

I knew Polodski was, or had been, married, as he was never without his wedding ring, but he lived alone, and there'd never been a hint of a romantic involvement with anyone, at any time—not even a visit to Dahlia's. And very few of us, if we were honest—male, female or other—hadn't done *that* at some point, the only other exception I knew of being Droopy Sykes, for reasons that should be obvious from his name and drinking habits.

Polodski had once described himself to my late friend Paul Manktelow as being a 'fellow widower,' but that was all anyone had ever known him say on the subject. Now, though, the alcohol seemed to have caused a benign short-circuit in the old man's brain, erasing the memory of his wife's death. Which meant he'd have more and worse than a hangover to contend with in the morning, assuming his recollections didn't improve before then. I hoped they didn't; he was hard enough work already without him breaking down in the middle of the street.

"We married—God! How long ago, now? It's difficult, reckoning time here, as you know. People come here from all different *years*, as well as places. Yes?" He wagged his finger again—first at Ahmed, then at me. "Seen a great deal happen since then, in any case. But anyway, the year was 1935. Just kids, both of us. From Toruń, where we both grew up. I was twenty-one, she was twenty-three. Yes! The older of us. Unusual back then. I was her toy boy!"

He laughed, stumbled, almost fell. Ahmed and I steadied him.

"I need to sit down," he said, sagging in our grip. "Just a moment. I'll be all right."

We exchanged glances, then lowered him to the kerb. He was heavier than he looked, and he'd be easier to move with his cooperation. He groaned, then breathed hard; Ahmed and I stepped back, thinking he was about to throw up, but he sighed and shook his head.

"1939," he sighed. "Married four years, and then the bastard Germans came. We ran, of course. Escaped. What else could we do? A near thing. Had to kill a German."

"That how you ended up here?" said Ahmed.

Polodski looked as though he'd been asked if he believed in the Tooth Fairy. "Of course not! We had many years left still, before all this." He gestured around him. "Besides, if the Closers were hunting killers, they were spoilt for choice, back then. Plenty of it to go round, and it had barely started. We escaped the bastard Germans, but fleeing them, we ran east—straight into the bastard Russians instead. People forget, people forget—Hitler, Stalin, they were like *this*, in '39." He held up a clenched fist. "One attacked from the west, the other from the east. A nutcracker. And Poland was the nut."

He sighed. "We were captured. Sent east. Siberia! That was no joke. Had to kill two men out there, just to stay alive. It was dog eat dog. Or whatever you could lay hands on—dogs, rats... and worse."

"So was *that* when you ended up here?" I said, hoping this would be the end of the tale.

He snorted. "Don't be silly, Tim! I told—it was *years*, before I ended up here. Far better pickings for the Closers back then, remember? And far more deserving cases."

Ahmed and I exchanged glances. We both knew—and so, to be fair, did Polodski—that what you deserved or didn't was immaterial. Serial killers and war criminals went untouched, while those trying only to avoid getting butchered themselves—like Sadie, again—had ended up forced to flee here.

He grunted. "Or I was lucky. Who can say? But in '41, the thieves fell out—Hitler invaded Russia, and suddenly Stalin was on our side. Sort of. In any case, there was an amnesty. A lot of Poles were set free—and that's how my Ewa and I ended up in England. That's how I survived, you see? How we both did. The love of a good woman. And of a good man, for her. At least, I hope...I tried to be..."

He gazed mournfully down at the cobbles. Oh Christ; he was about to turn maudlin. Tears before bedtime. I knew I was being uncharitable, but I was drunk and tired too.

Ahmed crouched beside him. "Feel up to walking, Jakub? Eh? Maybe a coffee?"

"Mm? Yes. Yes, of course." He patted Ahmed's shoulder. "Of course, you're right. You have beds to get to." He wagged his finger at me. "And your little Sadie, of course, eh, Tim?"

I forced a smile, nodded, and we helped him stand. I looked down the road, trying not to look into the black, open mouth of the viaduct or at the starless sky above. Streetlight gleamed on the damp cobbles. Bone Street isn't very long, but it felt considerably longer tonight. It also felt very empty: everyone else was in bed now, so all the inhabited buildings' lights were off, but I felt particularly aware of the untenanted ones, all the old shops that were boarded up and slowly falling apart.

Ahmed clapped me on the back. "Come on, my friend. Let's get him home."

"Good thinking," said Polodski. "Home is where the heart is. Yes? Homeward bound!" He sang a few bars of the Simon and Garfunkel song, then tripped and almost fell. We steadied him once more. "All right. Let's go."

I thought that had put an end to his ramblings, but a few seconds later he began again, a little more muted now, sadder.

"Poland," he said. "We never went back, you know, not even after the Communists left. We talked about it, made plans, but kept putting it off. We should have, really. I would have liked to. And Ewa. But there'd have been so little left of where we grew up. Our families, back in Toruń—both our families..." He shook his head. "The Nazis, the Communists—between them, our families were gone. But we should have gone back, just once. No excuses. The children were grown. We could have afforded it. Went abroad every year—Spain, France, Greece. We had a little shop, Ewa and I, in Manchester. Just like this one."

He pointed to the mini-mart, which we were finally approaching, although nowhere near fast enough for my liking.

"Got your keys, Jakub?" Ahmed asked.

"Mm? Yes. Yes. Wait."

He stopped again and ferreted in his pockets as we propped him up. He still couldn't stand unaided, but had no such problems with talking.

"I suppose," he said, "we were afraid of what we'd find. Or wouldn't. Too many memories, and nothing we recognised. And maybe, in our minds, we'd just written the old country off. Resigned ourselves to never going home. England was our home, now. Manchester. We probably knew Manchester, in the end, better than we'd ever known Toruń."

He scowled, looked around, then grimaced and spat on the pavement as if he'd tasted something sour. "Though we never heard of Bone Street, in all our time there."

"Yeah," I said. I understood that, being a fellow Manc myself: Bone Street is nominally part of that city, according to its street-signs and any written addresses you'll see, but you won't find it on any map of Manchester. Or indeed, any other. You won't find it at all, until the Closers come after you.

"Better, perhaps, if we never had," he said, then pursed his lips. "Although, of course, if not, we'd never..."

He trailed off, gazing upwards. "Jakub?" said Ahmed. "The keys?"

"Mm? Oh, yes. Yes." Polodski began rummaging again. "No, we never did go back. Maybe we would have, in time, but then—then Ewa, she got sick."

I tried not to sigh too audibly in relief when he finally produced his keys, and we steered him towards the door of his flat above the mini-mart.

"It was cancer," he said. "If we'd come to them sooner, the doctors said they might have done something, but we were both always raised to, to… endure? Yes. Stiff upper lip. Eh, Tim?"

"I suppose."

"You put up with pain, with discomfort, and soldiered on. Didn't make a fuss. And so she didn't, until she was in such agony she was crying out. And by then…by then…" His blue eyes were wet; he stopped and took off his glasses, wiping them on his sleeve. "I'm sorry. By then, she was… riddled. It was everywhere. Metastasised. The scientific term. Nothing to be done. Only drugs, to keep her comfortable."

He replaced his glasses. We guided him the rest of the way to his door, at which point he dropped his keys, then bent to pick them up at the same time I did and accidentally headbutted me. I rocked backwards, lost my balance and went sprawling on the cobbles.

The old man burst out laughing; even Ahmed was biting his lips in an effort to keep his face straight. Polodski wagged his finger at me again. "Too much to drink, eh, Tim?"

"Look who's talking," I said, more sharply than I really should have, but he didn't register it, just picked up his keys, swayed and again almost fell, till Ahmed caught him and propped him up—at last—against his front door.

"Ack." Polodski fumbled with the keys, peering at them myopically. "Now which blasted one is it?" It was a dismayingly large bunch of keys, and I was tempted to leave him to it. But I couldn't: Sadie would be furious if Polodski ended up sleeping on the pavement because we'd abandoned him, or injured himself—or worse—trying to climb the stairs unattended. And however tired and irritable and drunk I might be, I didn't want that happening to him either. So I sighed and let Ahmed help me up, and we watched and waited as he began trying every single key, one by one. Resuming his monologue as he did.

"There was a hospice," he said, over his shoulder; we mounted the pavement to stand beside him, so he wasn't distracted from his task. "But in the end, she didn't want that. She wanted to be at home. The home we'd made. Our little flat, above our shop. Just like here. Raised our children there, and after they moved out—well, we stayed. No point moving. We didn't want to retire. Keep working, keep busy. That's how you stay fit and healthy, in your old age. Only, of course, Ewa..."

He leant against the door, resting his forehead against the wood as he tried to fit another key in the lock. "It was just us. She had a morphine drip, for the pain. But even so, that last night..." He shook his head, without lifting it. "God, that last night. The way she breathed. Cheyne-Stokes, they call it. The breathing gets deeper, and deeper... sometimes faster and faster. Then it fades... fades... and stops. You think they're dead. And then—it starts again. Over and over and over. She just... wouldn't die. Despite everything. Until, at last—ah!"

A click, and the door swung open. Polodski stumbled through, groping for a switch. A very bright unshaded bulb came on directly above him, dazzling us both.

Beyond the door was a small vestibule, and directly in front of that was a staircase leading upward. Polodski flicked another switch, turning on a second unshaded light at the top of the stairs, then removed his coat, hung it on a hook beside the light switch and wove towards the stairs.

Here it was, the end of the journey. Only then he turned and plopped down on the bottom step, sighing. He looked down at his hands. His thumbs moved over one another.

"Jakub," I said, doing my best to keep my patience. "Come on. Let's get you to bed."

"There was a cushion," he said. "On my chair."

I heard Ahmed breathe out. Here it came; the confession.

"I stood and picked it up," he said. "I looked at it. It was old and worn. Faded. But so were we, it seemed fitting. I took a deep breath, steeled myself to do what had to be done. One last act of mercy for the woman I loved."

But the Closers didn't understand mercy, any more than they practised it. Or rather, they considered it irrelevant. This death, for whatever reason, had been the one that counted, and made Jakub Polodski their prey.

Except...

"And then," he said, "as I turned, she stopped breathing for the last time. I think, sometimes, she somehow knew. And decided to spare me the guilt." He chuckled, but his eyes filled up again. "One last act of mercy, indeed."

"So how *did* you end up here, then?" demanded Ahmed.

"Mm? Well... this will make you laugh. Or perhaps not. After she... after Ewa stopped breathing, I sat back down for... I don't know. The longest time, it seemed. I couldn't bring myself to call anyone. Not yet. Ambulance, doctors, whoever—they would come and they would take her away. Our quiet little place, they would come in, and there would be noise, and... they would take my Ewa away. And I just... wasn't ready for that.

"But I couldn't stay in the house, either. The silence in there, it was... oppressive. So I went out. If I'd just gone for a walk, it would have been different. But I took the car. I don't know why. Just drove and drove, around and around. Very late at night, like now. And suddenly, as I rounded a bend, a man—drunk, wandering home, like us—staggered out in front of me. And I couldn't stop in time."

Realising he was still holding his keys, he stuffed them back in his trouser pocket. "And that was it. Simple. Stupid. Random. He was dead, of course. Outright. I got out of the car, examined him, but there was nothing to be done. If there had been, I would have called someone immediately, waited with him. But there was nothing. And nobody had seen. So I drove home—I stopped at a payphone on the way and reported it, anonymously. I wasn't heartless, but..."

"But you'd have had to explain," I said. "Had to tell the police about Ewa, and then..."

He nodded. "I knew it was wrong. I knew sooner or later they must be told. That I must say goodbye. But..." He shook his head. "I couldn't. Not then. I wasn't ready. I didn't know when I would be. *If* I would be. But before that became an issue... the Closers came. I felt them. Their presence. *Closing.* Of course I knew I couldn't stay. And so I left."

He motioned around him. "And here I am. A refugee again. Eternal exile, this time—no chance of ever going home. To see the children, to see my homeland—Britain *or* Poland. Exile. But as I said before, Tim—you can bear anything, when you have the love of a good woman."

Which made no sense anymore, and I was drunk enough to say so, but thankfully Ahmed put a hand on my arm to shush me, as Polodski began to sing again, the same old love song as before..

"Let's get you upstairs, Jakub," he said.

"Mm? Oh, all right. All right."

It wasn't easy for three of us to negotiate the narrow staircase together, but we weren't leaving the old man to attempt it alone. I went ahead, holding his arm, while Ahmed—being the biggest and the bulkiest—followed behind, to catch him if he fell.

The landing carpet was threadbare, the wallpaper old and faded, but like the vestibule and Mr Polodski himself it was almost painfully clean, which made the smell all the stranger. It was dry and musty; caught at the back of your throat and made your eyes water. Polodski didn't seem to notice as he swayed along the landing, leaning against the wall, but he'd had a while to get used to it.

"I'm home, darling," he said, opening the bedroom door.

The smell immediately became so thick I almost brought up everything I'd eaten and drunk that night there on the landing carpet.

Mr Polodski just smiled and blinked sleepily at me, then switched on the light and tottered inside.

On the empty side of the bed was a neat, apostrophe-shaped indentation, worn into the mattress over time. On the other lay Ewa Polodski, in her white wedding dress. There was a veil, but it had been flung back across the pillow, exposing a face the colour and texture of autumn leaves.

Mr Polodski sat on the bed, trying with very little success to take off his shoes. The floor creaked and I heard Ahmed mutter "Oh God." The old man didn't notice.

All I could think of, just then, was how immaculate he'd always been. Always trimmed and shaved, always neatly dressed. How clean he always smelt. All the hours of washing, scrubbing, showering it must take, every day, to ensure none of us ever guessed what was up here.

"What do we do?" whispered Ahmed.

But he already knew the answer, same as me. This was Bone Street, after all: you didn't judge what others did to survive, as long as they harmed no one else. Polodski had been running the mini-mart for years, without a customer suffering so much as a day's illness that I'd heard of, and his wife was long past any kind of hurt. We'd do nothing, and we'd say nothing. We all had our secrets, and they were generally better off kept.

"We put him to bed," I said. "That's what. After that? Don't know about you, but in case you've forgotten I've got a wife of my own now."

"So you do." Ahmed half-smiled, then nodded. "All right. But—after you."

By the time we'd got Polodski's shoes off, he was practically asleep; after that, I eased him into the hollow his body had made in the bed over the years. By then Ahmed was already out on the landing; by the time I stepped out of the bedroom, he was halfway down the stairs.

I couldn't blame him; he'd seen enough. So had I, really, but I saw one thing more when I turned back to switch off the light: Polodski's bride, turning towards him in the bed, and reaching out to take him in her arms.

Simon Bestwick is a bisexual male author based in North-West England and the author of nine novels, seven under his own byline and two as Daniel Church. In addition, he's had five novellas and four full-length short story collections published; his short fiction has appeared in *Shakespeare Unleashed, ParSec Magazine* and *Nightmare Abbey*, and been reprinted in *The Best Horror of The Year*. His novel *The Ravening* has been shortlisted for the August Derleth Award, and his third Daniel Church novel, *The Sound of the Dark*, will be published by Angry Robot Books in October. "Polodski's Bride" is not his first visit to Bone Street. Nor will it be the last.

SCOTT J. MOSES

Other People

HONEY LAUGHTER FLOATS THROUGH the constrained bathroom, coaxing my gaze through the grimy window. The sun warm on my face. The lace curtains solemn. The dust congregated where the pane slips into the wood as if in reverence for today. I've never known why I notice these things.

The plastic tables end to end draped in white department store cloth, clustered balloons sprouting from zip-tied river stones before every other fold-out chair. Her parents' backyard. That would've made me feel a lesser man when I didn't know better. Back when an ex-girlfriend thought it was more about the presentation of the day, than the day itself, and said as much with her actions, though not her words.

See, we wanted to save money, inflation be damned, and with her folks offering—well, we couldn't pass it up. I silence the running tap, dry my hands on the beige towel.

A glimpse of my face in the fading mirror, memory assails me—

Me in a shoebox apartment, standing with a bowl of cereal cradled to my chest before a poorly mounted flatscreen. The dangling wires the mark of a true DIY job.

Just a kid, nineteen and newly out on my own.

I chuckle, adjust my black tie.

Come a long way from—

Dark threading reaches out to me from behind the blemish in the mirror—but no, it isn't growing at all. More *caught*, torn from a black suit or dress. The spider-webbed cracks exfoliating from the anomaly an infection. The mirror split up its center. The bisected halves of my face slid away from one another.

I blink, and the mirror's whole, as am I.

I run my fingers along the newly placed tungsten ring on my left third finger.

Must be stress...

We've planned this day forever, and now we're *here*. Another peek out the window, Kim's riverside-flowered veil on the table, her open-mouthed, red-lipstick smile as she touches a forkful of trout to her tongue. She in white, the north star to the others seated near her in black tuxes and ties, seafoam dresses as well. We wanted simplicity; I think we pulled it off. That joy of hers terrifying as the first day I laid awareness upon it. Knowing if I became attached, that given time, it'd be gone for the both of us. But also if I never asked her out on that rain-assaulted marina as some dorky college kid, the regret of not knowing her in this life would outweigh the inevitable loss of her, of something real.

A smile forms in me, and as I reach for the closed bathroom door, sharp pain shoots from behind my left eye. I wince, bring a hand to my face, the eye obstructed by thick gauze.

I stumble backward, dizzy with... *what is that?* Chamomile? Strawberries and cream?

Turning around, I grip the sink with shaky hands, stare myself in the face. Kim's smeared lipstick on my cheek and collar, signifying a beginning. How happiness is in this life, an abstract wish fulfilled. Something you never knew you wanted, needed, or ever deserved.

The pain claws behind my eye.

A waterfall to my rear as I hold Kim close. A picture taken there. Her dad smiling from behind the camera, pulling the trigger to hold captive this moment in time. He's smiling, as is Kim, as am I. The waters roar on to infinity behind us.

The split mirror, the gauze akin to a headdress on me, my suit-sleeve torn, frayed at the edge.

Her dad and I before the open trunk of a rusted sedan. The roaring water's descent the only constant akin to the first vision. He digs in and around the trunk, glances over to me, the vacant road. Worry seeping from his pores. Returning his eyes to me, he extends a revolver.

"They're coming," he says, pulling the slide back on his semiautomatic pistol, and turning to the jagged jaw of cliffs parallel with the waterfall's crest, he waves to the assumed nothing. The reflected glint of a scoped rifle winks back in the burgeoning sunlight.

I blink the memory away, and rubbing my temples, shake off the wrongness clambering over me. But no… it's the heavy stillness, the *quiet.* The celebration suffocated, and though intuition pleads against it, I pull back the curtain of the lone window, to their void stares. Some open-mouthed, all statuesque but for the occasional twitch of a jaw, a finger, or shoulder. These no-longer uprights a dry-rotted fence in how little they move. Placed long ago, though not meant to last the winter. How unalive they are.

No wind.

No birds.

The parallel slits in Kim's neck inhaling, exhaling, expanding, contracting. Her father's face sagging off another beneath. An ill-fitting bag draped over one desperate to see.

I jerk back and my elbow collides with the sink. The biting pain an exorcism.

Kim's dad and I firing the pistols at the black semi-circled SUVS pinning us there behind the bullet-shorn sedan. The waterfall at our back, all but drowning out the guns' clamoring screams.

He glances to the hill where another SUV climbs the winding mountain path.

Kim.

Her dad looks back to me with tears in his eyes, says, "They can't know. They can't."

And as the doors open and close from beyond our pinned view, and the heavy, rapid armored footfalls from those therein advance, bullets dinging off our shorn shred vehicle, he puts the gun to his head, pulls the trigger. They find me against the car's rear wheel, knees to my chest, pistol to my head, hesitating, staring at the hill where my beloved might rest.

The eruption of gunfire. The oil crows fleeing the trees. Their cawing the catalyst to some caged madness within me.

Hands seize my arms, but my pistol's long gone.

Tears in my eyes? Pathetic. They're made of stronger stuff, Kim and her father. And he never knew what she saw in me anyway.

A knock from beyond the bathroom door. The tap's hissing.

Didn't I turn it off...?

"Hey, you alright in there?" a muffled voice asks. "Not getting cold feet, are you?"

I turn from the door, reaching to the small of my back for the nothing now there.

What is this?

The knock again. Strawberries pungent in their colonization of the air. My throat's raw with it, gaze blurring.

That thread in the mirror's grasp.

My father peering up at me from his wheelchair, tears lining his eyes as Kim and her dad wait outside in the rusted sedan.

"I only wish I could see you do it," he says, and we shake hands.

I turn to leave, and he inhales, a whine therein. "Don't give the bastards nothin', hear? You go down like a wild beast, but a mute one at that. You make them regret crawling up from the sea, hear?" I follow his gaze to her picture on the nightstand. The only one in the room worth remembering. This no-longer-home. Her tight-lipped and staring off a balcony before the world changed. "Your mother deserved better."

I nod, and his grip tightens on mine before he releases me. Ending the closest thing to an embrace we've ever had. The car horn chirps, and turning for the splayed front door, I catch the desecrated one on the surgical slab in the room's rear. The metal gurney lowered to where someone sitting would have fair vantage. An array of tools spread between the creature's bipedal legs. The humanoid's blubber splayed as if a flower blossomed from its chest, as if it the flower itself. The intended design always meant to bloom, to die. Like us on the outside, unless you know what to look for.

The yellowed, pinned newspaper clippings on the corkboard atop the shorn creature. The dank, musty basement. The brine tang of the gutted creature behind my father in his workshop. Beside it there, the poorly rolled face of a woman, who lived once, walked around as you or I in the days when they tested land. Blending in. Their oceans simmering. Their ecosystem damaged from our selfish tendencies. And now, perhaps for the betterment of all, there are so few of us left.

A knock rattles the bathroom door in its hinges.

"Okay in there, Bill?"

Another now, less fist, more kick. The mirror beckons me. The torn threading from the sleeve of my wedding jacket a siren's song. The crater large as a clenched...

I punch the blemish in the glass, and blood seeps from my knuckles swarming the splits in the mirror. The pain awakening something in me. Drawing back, as the door behind me convulses, I strike it again *again*. My lipstick smeared cheek transfiguring in Rorschach, and where once the lip stain of my beloved imprinted the skin, three curved splices reside. As if the devil kissed me with upturned fangs, but at least *he* is known to us. These... well, they are beyond.

My hand screams, and dark walls intrude in my vision's periphery. Water pouring in from somewhere high. This place much unlike the bathroom some part of me still stands. The water, ravenous and to my neck now, my wrists and ankles bound to a chair, as I extend my chin high, though the pooling surface laps at my Adam's apple. The boy looking up at me, his milk-poured eyes as globes beneath the water's surface. Distorting my view of him as he undulates in mirage.

The others obstructed by one-way glass, huddled together, though I can't tell how many. The singular one, closer than the rest, pacing the confines of the one-way visage. It pauses, faces me from across the room as I strain to keep my head above the licking, brackish torrent, and bringing an appendage to its head, the boy that is not a boy rolls dead eyes back into his skull, and nods, returns them my way. And though his lips part, slits in his neck pumping beneath the rippling water, he speaks to me with his mind, as he has done before.

"They ask, is this not what you wanted? Tell us, then you may live in the dream made for you."

Kim's dad places his Glock to his temple, his eyes begging me to do the same. Kim's rifle erupting from the cliffside.

Head craned, I grin. My urine flowing into the rising water.

"Tell me," I say, smirking despite the angle. "As an outsider, what's your view on intelligence?"

His gills open, stiffen, and his eyes don't leave mine as the entity beyond pounds the glass. The hollow *thump-thump-thump* drowning out a language I'm sure I wouldn't understand.

Though he hasn't need to clear his vision, the boy blinks up at me from beneath the water, rises to his feet.

"Why turn away the only one here who looks out for you?" he says in my mind, gills fluttering. *"Who's taken pains to get your wife's scent right?"*

And as he closes his eyes, strawberries and chamomile permeate the room, kissing my face as acid rain from the ceiling. The room falls away with a whisper on my mind's ears.

"This is your last chance," he says. *"If not now, they will treat you as your father did us. An eye for an eye, a skin for a skin..."*

"She never smelled like this..." I slur with a smile through tunneling vision. "How little you know us."

The tall one places his hand upon the glass, its fingers quadruple-jointed and on the opposite side of our own. More immense fin or wing than digits. The static in my mind rises.

"E...*nough*," The tall one says in my mind now. Its voice deep, grating on my brain.

Do not forget...

The stench heavy in my lungs, my eyes burning.

"The answer... is no... longer worth the eff...ort. You disgust... us. Reek of your... father, and because... of this, you... will die twice."

Do not forget...

I'm thrust backward.

Do not forget...

...the words a one-line chorus in my mind.

The tap runs as I dry my hands. My wife's laugh on the wind beyond the closed window where the sun bleeds through laced curtains. I never thought I'd be here. Hell, I always thought marriage was for *other people.* Maybe, I was right.

A light knock on the door.

"You okay in there, bud?" a voice asks, chuckling now. "Your wife's wondering if you fell in."

My wife. That'll take some getting used to...

The chamomile on the air begs me to remember how we met. An itch in the small of my back, some unknown vacancy. The hissing tap behind me. My unbuttoned suit jacket floating at my sides as if I'm levitating. My head craned up as I spit up sludge from my lungs, coughing.

Shattered chaos beyond the window. The pounding on the door. How it shakes as I reach for the loosed shard knocked into the sink. It tearing into my palm as I clench down. I don't know why I'm overcome with the urge to hurt myself. Maybe it's to know this marriage can't go bad if I end it here on our wedding day. If I sell when the market's high.

The window shatters inward as webbed hands claw through the wall's opening. Green water swarming in from the backyard. The half-split door giving way as the crimson slides down the vertical slit in my forearm.

My wife's hands to her mouth as a man with sagging face and gills wrestles the glass from my numbed fist. I collapse, smiling, though I don't know why. My head craned upward, held aloft by some reverse gravity. And though my hair floats, I cough and hack as panicked bubbles flee my lungs, this dying vessel. Kim looks down at me, and as she pulls her hands from her face, disappointment overtakes her features.

I know now that she realizes we've grown apart. That she's different, as am I. That... *no*, my wife, the woman I love, is up on a mountain somewhere. Watching over me through the scope of a rifle. The wink of the sun across her view, as we give this a real go.

My lungs fill with brackish water as the blood leaves me entirely. This willing transfusion. What did the pastor say in this twilight daydream? Something about the marriage of two beings casting themselves aside to become one flesh. A new creature. But if we're truly *one* now, what becomes of the husks of us? You'll have to tell me, when this life-worn shell rejoins yours in that fabled place we all know we're going, yet have never been.

Show me the ropes, Love. I'm sorry, I'm new at this... being dead, though I'm an attentive scholar. See, I've been dying a while now without you here.

Scott J. Moses is the author of *Our Own Unique Affliction* (Shortwave Books). An active member of the Horror Writers Association, his work has appeared in *Cosmic Horror Monthly*, *The NoSleep Podcast*, *Planet Scumm*, and elsewhere. He also edited *What One Wouldn't Do: An Anthology on the Lengths One Might Go To*. He is Japanese American and lives in Maryland. You can find him on Instagram, Bluesky, or scottjmoses.com. He is represented by IAG for TV/Film.

JOE KOCH

Starving Stones, Speaking Stones

WHEN THE HIGH-PEAKED CHAPEL with its mottled grey stones settled into the cleft of the mountainside, Daniel enjoyed a deep, satisfied breath. The air at high altitude was free of the grit of the desert or the lurid dampness he disliked in the swamps. He stepped out through the ancient arch of the doorway and blinked at the gauze of snow on the rocky ground and the searing blue sky beyond the pines. Somewhere near the Rockies, he supposed, though he didn't know why.

Searching for some memory to verify the impression, he came up blank.

Perfect, he thought, nodding to himself.

Pastor Dan wasn't a man of faith, not exactly. He didn't imagine any god or spirit world, not unless memories were ghosts and faith a capitulation to history: the past's follies of ambition, the future's treachery of hope. No, he was a practical tradesman, pleased to live forever in the present moment, stirred by his freedom from tethers to start clean again, and again.

How many times had it been? Did it matter? He was content to land on this mountain cleft, to breathe the pristine air that left his chest lighter, his lungs more youthful and expansive. He returned through the looming grey stone arch, the heavy wooden doors groaning closed behind him, and set about with his usual preparations before the next hopeful couple arrived to be wed.

Inside, the chapel was windowless and murky. Ancient masonry waited, alive with an eternity of ransomed memories. Microorganisms in the mud and pores of the brickwork might have recounted the history of human matrimony if the starving stones had chosen to speak. Listening patiently for the intonation of vows, they survived, for what was gained by wedding celebrants always entailed a certain degree of loss. No commitment occurred without compromise, and over time, enough small sacrifices amassed into a feast. The starving stones might have spoken of many devoured lives to Pastor Dan, but they did not. Secrets ruminated in the rock.

Accustomed to the cool reticence, Daniel steadied his steps by touching the wall as he descended into the deepest crypt. He was no longer young. His left knee rebelled against each drop. He worried he'd wasted too much time outside. Perhaps the chapel listened to his thoughts through his fingertips and forgave his shaky pace.

Reaching the dirt floor where the cramped stairwell curved into a subterranean alcove, he gathered the tools of his calling and hurried them upstairs. Book, candles, dagger, and a small crate that remained always closed, its double seams of pink velvet piping pursed like the dusty lips of a corpse beneath its rusted lock.

He filled candelabras with fresh tapers and straightened those not yet spent. With a jab to the third finger of his left hand, he lit each tallow candle with a drop of blood. He squeezed his finger, and a sigh hissed upward as another wick ignited. The chapel walls came alive.

At the tip of each flame, smoke ascended into nothingness, releasing another flash of distant thought in Pastor Dan that flickered into absence. He tingled at the back of his neck with each small, sweet loss. That brief physical sensation, like his skin's response to a lover, was all that remained after each memory had fled.

He heard a dog barking at age twelve, vaguely aware that he should know its name. A punch missed his jaw outside of a dive bar, and as he dodged the fist, he heard a woman yelling as he fell and sprained his wrist. Then the smell of green curry cooked on a stove, a hand he could no longer attribute stirring it excitedly as the bubbles whispered and popped. Although the dish was prepared in celebration and the hand merged toward a younger version of Pastor Dan with affection and joy, he didn't try to grasp it. He let the luscious smell and the impassioned stirring go up in candle-flame with all the rest of the remnants of his past.

Next, he read aloud a formula against the future from the ancient book. Muscle memory served him where the gift of perpetual obliteration had stripped most words of meaning. Enunciating the present toward the precipice of a single eternal void, he paused in confusion, his mind going blank. Frozen in quiet panic, in the sudden blackness of the moment, Pastor Dan was struck with total consciousness of his not-knowing, his absolute loss of self.

A question like a slap in the face: *What year is this?*

In his hands, the book had become an unrecognizable artifact. Overwhelmed, he stared at its oblique configuration of lines and dashes as the candlelight wavered, casting shadows on the ageless stone that gestured at him impatiently to finish. Over his muteness, the sounds of cheerful voices from outside approached. Laughter ascended the chapel steps.

No, no—it was too soon. He had to complete the... what was it, a prayer? But Daniel had never been religious. Why was he here? Who was opening the great double doors of this archaic, cavernous structure where he found himself trembling idiotically, as if deposited mid-nightmare?

A window had fissured open in the rafters, sending a shock of sunlight through the dim interior. Trapped in the startling beam, the book closed—*Daniel* closed it, but it felt like someone else worked his joints and muscles where his ego found no purchase. To the small and disparate particles of Pastor Dan, it seemed an outrage that the closing was too casual to match the severity of the rift above. The chapel roof cracked asunder into a prismatic skylight, opening up a distorted reality that somehow imitated elaborate stained glass.

The doors groaned open. Chatter and exclamations of awe echoed around the stone walls. The couple—no, he counted three people, then four, and then five in all—entered with backpacks, clad in colorful hiking gear. They looked unbelievably young to Pastor Dan, radiant from sun exposure and freshly exhilarated from their climb up the mountain.

"Stunning," said a stately somebody with long dark disorderly hair. They tilted their head at the ceiling. "How did you say you found this place?"

"Wasn't me. Mel gets all the credit on this one."

The answer came in a resonant, gravelly voice from a short, hefty pale-skinned person in a rainbow-striped cap whose backpack seemed twice their size. They handed a half-gallon repurposed jug to a strong-looking woman in shorts and a sleeveless crop top. Her outfit showed off a panorama of colorful tattoos. Presumably Mel, she flipped a ponytail with pink highlights and took a swig of the sepia-tinted liquid. "Nope. Had to be Petra's great-aunt. Wasn't she here in the seventies when it was all weed bikers and psycho killer hippie cults?"

"Not according to Petra. I could swear it was you who found it."

"Doesn't matter anyway." Mel spun in an awkward, exultant pirouette. "Fucking wild. This place is old as shit!"

Catching sight of Pastor Dan behind the altar with the incomprehensible book folded in his arms across his chest, the pain of confusion and subdued panic in his eyes, she stumbled to a halt. "Oh, sorry, Father. I didn't see you over there! How are you?" She linked the short, hefty person's arm in hers and approached, offering Daniel the jug. "Do you partake?"

Her companion snorted and looked down. "Cut it out."

"It's a valid sacrament. You're not a priest. You don't get to decide."

The party converged on the altar, gleefully loud, removing backpacks, stretching, rubbing each other's sore shoulders, and surrounding Pastor

Dan with such unabashed warmth that he fumbled as he dropped the book from his sweaty grip to accept the libation.

"I'm not a priest." He indicated the crimson embroidery on his black robe that looped his neck in arcane script instead of a traditional white clerical collar. "In fact—"

He stopped. Should he admit that he didn't know his qualifications, or how he got here, or who he really was? Beg these people for help? Befuddled, awash in the group's contagious glow, Pastor Dan didn't want to be a disappointment and ruin their celebration. They seemed so delighted, had hiked all the way up the mountain to get here. He didn't want them to leave him alone. "Please, uh, don't call me Father. Daniel or Pastor Dan will suffice. Thank you for this."

He raised the jug in a toast.

Taking a sip to be polite, he tasted honey and ginger, a pleasant surprise instead of alcohol. After a second and much bigger swig, the party began introducing themselves in a flurry of names that Pastor Dan couldn't keep organized. Their energy overwhelmed him, flooding the hungry, silent space with more life than he imagined the starving stones could swallow. The group's camaraderie felt wonderful and strong. He basked in it, telling himself it was powerful enough to make them immune.

A sudden sense of longing arose in him, strangely akin to jealousy. As they passed the jug around, including Daniel as if he were a long-standing member of their circle of friends, he drank and listened with guarded pleasure, enjoying their shared chatter and unreserved affection one moment, painfully aware how different he was from them in the next.

It wasn't just that he was older. He was less vital, less his full self.

Unsettling, this sense of shattered recognition, of being someone and somewhere he'd forgotten, a whole lost existence like a word on the tip of his tongue. The stately person—already Daniel had misplaced their name in his confusion—whose height and austerity contrasted so charmingly with their unruly hair, questioned him enthusiastically despite Daniel having no answers.

"Did someone move the whole structure brick by brick?" Bending, peering, touching, they examined the chapel walls and carved stone altar. "The masonry seems pre-Roman, but that modernist glass can't be original. Was it done during reconstruction, maybe to hide some damage during transport?"

Daniel said, "I have no idea."

"The chancel looks Gothic, and yet the shape of those arches, do you see? Not typical for the period. None of these materials and styles make sense together. It's astounding. The more you look, the more anachronisms you find."

"I'm at a loss," he said.

"But surely you must know the origins of the chapel, who established it or rebuilt it here. Tell me: is it really authentic, or some expertly wrought folly?"

They were so insistent, and his ignorance so total, and yet his pleasure at their company so unexpected that Daniel almost wanted to laugh. He winced and squinted up at the skylight, the flawed and rupturing reality that the visitors viewed as art. Was it some sort of omen? He felt a sense of hysterical amusement bubbling up around the needling terror that he had forgotten something—or many things—of dire importance. "I suppose in here..." he said, and paused, lost for a split second. Then it came to him.

"...we exist outside of history."

"That's so *cool*." Mel spoke before the wild-haired hiker could question him again. "Like how cool that you can just walk into a sanctuary and *boom*." She clapped. "Eternity!"

A muscular blonde with large, dangling earrings—Daniel was fairly sure that was Petra—began clearing the backpacks and gear away from the altar. The shorter person with the gravelly voice and striped knit cap helped, moving everything onto a rear pew out of sight. The fifth member of the party, a young man with a slight frame, sparse beard, and nondescript hair and eyes, put a protective arm around Mel. He muttered to her with a subdued, mischievous gleam in his eye.

"I don't think that's what the word means."

She gave a gentle shove. "Maybe things mean something different in here. That's what churches are for, right Father? Oh, I'm sorry, *Pastor* Dan. It's cool we have two Daniels today." She nudged the bearded man again and turned to Pastor Dan, grabbing his hand. "Does that mean we're super extra double blessed?"

He and the young man both laughed, but the echoes ended abruptly as Daniel's heart leapt into his throat. For a moment, he couldn't breathe.

He yanked away his hand.

Stressed by questions for which he had no answers, questions that prodded at the edges of a vast, creeping uncertainty, for not only did he not know where or when the chapel had originated, he also had no idea how it moved and situated itself in different places and times, or why the stones had seduced him into mindless service with their blissful draining. How they listened and absorbed his innermost thoughts, erasing desire and fear; except when the mysterious communion failed and his serenity cracked and Pastor Dan *remembered*—

No. He would not allow it.

His voice shook. The ceiling stretched higher, striking the grey stones with emissions of irregular multi-colored light. Colors danced on Daniel's black robe. He said, "Are you the happy couple getting married today?"

"Oh, no," Mel squawked. "Nothing like that! You have to give me away, I guess." She hugged the friend—perhaps brother—beside her as she cackled.

Turning back to Daniel, she took his hand again as if he were a beloved elderly uncle to be indulged. He flushed with anger—he wasn't *that* old—and shame for his ignorance. He had nothing to show for all his time serving the chapel. Something about her touch told him it had been a very long time.

"Falton, me, and Loom"—here Mel nodded toward the stately person with wild hair—"are doing our commitment ceremony. We've been together three years. It's not a legal marriage, of course, but my dad's an attorney and he figured out we can incorporate like an LLC to share legal rights as partners. You know, buy a house and all that. Deal with custody rights and estate planning for kids. You're not breaking any laws by holding the service here, I promise."

That visceral sense, once again, of isolation and recognition, of invasive thoughts erupting with simple, ridiculous, and yet elusive clarity. Had he always been such a fool? He adored Mel almost instinctively, angrily, with a jealous hope that had no conscious object. An abstract rage at being cheated. Yet he felt strangely protective, too.

Loom tossed their hair, straightening up after inspection of the chapel's architecture. "We'd like to include a drumming circle. Would that work better for your process after the vows, or do you recommend it for opening the ceremony?"

Falton, the shorter person in the knit cap, scurried from the rear pews, waving papers they pulled from a pocket of their hiking vest. They hadn't removed any of their outdoor gear. "Vows first. We've been over this." With a chastising glance, they handed Loom a page. "Here you go."

Mel broke away from Daniel to snatch her vows. Falton taunted her and whipped the paper away, inciting a game of chase. Loom rolled their eyes. Mel caught her page by darting behind Falton's back and raised it up in both hands. Beaming, she bounced on the balls of her feet.

"I'm so excited!"

Loom towered over Falton imperiously. "You can't just come into the poor little man's parish and boss him around. Show some respect."

"Honey," said Falton. "Once the drums start, no one is going to stop and chill for all that, and you know it. We'll read first."

"Honey? Really?"

Mel shimmied up in between Falton and Loom, jiggling against Loom's shoulder. "Especially not this bitch."

"Stop that. Well, I suppose it *is* the natural progression." Loom turned to Pastor Dan. "Would that be amenable? We've written our own vows, but if you have certain traditions...?"

He stared. When contact had ceased with Mel, Daniel realized the stones had leached no life through him. He couldn't understand it. Instead of serving as a conduit via physical touch, he'd been connected to her, experiencing his own responses, a confusion of warmth, wonder, jealousy, misplaced rage, unmoored yearning. Emotions he didn't have names for.

Nothing felt right anymore. The party seemed to be waiting for him to do something, but a subtle, piercing, sound had invaded his head, a sound like distant infants screaming. The screams brought images, cascading daydreams that shook Daniel with horrible certainty.

A dog's playful barking, hours spent inseparable in summer, on weekends, and the musky scent of comfort overriding his mother's detergent fragrance on clothes and sheets. The tattered blue collar and tags he'd kept as a treasure when his friend's short life had come to an end.

"*Ranger,*" he said, reading the engraved name.

The stones were no longer silent.

Pastor Dan grabbed the book from the altar, crumpling its pages in a rush to find the right chapter and finish the failed reading. The starving screams assaulted him with memories. All he'd willingly sacrificed now shoved to get back into his mind. The rift in the chapel's expanding rafters shone. All logical proportions had been transgressed. Polarities had switched.

Haltingly, he stuttered through his resurging comprehension. Syllables gained meaning and combined into words; the sentences they formed made horrid sense. As the incantation turned to ash on his tongue, the rift opened further, madder, and brighter. Its colors rained down in a shimmering mist of catastrophic light.

"We have to get out," he said, looking up from the useless book like a child. "It's too late."

Mel took his elbow and rubbed his arm. More emotions, more memories. The young people gathering around him didn't hear the screaming of the stones as memories disgorged. He wanted to pull away, and yet he wanted to stay with them, be with them. He wanted to be one of them.

Mel said, "It's all good. Relax and have a nice trip with us."

The bearded person pulled the book quietly from his clenched hands as Petra set up several rustic handmade drums. Loom cocked their head at Daniel and waved Falton over. "Oh, you poor thing. Yes, get him some water."

"No pressure to perform," Falton said, offering a thermos. "Stand in our circle, as a witness. We didn't really need a minister, anyway. You just, uh, kind of came with the place."

They grunted apologetically. Pastor Dan stared at the thermos, dumbfounded by full awareness that he was not a pastor, not at all, and never had been. He wasn't even religious.

He saw the chapel from the outside at a slight distance. Visions flashed through him of finding it, entering it; glad voices, cheerful expectations, a day of celebration. He had come here young and hopeful like the hiking party, attending a wedding with cherished friends. He felt warm and close to the people around him, both in the vision and now. How good to be part of a love that was bigger than craving, beyond mere *need*, that flowed so bountifully it encompassed many instead of one. How caring the young people tending to him now, especially Mel with her encouraging touch. Even Petra softened and drew near to reassure him everything would be all right.

It was achingly familiar, an archetype of all he'd lost. He turned to Mel stupidly, searching—for what? His mouth felt burnt and chalky.

Beside him, the bearded person, like a youthful shadow. Same height, same nondescript hair and eye color, and hadn't Daniel once worn a shaggy, sparse beard when he was finally able to start growing one?

Mel released him as the vows began. Something inside his chest went cold and plummeted into his stomach like a stone. He had come here like them, yes; come here young and never left.

No, none of this was real. His sense of impending doom, his gut twisting with urgency—merely the effects of some drug. It was all an illusion. It had to be. There were no hidden memories to haunt him, to warn him, to save him. Let the stones scream; he would not listen.

Let them scream. Let them starve.

The chapel was situated outside of time, the celebrants mere ghosts. And although what Daniel envisioned couldn't be real, in an agonizing rebirth of lost images he saw very clearly that Mel's hand stirred the fragrant green curry and reached for him with affection.

She was a man in the memory, and it was the day Daniel came out. Mel was the first person he risked telling. Beyond the gift of her acceptance, she insisted right away on making a big dinner to celebrate. She said she'd wondered why he was so much hungrier lately. She'd make sure there were plenty of leftovers. The green curry was delicious, and she made a terrible mess.

The world opened up after that. They shared courage and resources to cope with parents and old friends, made new friends like Petra, Loom, and Falton—and yet, Daniel knew there was no way this found family in the chapel could be anything but a fantasy of a life he never had.

As if to insist upon her veracity, Mel graced him again in flashback, as lively as the woman now reading her vows. Early in her transition, he defended her against a slur outside a favorite dive bar. She yelled. Daniel dodged a fist aimed at his jaw. He'd never been in a fight before. Falling, he sprained his wrist, making himself bloody enough to satisfy the frat boy. Mel teased him later while they waited at the ER that his incompetence saved him from worse injury.

"Seriously," she said. "Don't ever do that again. Not with the way people are these days."

"It's not right, though."

"Who do you think the cops are gonna throw in jail? You or Mister Trust Fund?"

"I don't care."

"Look, I'm proud of you. And you know what? You did better than most guys, just a few scratches. That's, like, fucking awesome! But I need you alive. Deal?"

A white web of old scar tissue on the meat of Daniel's thumb proved the injury was real. He rubbed the familiar rough ridges as the stones screamed and the chapel flickered in and out of eternity. Memories of the future mimicked the dance of candlelight on grey walls. As the ceremony ended, Daniel took the young bearded man's hands in his and checked for scars.

He held on too long. More than anything, he wished that he could stay here forever, poised in this memory of shared happiness with the wedding party, and forget in bliss.

The bearded man laughed awkwardly and shook Daniel's hands as if receiving congratulations, clapped his shoulder, and pulled away. Petra started drumming. Mel tittered with joy, their pink ponytail bouncing as the three celebrants hugged. Loom's usual austerity melted. They fanned away tears as they kissed Mel and then yelped as Falton grabbed them in a bear hug, lifted them up, and spun around.

Outside the circle, Daniel reached for the dagger on the altar. To his alarm, the lock that had been rusted shut on the small crate beside it was sprung. Using the tip of the dagger, he opened the lid. Within, the dusty pink velvet lining cradled a bone with one knobby end on fire.

The flame consumed no fuel; not fabric, wood, or curious fingers when Daniel tested its heat. It seared him with pain, and yet no mark appeared on his skin. Daniel picked it up by the shaft like a mace and raised the dagger in his other hand.

"Leave," he said, trembling behind the altar. His voice was weak. He tried again with more force. "All of you need to leave here. Now. Go. Get out!"

The drumming stopped. The dancers paused before their revelry had begun, more puzzled than fearful. Pastor Dan bellowed with all the fear and love breaking his heart, a mad black-robed evangelist brandishing both dagger and flaming bone mace. "Listen to me: I said you have to leave this place!"

On the opposite side of the altar, the young hikers may have questioned him or tried to talk him down. Their voices were subsumed by the screaming of the stones. As old as Gehenna, ashes in the mud and lime binding the masonry with burnt offerings, divinatory vivisections on ancient altars, the agony of stolen and forfeited brides, children; the bitter discipline of seers who read erupted bowels before the fires were lit. Their wailing blasted his ears.

They were all Daniel could hear as his creeping omniscience slowed time into a single, inescapable point.

First, he felt something like a giant insect buzz his face and bite his cheek. A wet sensation woke him to the realization that he was bleeding. He recognized the wound with sudden paralyzing urgency. His thoughts flailed. It was as if his mind mocked him with the most useless of gifts, remembering events at the exact moment that they happened, no better than extreme *deja vu*.

Next, Mel's crop top bloomed crimson across her chest. Her tattoos were splashed and quickly saturated as she shuddered, grasped at nothing, and stumbled. With a baffled expression, she collapsed toward the altar, leaving a stain on the ancient grey stone where her head bounced.

Petra had already fallen. They lay twisted across their drum, arms tangled and inert. Loom and Falton scuttled low to the ground, gasping in panic and pain, huddling together behind a pew in a growing pool of red that formed dark branches across the veins of the mortar. As one went limp and the other gave out a cry of grief, they slumped into silence. The stones flooded with color.

Daniel didn't take cover or search for the bearded man, his young doppelganger. Instead, he stared dumbly at the open doorway of the chapel, shocked with recognition. Despite the colors erupting from the false skylight, it was night outside. Framed by the mountainside forest's snowy glint of moonlight, yet another double, a hoary old man in tattered robes, paused on the threshold and lowered the long-barreled firearm he'd been aiming at the altar.

He took a step forward and grinned at Daniel. His teeth were dark within a disheveled beard, his hands and stance gnarled like a diseased ash tree. His dusty black robes had faded in spots to mottled grey, matching the chapel's ancient stone. If he hadn't grinned and held the gun, he'd have been so nondescript that he might have faded like camouflage into the chapel's walls.

Daniel wanted to ask why. He wanted to scream at the man, to destroy him and punish this imposter for what he'd done. He stuttered forward from the altar, halting when he had to look down to avoid the bodies. It didn't make sense. Nothing made sense. He wouldn't do this. And how had these wrecked and strewn things so quickly replaced the people he'd seen dancing moments earlier, the people he'd chosen and loved?

"Get down," a voice hissed.

The slight, bearded man was wedged underneath a pew. Daniel knew instantly that he was unwounded. It was his desperate voice, the changed light of the open doors, the endless wailing of the stones, the smell of cordite and cold pine, as if every second triggered new memories of this impossible conflation of past and future.

He remembered holding Mel's bloodied corpse and crying, mourning the loss of his friends while isolated in the silent chapel. Once again, the ancient masonry had dimmed to a damp grey in need of candlelight. No radiance cascaded from above. Satiated, the stones refused to speak.

"Never again," Daniel said to his younger self, who begged him from beneath the pew to get down and out of the line of fire.

The grinning gunman looked at his weapon, nodded, and then turned and chucked it outside through the chapel doors. Facing Daniel once again, he spread his arms wide, inviting attack.

Possessed by frustration and guilt, trapped alone long ago with corpses of the beloved that were, to his horror and disgust, not inured to the passage of time, perhaps his grief had been so rooted in those dear to him that he'd once willingly accepted what the abyss had asked. This time, he would fight back. He would wreak his revenge and change the past.

Daniel hurtled forward and plunged the dagger deep as he tackled the old man. The two of them tumbled down the stone steps. The blade burrowed into the gunman's abdomen. Outside in the rocky dirt, the sound dampened by the moonlit gauze of snow, Daniel scalded the man's tender exposed entrails with the ever-flaming mace, burying it deep with his clenched fist.

As the flame snuffed out, the dying man wailed and cackled up at Daniel, his face more hideous and familiar than before, his features contorted with a mad, satisfied, and perverse joy.

The darkness outside shifted toward a more monochrome blue moonlight. Screaming and shaking the dead wretch, still demanding to know why, Daniel suddenly recognized his surroundings and froze. The woods, the scent of pine, a place once full of hope.

He remembered everything.

He leapt up, but before he could shout or clutch the arm of the weeping young man framed in the chapel doorway by brilliant, cascading light, the night sky on either side swept closed like a zipper from the mountain to the moon, and the chapel vanished from sight.

Joe Koch writes literary horror and surrealist trash. Their books include *The Wingspan of Severed Hands, Invaginies, Convulsive,* and *The Couvade*, which received a 2019 Shirley Jackson Award nomination. His short work appears in *The Best Weird Fiction of the Year, Southwest Review, Nightmare Magazine, Vastarien,* and many others. Find Joe (he/they) online at horrorsong.blog.

J R HARLOW

The Dead Do Not Want

IN THE BEGINNING, THERE was the smell of pine alone. I guessed I had been saved, because, to me, our savior always smelt of pine. When I used to look up at the broad, carved crucifix on the towering stone walls of our church, I saw His arms become one with the protective limbs of the cross. His serene, benevolent face reminded me of a pine forest at night too—slumbering but watchful, ever-comforting.

Later, another smell overtook the sweet pine: damp earth. Then sinewy worms, and the wet warmth of the pulsing world as it pressed down over me. I felt the lace at my wrists and neck, satin flowers on my bosom, and a darkness so absolute that no eye could penetrate it.

That evening, Radu sat across from his sister Andra in their dining room, their chairs flanked by dusty furniture. On the long table; time distorted silverware glinted between murky stains of green tarnish, oddly offset by a long flotilla of pale carnations and huge, showy lilies.

A stack of leather-bound encyclopedias leaned sickly beside Radu's chair, threatening to topple in a cloud of dust. When their parents died they'd left the house and its contents; nothing more.

Over Andra's shoulder, a grease-glossed old canvas showed Christ healing Lazarus. The old man in the painting gestured outwards, seemingly at a tureen of boiled winter greens.

Neither sibling commented on the rhythmic scrape and bite of shovels coming from the churchyard across the way, but Andra broke into it.

"How fortunate it is," she said, "that the bride's family pays for the wedding."

Radu's spinster sister, nine years his senior, always reminded him of the nuns at his Catholic school. She was handsome but plain, thin-lipped and fussy. She picked at her food with poised fingers, tearing gristle from sinew. The bird she'd prepared for the table was one of the fowl the butcher normally reserved for his dogs. It was all they could afford.

"There is talk of venison for the main course..." she added happily.

Radu was due to be married in three days' time. He had never met his bride, but this did not cause him any concern. In fact, an arranged marriage was a simple pleasure for him. He'd never experienced that rush of undignified ardor that other men felt. When he saw a beautiful woman, he experienced her only as one sees a lovely painting and appreciates the brush-strokes, or admires a flower for the gentility of its blushing pink.

Neither was he drawn to his own sex. He had examined the theory and had come back lacking. No. Radu did not covet the pleasures of the flesh in any form. But he would like to have a woman about the house; a sweet, gentle woman, with her eye for making a house homely. Someone to converse with in the evenings, a pretty face to come home to.

So it was that their marriage was arranged. Radiana was her name; perhaps the long-lost twin of his soul. He had a cameo portrait of her in his dresser drawer that he would examine in the lonely candlelight of his evenings. Young but dignified, she stared straight at the painter, unabashed. Her posture was immaculate, her back straight, hands crossed daintily across her lap. Her face was long but not overly so, and her features well defined.

Aware that no-one had spoken for a while, and partly to fill the silence, Radu said:

"Andra, where will you live when I am married?"

His sister, wiping her hands daintily on a napkin, smiled amiably at him. "We'll open up the East wing," she replied, "and I'll live there."

"But we'll still dine together, the three of us?"

Andra collected up her cutlery again, nodding. "If you wish."

Her ambivalence must have stirred a mild anxiety in Radu, because he voiced a thought that had never come to him before.

"I think, perhaps, I should like to meet her, after all."

Andra dropped her fork and Radu started in surprise at the clatter. Then she made a sound that approximated a hiccup, daintily picked the fork up again, and reached for the water jug, covering her mouth with one hand, her eyes bulging slightly.

"I thought you had no wish to meet her before the wedding" she said, unhappily. She poured some water into her chipped wine glass and drank most of it, letting the last puddle mingle with some coagulated wine at the bottom. Then she added, more sternly:

"Do you not trust my judgement?"

"No, it's not that at all. Only…"

He stared into the table decoration between them. Beneath one of the gaudy lilies, yellow pollen stained the table cloth. His sister spoke again, defensive.

"She's very refined, you know. A distant relative of Count Botezatu. Lovely girl. You're very lucky to make such a match, especially in our situation."

The way her eyes lowered as she said it made him doubt quite how special Radiana really was, but his sister was right about the fortunate match.

"We don't want to seem ungrateful, Radu."

"No, of course not. I'm sorry."

Andra played with the stem of her wine glass for a few seconds, gazing listlessly into a protruding thigh bone on her plate, and Radu had to move one of the fleshy leaves from the table decoration aside so that he could see her face properly.

"If she is half the woman you are, sister, I will be a very lucky man" he said.

She smiled at him, relenting a little. "She's a sweet, innocent creature. She'll be a good wife. She'll keep you company, *fratie*" she called him that as a pet name, a silly corruption of the word for 'brother'. It was probably Andra's only concession to frivolity, and it was special because of that. He reached over and gave her hand a quick squeeze.

"Thank you, *soră*... I trust you, and if you think she is perfect then I'm assured of it. You know that I cannot talk to women, and you saved me that. So thank you."

She flashed a smile at him and gestured towards his plate. "Won't you finish your duck?"

Radu picked up his cutlery again, wondering which of the scraps he'd torn from the bone was most edible. The strings of gristle were interlaced with translucent lumps of fat.

"Certainly I will. You've done so well with the food. And the center-piece is immaculate, too. However did you afford it?" His voice trailed off as his sister abruptly got up from the table, clumsily pulling at the table cloth and making the cutlery clink.

She shut the heavy dining room drapes against the scrape and bite of the graveyard. Radu found his eyes drawn back to the centerpiece, seeing it for the first time with new eyes. The pale, cold carnations, close to wilting. The dour sprigs of grey-green foliage, the drooping heads of morbid field daisies—and those grotesque white lilies.

When he looked back at his sister she was pale, clutching her long hands together with her back to the closed drapes.

"The dead do not want for flowers" she said bitterly, by way of explanation.

Radu's legs propelled him up from his chair and she let him steer her, by the elbow, back to her own seat, so that they were staring at each other once more. He could feel his heart beating in his ears to the rhythm of the shovels outside, but he let her continue.

"I want for so much, *fratie*..." she said in a low voice, as though not to be overheard. "What should it matter if these stalks give us the slightest bit of pleasure? The dead have no use for them—" She broke off and fiddled around the high neck of her dress for a thin, copper-colored chain, which she dragged out, producing a small cross dotted with tiny dark rubies.

"God help me," she whispered, letting the little cross dance from her index and middle fingers. "But the dead hold sway over the living far more than the reverse."

Radu felt a depthless feeling of foreboding. Andra must have been desperate to take flowers from a grave, he reasoned. The churchyard was too close, too inviting. Surely the good Lord would forgive this indiscretion.

Reflexively, he crossed himself. "God will forgive you," he said. "You should get some sleep and take them back in the morning."

"No" she said abruptly, slapping the table. "No. You don't understand, Radu. You were never there on those nights in the old village. But I was. You never saw those horrible things..."

Her eyes glazed and seemed to fix in place. She was still holding the cross out in front of her and staring into a point somewhere below Radu's open neck-tie.

"Whole families dropped from plague, one after the other. Little children, strong young men... all taken. The dead take from the living, *fratie*. They have no mercy. Why should we not take from them?"

Radu burbled something, weakly. "Poor sanitation that caused the plague, *soră*. Peasants living cheek by jowl with dirty farm animals. Old food, kept for too long..." He was suddenly feeling that he needed more air, as if her words were suffocating him. He tugged at his open neck-tie and undid it, flopping it onto the table after wiping his brow with it. Then he pushed his plate away and propped his elbows onto the table.

"You don't know," Andra said quietly, her voice trembling. "You don't see. But you will."

Radu's sigh eased into all the corners of the room, stirring the pollen on the table cloth. He closed his eyes for a few seconds, recalling how their father used to watch the graveyard by night, guarded and suspicious, and he wondered if there was any truth in her stories.

Then he dismissed it, and got up from the table.

"I will retire" he said flatly. "I need to harvest the rest of the potatoes tomorrow."

I remember being afraid at first that the pox would ruin my looks. How silly. How like a girl to fear that marriage would never come to me. But then, as I lay dreaming, they dressed me in the most exquisite dress of silk and lace, with pearls at the neck and a veil of gossamer that lightly brushed my cheek.

My heart rejoiced even as my mother wept.

But now, that same lace and those hard cold pearls bring no comfort. Hard diagonals of wood press down upon my shoulders. My slippered feet cannot wiggle upwards or even slide to one side. Itches that cannot be scratched burn on my skin, and the silence, oh, the silence is the worst of all.

I never lived alone, never slept alone, was never left to the cataclysmic thunder in my own ears before. I cannot sleep without my sister's warmth beside me, so I lay awake, and I pray.

In Radu and Andra's home, it was dusk, with just the familiar scrape and bite, scrape and bite, of the shovels in the churchyard for company. Andra was running her errands in the buzzing September drizzle. Over the way, the grave diggers still worked, under a saltpeter sky with yellowing mists cast by the lamp-posts.

Glad to have got his bounty safely into the barn for the night, Radu scrubbed the dirt from under his fingernails, watching the veins stand out like throbbing canals against the white of his hands and his chafed red knuckles.

It had been a good day's work, like panning for gold. Each time the earth tumbled from his questing fork, beautiful oval treasures like golden eggs popped joyously from the soil. Some were speckled or pitted, some perfect and unblemished. It was a good potato harvest this year. Each time the steel tines probed into the mounds of dirt, up surfaced another pale dome, like the crowning head of a new-born baby.

Or a skull.

The scrape and bite continued outside, and from his grimed window with its single pane, Radu watched a huge moth swoop onto the lamp outside, the furry wings spread wide. Not wanting to see the inevitable immolation, he drew down the blinds, set the little brush back on the chipped basin, and shook the droplets from his hands.

He would light a fire now, he thought, and practice his vows again.

I thrashed, I flailed, as my world caved in above. There were gritty blows that fell dully on my solid sky and rains of pitiless dirt, peppered with sharp shreds that bit into my face and hands. I heard voices too, harsh but wavering, angry and afraid and hurried.

After what seemed like eternity I was lifted up, perhaps by our savior's welcoming arms.

Then I was free.

I burst into the cleansing cold, choked and spasmed, and sat upright, with His name on my lips. I was reborn, like the Lord Hristos himself, to a hushed gasp.

When my eyes finally opened, stinging with dust and grit, I was surrounded by men, all grimed with dirt and holding shovels and lanterns. When they saw me shiver into life, they clamored to cross themselves and their lips moved in blessing and prayer, as if they had witnessed a miracle.

"Zeu salvează-ne..." they said, in unison. God save us.

Exhausted by a day of digging, Radu slept soundly, as if in a stupor, with his mouth half open and his neck contorted where he had lost consciousness shortly after falling into his bed. But his sleep was pierced by odd noises and disturbing visions.

Sometimes he saw the ill-fated moth consumed by flames, sometimes the ringing of a bell in the solemn lych-gate of the church and visions of his parents' bodies being lowered into the grave. He saw Andra kneeling to steal flowers from the graves of children. Flocks of crows rained down on him, their wings clapping against his head in fury, and all to the steady sound of the scraping, biting shovels.

Then he saw a creature, frail like a child but feral like a beast, crawling towards him on all fours, leaving a trail of dirt on his bedroom rug.

Powerless and paralyzed by fear or by sleep, Radu could only watch in horror as the creature dragged itself up onto his bed and swarmed over him, subsuming his legs and pelvis and leaving an unearthly warmth there. It crept further up until it was pressing against his chest, and he could see the pale, winsome features then, and feel the feather-soft tresses of hair falling across his eyelids and mouth.

He felt the wraith smothering him and his breaths became shallow.

"Husband..." the creature said, a sinewy tongue rolling over pink lips. He recoiled in disgust as a dreadful, savage kiss, the first he had ever received, made his lips burn and blister.

When he woke, he found a muddy trail of well-worked soil stretching from his open window, across his rug, and up to his bed.

They left no lanterns, no light for me to see by, and compared with the damp warmth of the casket, the night was cold. Alone, and afraid, I went out into it. I went out to seek a salve for my aching heart and my lonely soul, to find some company.

I tip-toed like a ghost around the slumbering village, watching the rise and fall of peaceful sleep in myriad forms, and I envied that.

But there was something else, too... a bristling desire. A desire to consume. Like the earthworms or a flame. It called me to take a sleeping man and rip him up at the roots, like my stolen flowers.

That morning, Radu brushed past the dining table. A reflexive shiver went through the dying flowers in the centerpiece, and a shower of crisped yellow petals fell away onto the stained table-cloth, leaving just the bare and slightly obscene stamen of the lily, quivering and long-since denuded of pollen.

He noticed Andra in one corner of the kitchen, mixing flour in a huge earthenware bowl. The morning light cast a dim glow onto her brown hair, picking out strands of white in a surreal dawn-pink. "Why did you not take them back?" Radu asked, pointing at the flowers.

She sighed and shrugged, looking tired. "I don't have time, *fratie*. I am making your wedding pastries. They will not be missed." She went back to mixing, the muscles on her forearms standing out like snakes. "Besides," she added, as Radu swept some of the fallen pollen into a little pile with the curled petals, "they're already dead. Pass me three eggs."

Radu opened the pantry door and stared into the half empty shelves. He thought there might be a small pile of mouse droppings on the flagstones, but he tried to ignore it. "There are only two left," he said listlessly, carrying them over to her.

"Break them in," she ordered him, proffering the side of the bowl. As the yolks slithered into the flour he asked her if she had heard anything in the night. "Nothing" she said. "I think I am too busy worrying about the wedding to notice anything."

Out of the window, Radu could see the shovel handles starting to bob over the walls of the churchyard again as the gravediggers went to work. They disturbed a flurry of birds that had been settled on the bare ground and they flapped up to the highest reaches of bushes and towers to wait.

The birds waited when he dug for potatoes, too, watching him with intelligent, beady eyes, waiting for the twisting coils of worms that he tossed to them.

"They're busy over at the churchyard again," he said. "They've barely stopped for days."

Andra was furiously beating the eggs into the flour. "The first chills of winter," she said matter-of-factly. "Fevers, agues and the like. The weak are first plucked out, like your failed potatoes." He nodded, thinking of the tiny, bud-like green tubers that he tossed away, ridding the soil of their pernicious frailty, so that the other tubers might grow and thrive.

"*Soră*," he asked, "What did you mean when you talked about those nights in the old village? What did you see?"

Her eyes scowled when she looked up from the bowl. "You would not believe it if you knew," she said. "You were lucky. Father never took you. He said you were too young. But I went. He made me hold the light as he worked." She slapped the bowl down onto the counter so hard that he feared it would break, and wiped her hands angrily on her apron. The cold weather and harsh carbolic soap had taken its toll on her hands and as she wiped, her cracked knuckles left streaks of fresh blood along the fabric.

Seeing it, she laughed, without mirth. "Only the living bleed, Radu. But you did not see old Laszlo's face, drenched in blood, weeks after his death. He came back to visit his wife, in the night, and took her with him. Back to the grave."

They looked at each other for a few seconds, Radu not daring to speak. A flicker of movement caught his eye and he noticed a large moth, struggling in a puddle of spilt water on the draining board, leaving dusty marks from the shed coating on its wings.

"Fetch the milk jug," Andra said flatly. As he moved past her, he asked one more question.

"Why did you never marry, *soră?*"

On the morning of his wedding, Radu could hear a fountain of inane chatter coming from the dining room. It was dizzying, like a screeching flock of birds.

The house was so full of people, in fact, that he immediately left. Radu was not used to so many people, so much human noise. He ran outside, gulping down air.

As he was stooped over on the porch, waiting for the dizziness to settle, the priest walked slowly up to him.

"It is normal to feel apprehensive," he said, without smiling. His jaw seemed oddly tense when Radu looked up at him, as if he was clenching his teeth.

For once, the graveyard was silent.

They came to find me in the bright morning, and led me to the church. I went happily. The building loomed like a glorious piece of heaven before me.

A stirring wind fingered the petals in my hair and my painted lips quaked. My eyes burned with happy tears as I clutched the bouquet to my stomach, and I took my patient steps towards the priest, trembling and filled with hope.

Oh, but the Lord blesses me! What happiness I shall have—a whole life stretching out before me when I thought it had been taken away.

Under the arched porch I walked, a crown of undulating spires above me. But try as I might, I could not enter the comforting womb of the nave. It repelled me. It was like walking into a wall of stone. I glimpsed the warm candles and soft prayer cushions inside; the blessed font rising from the flagstones, the patterned glass awash with glowing blue and gold light, and yet I could not enter. Not even on my wedding day. My stomach ached with grief.

Then a hand gripped my arm and pulled me aside. It belonged to a tall man with an unkind face. "It cannot enter" he said, and then he dragged me into the windy churchyard like a stray dog, and cast me against the hard gravestones. "The strigoi cannot enter a church. We must do the ceremony here."

The word struck me like a blow, bleaker than the gravestones, more callous than the man's cruel hand. For now I knew the truth. I was not reborn, like our Lord.

I was strigoi. The undead.

"You have tricked me!" Radu cried.

Andra rushed to him, dressed in her old communion gown, the re-stitched sleeve barely showing. Her cheeks were flushed.

"I am so sorry, *fratie...*" she squeezed his arm and he saw tears in her eyes and regret twisting her mouth. "Please forgive us. We did what we must."

Further off in the graveyard there was a dreadful clamor of raised voices and cries of subdued terror from the women. The priest stood a little way off, his prayer book clutched to his stomach, watching.

"What is that girl?" Radu whispered, feeling weak.

"Your bride. A descendent of Count Botezatu. All that I told you was true..."

"With one omission!" Radu roared. He had never been so angry in his life.

"She died, *fratie*, before she could ever be married. We knew that she would return. She must return, out of loneliness, to make a union with a man from amongst the living." She glanced nervously behind her at the priest and then to the crowd between the graves. They seemed to be struggling with something, fighting between themselves.

"If we couldn't give her a husband, Radu, she would take one. By force."

Radu stepped back, shaking his head and swaying on his feet. He thought he would faint. He believed his sister, for the first time.

"So you offered *me* to the Strigoi? Your own brother?!" He felt the rage coloring his cheeks, but there was another feeling mixed in with it. It was sadness, so acute that it stabbed like grief. It was the loss of that delicate trust he had placed in his sister. His only living relative.

"You must understand..."

Andra tried to close the gap between them but he retreated again. From the corner of his eye he saw two of his groomsmen approaching, silently, gripping a slight and drooping figure between them. For a moment she resembled, in Radu's tortured mind, one of the dying lilies in his sister's stolen center-piece. Her face was mercifully hidden by a long veil, but there was mud smeared along her wedding dress.

"You were the only choice, Radu" Andra said, calmly now. "You told me yourself that you never desired a woman. You only wanted a silent companion—serene and beautiful, like a painting. Radiana is perfect for you. She'll say nothing, desire nothing from you. Nothing but your hand in marriage. And she *was* beautiful once..."

The groomsmen brought the creature to his side, and raised one of her long white hands. The lace at her wrist almost reached far enough to obscure her torn fingers and bloody nails. He wondered if, beneath that grubby veil, a long tongue rested between swollen pink lips.

"She'll want nothing from you," Andra said, her words curving in his ears. "The dead do not want, *fratie*. The dead do not want."

J. Rosina Harlow/**J R Harlow** is a regular contributor to the *Dark Lane* anthology series. She has also appeared in *Adverbially Challenged* Vol. 2, *Holidays: Straight Up or on the Rocks, Stygian Lepus* magazine (AUS), *The Ghastling* magazine (U.K.), U.S. anthologies *Grimm Retold* and *Strangely Marvelous Creatures* and the British anthologies *Infernal Mysteries* and *Tales of Folk Horror*. She was longlisted for the To Hull and Back competition in 2019, won third prize in the CAS short story competition in 2022 and was a winner of the Philip LeBrun prize for creative writing on graduating from Chichester University back in 2005. She is a professional musician (under the name Jo Harlow) and currently lives in Kent with her husband and just the right amount of cats. Find her at facebook.com/JRosinaHarlow.

JACOB STEVEN MOHR

Samanthas

Around two a.m., my best man crashed out of the Opry Hotel bathroom rubbing his top gums with one finger. That was bad omen number one.

Our suite was a dozen floors over the Nashville strip. Picture neon cowboy Disneyland with tassels and a lift kit, the same electrified four-piece country/blues blasting out of every door we passed. We'd drunk at Rainbow Room; we'd drunk at Redneck Riviera... Gordie, wiping sweat off his glasses, swore up and down he'd clocked Kid Rock waddling out of the john at the tip-top of Nudie's, but none of us much believed him.

The night heat was a fever. Two hours ago, we'd been Bad Hombres, with hot blood bulging our arteries and overpriced ten-gallon hats on our domes. Now we were just five sweaty, heavily liquored thirty-somethings stinking up our hotel suite's all-linoleum kitchen and wishing we were about ten years younger.

Gordie squatted in front of the fridge, handing back the beers we'd grabbed right when we touched down at BNA. Tanner and Cliff belched out a toneless rendition of "Red Solo Cup" with their hats pushed way down over their eyes. I stood over the sink, watching water swirl down the throat of the drain and trying not to think about puking.

The atmosphere was woozy and thick—the room seemed to collapse in and out, like inside a beating heart. And as I listened to my friends bellow: *"I fill you up, proceed to par-tay-y-y..."* I realized the booze had us right in its clammy palm, and the night was probably one pair of novelty spurs away from getting catastrophically stupid.

When Ceejay found me, I was seriously toying with the notion of toppling onto the loveseat and letting the room spin me to sleep. But one look at his wild eyes and the white snow still crusting his mustache and I knew I'd have to soldier on.

"Manny," he huffed. "Man oh man. Some party."

I jerked my chin at the powder under his nose. "*Jee-zus*, Ceej. You flew with that?"

He nudged me aside and blasted the faucet, dunking his skull under the stream. His hands scrubbed over his face, then he came up spluttering, his eyes bulging and pink.

"Gotta keep the party going," he muttered, seemingly to himself.

Then he clapped one damp hand on my shoulder, fixing me ferociously with his eyes like he had to make certain I was really there in front of him.

"Listen," he said, breathing uncountable whiskey shots in my face. "You having fun?"

I felt myself nod. The unvarnished truth—I hadn't wanted a bachelor party. Maybe if we'd all still been twenty-five, I could've drummed up a little more gung-ho. But at thirty-one, bacchanalia felt like dress-up, one step off from the midlife crisis I'd felt looming ever since I started wearing a tie to work. But when I told Ceejay this, he'd looked at me like a puppy I'd just kicked in the ribs.

So I said, "Time of my life," and tried like hell to mean it.

Ceejay smiled in relief, casting his eyes around the room. The others had shuffled in front of the big hotel TV and were rock-paper-scissoring for something. Tanner threw rock; Gordie threw paper. They busted out laughing and swapped cowboy hats.

"Red solo cup, I fill you up..."

I couldn't tell which of them it was singing.

A yawn twitched in my jaw. Ceejay glanced furtively at his phone screen, then back up at me. He showed me his teeth and reddened gums.

"Don't get sleepy yet. Got a surprise coming."

"Your nose is bleeding," I told him, pointing.

Then the hook sunk. "No, Ceej," I said. *"Uh-uh.* We talked about this."

A beer appeared in my friend's hand—he pressed it into mine, cold and sweating from the room's heat. Somebody had cracked the balcony door, just enough that a banjo's high amplified twang sifted in from the street, miles below.

"Hey. All cool," Ceejay assured me, like it settled everything.

Then he sniffed, eyes darting to the door again. "It's your bachelor party," he explained like I was nine years old. "You gotta, you know. Party. Or else it doesn't count. I'm the best man—I'll take the heat. You didn't know anything about it."

"Ceejay..." I warned.

But he was already drifting off, back towards the middle of the room. He slapped Gordie hard on the ass as he wobbled toward the door—like a magic trick, a hand knocked hard just as he reached for the knob. He yanked the door open with a flourish.

"Hey, you animals," he called back to us. "Look who's here."

I saw them first past Ceejay's shoulder. Three of them, clustered on the plush carpet, close like bowling pins. I could see only the tops of the girls' heads at first—hair all colors, red then black then platinum blonde—a nightmare stoplight. I heard high girlish giggles but no words. I could smell cheap perfume from the kitchen.

I grabbed Ceejay's elbow just as he was ushering them inside. "The fuck is this?"

He offered a blank look. "Your surprise."

"I promised Heather," I hissed. "You asshole..."

It was only half a lie. I'd said next to nothing to my fiancée about the trip, and she'd seen me off at the door with a kiss and an *I don't need to know* wink. But there'd been something beneath this as well. A certain guarded nature—in the inquisitive curve of her mouth, in the hand that lingered, trembling, on my hip just a hair-second longer before I slipped away to the Uber XL idling in our driveway.

Who will you be today? her eyes seemed to ask. *Who will you choose to be?*

"Will you cool it?" Ceejay hissed, sniffing again. "It's not what you think. I bumped into them in Nudie's. Told them all about the suite, said we had some good *tequila...*"

"Uh-huh. Sure."

The other groomsmen had gaggled around them like panting dogs. They were younger than us—mid-twenties at best, but made up so heavily they could've been five years upstream or down. At least they were dressed like tourists instead of strippers. They all had on the same tassel jacket cut off above their belly buttons, and Technicolor cowgirl boots that still had the tags dangling off the heels.

And there was something about their faces. Tanned and smooth-cheeked, but with some mis-alignment of the features that made them look like they were forever tilting their heads to the side, like they'd missed something you'd said.

Outside of their makeup and various hair colors, they might've been triplets.

"Your names are what?" one of them asked, in an accent I couldn't place.

The guy shouted theirs out as the girls peeled off their jackets. They matched beneath as well—jet-black halter tops with V-necklines so deep they seemed to split them in half, right down the middle. "What about you?" Gordie hollered, too loud.

The blonde pressed a hand to her chest and answered. The word she said sounded like *Samantha*, but in her tonguey, hollow accent, it could have been anything.

The other girls repeated the gesture. Each said a name that was, or wasn't, Samantha.

"You girls like to party?" Tanner asked.

Ceejay looked so pleased with himself I almost wanted to laugh—or shoulder-check him right through the suite's popcorn wall. Instead I just said, "I can't believe this."

"Look," he replied, putting himself between me and the mingling group. "What's the big deal? You're just looking at the menu. Nobody's making you order. But if you're going to live the rest of your life like some appendage, you owe this to yourself."

He patted my shoulder in a *poor you* kind of way. His eyes had stopped bugging, but they were still round, still searching—for what, I couldn't know.

"Besides," he said. "Who's telling Heather?"

One of the Samanthas appeared at Ceejay's elbow. Like instinct, he slipped his arm around her slender shoulders and thrust his chin at me leeringly. She looked me up and down—she was the blonde, seemingly the leader of their pack. Now I was certain they were all related. Down to the beauty mark just to the side of her right eye, this Samantha was nearly the perfect mirror image of the other two.

"You are the groom," she said. Her voice was dusky and low.

I looked helplessly at Ceejay. "You told her that?"

"Mister Ceejay tells me everything. He say you will be big married man."

She tweaked my polo collar with long fingernails, then pushed her nose into the hollow of Ceejay's neck. "What do you think?" she purred. "Maybe he marry me instead."

Ceejay mouthed silently at me: YOU'RE WELCOME.

Then he steered Samantha-or-not back toward the center of the room. I cracked my beer open—cold white foam erupted down my wrist. Images flashed... the two-day conference in Philadelphia. The clumsy flirting at the hotel bar. The keycard slipped into my breast pocket. The wine-red lip-print on the cuff of my only clean white shirt.

I pressed my mouth to the skin just below my thumb, slurping up the spill, the wheat-y taste pooling on my tongue. Then I followed after my friend.

Music, perfume, booze, sweat—the suite became a clumsy ballet of limbs as we crowded onto the tiny couch and loveseat and two narrow armchairs that came with the room. Gordie had his Bluetooth speaker cranked as high as it would go, so we had to shout over each other to be heard. It was almost two boys to a girl, but the Samanthas seemed to take up the champion's share of space. They sprawled across laps, leaned against shoulders… when Samantha Red tried to drape her legs over my knees, I stood up and kicked Cliff out of his chair.

He took my spot on the sofa, all too happy to swap.

Ceejay hadn't lied. There *was* tequila—Jose Cuervo Gold, which got passed around in a big loop. The guys made sure the girls got ample time at bat. Soon they were singing along to Gordie's Spotify mix and jabbering animatedly at each other across the room, half in English, half in something that hardly sounded like words at all.

Samantha Red sat between Gordie and Cliff, one hand resting on each of their thighs like the armrests of a throne; Samantha Black had one long, tanned leg draped over Tanner's, her calf dangling between his knees; Samantha Blonde clung close to Ceejay, but she kept glancing in my direction, eyes flashing under nearly-white bangs.

Somehow, "Red Solo Cup" came back around in the rotation. Again the room burst out in drunken bellowing by the time the chorus arrived. I expected the girls would join in, but they sat still as paintings, nodding slightly during the verses and mouthing the chorus when it came back around a second time.

When it was over, Samatha Black said, "Is good song. We are like this Red Solo Cup, yes? Empty, seeking to be filled. Always looking. Always seeking."

"I'll drink to that." Ceejay turned the Cuervo vertical so it bubbled.

"Wait," Tanner was saying. "Wait, wait, wait. Repeat that for everybody."

Samantha Black had just whispered something in his ear. Now she crossed her arms and pretended to pout. "You are make fun of me," she said. "You think I am big joke."

"No, no." Tanner pulled her tighter to him. She smiled felinely and let herself be pulled. "I thought it was awesome. I want the others to hear it."

"Maybe it was secret," she said.

But then she shrugged, and leaned forward to address the whole room. *"The night is an ocean,"* she said. *"The earth is the shore..."*

Serenely, the other two Samanthas answered:

"...and the voyage was long and lonely."

All three fell against the guys beside them, giggling into their hands. Tanner looked around like he expected applause. "How crazy is that?" he kept saying. "I mean—holy shit. What *is* that? What do you *call* that?"

"Sounds like Smashing Pumpkins," Cliff put in.

"It is truth," Samantha Black intoned.

"It's poetry is what it is." Ceejay grinned at me, then nudged Samatha Blonde, still hanging off his arm like a cloak. "You know, babe—Manny here used to write poems in college. Won a campus competition once."

Samantha Red clapped her hands once. "I want to hear poem."

"She wants to hear *poem*," Ceejay said, lilting the last word, his own approximation of the girls' accents. I felt a flash of hatred for him—grinning at me across the coffee table, he looked like the joker in a pack of cards. I spotted a little dried blood peeking from his left nostril. Samantha Blonde didn't seem to notice.

I waved them off. "Not tonight." Samantha Blonde cocked an eyebrow.

"He is shy?" she seemed to ask the whole room.

"Just not in the mood," I replied.

Ceejay curled his lip at me. "Not shy. Scared of his *wifey.*"

My face got suddenly hot. "Fuck yourself, Ceej."

But his sneer only widened. "You think she'd like it, knowing you've got company?"

"Ceejay, come on, man…"

That was Gordie, or maybe Cliff. Their eyes flicked to me, showing the whites. The music had hit a lull—Spotify was playing an ad for some kind of meal prep kit.

"No, no," Ceejay said. "This is bullshit. She's got his balls—" He made a fist, clenching it hard, "—rolling around in a jar. And we're not supposed to say anything?"

"Ceejay," I said carefully. "I mean it. Shut up."

"Sure, sure," he said. His eyes were too white. "With us, he can be a tough guy. Come on then, big man." He leaned forward, pulling free of Samantha Blonde's grip on his arm. "Go on and make me shut up."

I stood up quickly—I think it actually spooked him, because he sat right back against the back of the loveseat. The meal prep ad ended; improbably, the jangling opening notes of "Red Solo Cup" began to play for a third time.

I looked around the room, the bottle of tequila dangling from my fist.

Six pairs of eyes blinked. I breathed deep—in, and out, and in.

"I'm getting some air," I said. "When I get back, *play another fucking song.*"

The balcony door didn't keep all the noise in.

Even after I'd shut it, I could hear muffled conversation start back up, and an acoustic guitar come in sparse and slow, playing some soppy cowboy ballad. I had the tequila with me still, but didn't feel like drinking more of it. Below me, the strip was finally closing up shop. Neon horseshoes and lariats winked off, one after another. The heat was finally lifting off the city, and there was wet in the air.

It made something ache and yawn in my chest—like thinking about the end of the world.

I fished in my pocket. No texts or calls, but I'd had my phone on airplane mode since we took off from John Glenn. I had just started punching in a number when I heard the balcony door whine open behind me, then close again.

"I'm fine," I grunted. "I'll come back in a minute."

But it wasn't Ceejay, or any of the guys.

Samantha Blonde didn't look at me at first. She stepped to the rail, wrapping her hands tight around it like the wind might carry her over the side. Her hair moved stiffly in its breath—for the first time, I realized it might be a wig. She stared down at Nashville's shutting eyes, then up into the dark mouth of the night.

She said, "You should not be alone."

Her eyes cut sideways to me, half-lidded, her gaze cool and measuring. Perhaps I'd imagined the strange twist of her features before; it was like the two halves of her face had settled somehow, jigsaw pieces slipping finally into their grooves.

"Well that's, like, your opinion, man," I said.

She didn't laugh, or even acknowledge the joke. I felt her eyes like cool dry hands, moving up and up my body. In spite of the heat it made me shiver.

"Ceejay sent you out here?" I asked.

Her head shook slowly. "Mister Ceejay, he busy."

She rubbed her finger under her nose, sniffing loudly.

"Uh-huh." I felt caught. I didn't want to go back inside with the others, but I didn't want to be alone on the balcony with this girl either. I kept my eyes locked on those lit windows, imagining other parties winding down, other versions of myself hating them.

"I make you uncomfortable," Samantha Blonde said.

"Oh. Uh…" She'd given me an out. But before I could take it, she continued:

"Being alone. That is uncomforting," she said. "It is making the skin squirm, the flesh ripple. Before I came here, I thought I would be alone forever. Everything was oceans, reflecting darkness, reflecting stars. But that was before. Life is happier now."

"I guess you like America, then."

"It is like other places," she replied. "But yes—very much."

Now she was really measuring me, looking me up and down. I imagined instruments, dials and meters ticking up, up, up as more and more data poured in.

"Where'd you say you were from?" I asked.

She laughed ruefully at this—an odd sunken sound, more a yawn than a laugh.

"I did not say," she replied.

But then she spoke a name I assumed was a city. I imagined some tiny town in Eastern Europe, or even south of the equator.

"I've never been there," I said.

"There is nothing there for us now."

She said this with such faraway sorrow. I remembered I still had the Jose Cuervo and offered it to her. She unscrewed the cap, put it to her lips, then took a few big swallows. Then she wrinkled her nose and pushed her hand against her stomach.

"It is not the same," she murmured.

I took the tequila back. "Well, there's beers in the fridge if you want." Samantha Blonde didn't reply. She stared outward, gripping the rail so tight her knuckles went pale.

I searched for something else to say.

"Listen," I said at last. "I was rude earlier. I thought you were—well, I don't know who I thought you were. It seems silly now." I wiped my hand on my jeans and put it out towards her. "I'm Manny. I'm, uh. I'm the groom."

She smiled and took my hand in both of hers. I was instantly aware of how sweaty my hand still was—and how smooth and dry hers were by comparison.

Again, she said a name that was almost Samantha, but not quite.

She let me go, and I thought she'd go back to staring down at the dark city, as seemed to be her habit. But instead her features shifted into a studying look—the light was bad on the balcony, they seemed to almost rearrange on her face, like tectonic plates. She almost looked like a different girl altogether.

"But I have a different name," she said. "If you want it."

Her features shifted again. She angled forward—and forward and forward...

And suddenly Ceejay slapped the sliding door, pressing his nose against it.

"Hey, earth to Manny," he called.

I shook myself. I felt like I'd stepped off the plane again, touching down from a thousand miles away. Ceejay cracked open the balcony door, peering strangely at me. The bottle of Jose Cuervo was still in my hand. But Samantha Blonde had vanished.

The moments that followed blurred like rain on a windshield. Ceejay propelled me inside, taking the tequila from my hand. He led me—pushed me, rather—not back to the sitting room, but to the shared bathroom that connected to one bedroom as well. But I had time to see the den as I passed by. Cliff sat with his back to me on the loveseat, beside a kneeling Samantha Black, whispering intensely in his ear. Samantha Blonde stood by the fridge with a beer in her hand, watching me.

One bedroom door was shut.

Gordie and Tanner were gone. So was Samantha Red.

Out of the corner of my eye, I thought I saw Cliff's head lean back, Samantha Black's face dipping out of sight behind the back of the loveseat, toward his lap.

Then the door of the bathroom shut behind us.

Ceejay paced in front of the mirror, running fingers through his hair. On one end of the counter was a pile of towels, lumpy and still damp, dripping down the drawers and onto the slick white tile. Near the sink was a hand mirror, lying face up. Two lines of white powder were measured out there, as well as a few leftover crumbles.

"Don't be mad," he began.

I *had* been angry still—but when he turned to look at me, it all went up like mist off a hot street. He looked *scared*, of what I couldn't say. But he needed something from me right then, and all I could do was give it.

"I'm not mad," I said.

His eyes flickered, toward the coke first, then to his own reflection in the mirror. Then his attention returned to me. "I fucked up," he said. "I think I really fucked up."

"Lay off the powder," I offered. "Might help."

He rubbed his eye with the heel of one hand. "Sure, sure."

Then through some massive effort of will, he seemed to get his feet under him. "Listen," he said. "The girls. I didn't meet them at Nudie's. I didn't meet them anywhere."

"Yeah, no shit." I leaned against the counter, careful not to disturb the coke or the mirror beneath it. "Then where'd they come from? They didn't fall out of the sky."

Ceejay's face screwed up. "That's the thing," he said. "I don't know where they came from. I got a call from the... the service about a half hour ago. They said there was some kind of mix-up with the hotel address..."

"The service?" I felt my rage rush back into me. "Ceejay, they're..."

"No! No!" He held out his hands, a shield between us. "I don't know *what* they are. I think they're just... well, anyway, what does it matter? They're here. And they're cool, aren't they? Everybody's having a good time."

He gave me that kicked puppy look again—only this time, there didn't seem to be any artfulness to it. He looked desperate and scared and sick.

"I kind of thought," he mumbled, "something might happen. With me and Samantha."

"Which one?" I said—and Ceejay let out a choking laugh.

"Yeah. Yeah. Which one." He rubbed his nose, sniffed, and rubbed again. Then he looked back at me, leaning heavily against the counter.

"You're having fun, aren't you?" he asked.

"Why's that so important?"

"I'm your best man," he said automatically.

Then he shook his head, setting his jaw like it was carved out of wood. "No. Fuck it. I'm done covering for her. Marry her if you want, but you owe it to yourself to..."

"Ceejay," I said, calm as I could. "It's all right. I know."

His face sagged suddenly. "You know?"

I nodded. In truth, I didn't know what I knew. Only that Heather had been in the shower when a text ghosted across her phone screen as it lay on the bed. I read the preview again and again until it faded, while my fiancée toweled off, singing Gin Wigmore, her voice echoing off the tile walls. Then it was gone forever.

"I mean..." I said. "What else could it be. You know?"

Ceejay stepped back a pace, almost missing the toilet as he sat down.

"Jee-zus," he breathed. "You never said—"

"What would I say?"

"Anything. Literally anything."

Images in my head—*hotel, lipstick, fumbling in the dark.*

Heather, looking up from her laptop, finding her glasses to really see me...

I shrugged. "I love her. Somebody had to be the bigger man."

"Holy shit," Ceejay said. "Ho-leee shit." He combed through his hair again with his fingers, then looked up at me hopefully. "I'm sorry, you know. About before."

"Don't think about it."

"It's the stuff. You understand, don't you? I'm trying to lay off, but..."

The Jose Cuervo was standing on the back of the toilet. I reached past Ceejay for it, unscrewed the lid, and drank. Liquid fire going down—it woke me up like a hard slap in the face. Then I handed it to my best man.

There was enough left in the bottom, just enough.

"Don't think about it," I repeated.

When we left the bathroom, the suite den had changed again.

At first, it was total darkness. Only the little blue light from Gordie's Bluetooth speaker punched through, as well as a bar of yellow pushing in under the door from the hall.

Then our eyes adjusted to the black.

I couldn't be sure at first which Samantha sat on the sofa, staring into the dark void of the television. Only when she turned did I realize she was the blonde from the balcony.

"I have waited," she said. "I think to myself, maybe he does not like me."

I couldn't see her eyes, so I had no way of knowing which of us she'd addressed. In that moment it hardly seemed to matter. Beneath her flat tone there was a buzz of naked desire—for either of us, for both of us. It was immaterial which.

"Where are your... friends?" I almost said *sisters*, but held it back.

"Where's Cliff?" Ceejay asked.

Samantha Blonde shrugged. "Cliff, he say he want privacy." She giggled, then angled her chin at one shut bedroom door. "But there is still another room, yes?"

"Aren't Tanner and Gordie in there?" I asked.

Samantha Blonde cocked her head. For the first time, she seemed lost for words. I watched her roll her lips into her mouth, nibbling them with her teeth, seeming to search for an answer. But before she could speak, the other bedroom door creaked open.

Samantha Red stepped out, moving nimbly through the dark.

"Your friends got very tired." She addressed this half to us, half to Samantha Blonde. "I am feeling sick in my stomach. You stay—I will go."

To demonstrate, she laid one delicate hand across her exposed midsection.

Samantha Blonde stood up from the couch to meet her. They put their heads close together, whispering in their own language—I thought, in the dark, I almost thought I saw some small inscrutable object pass between them, from one mouth to the other.

But it was the light playing tricks—of course. The Samanthas disengaged; Samantha Red beamed at Ceejay and me, showing every white tooth.

"Manny," she said. "A wonderful party. Thank you."

Then the door to the hall opened, flooding the suite with light, then shut again.

Samantha Blonde faced us, smiling.

Ceejay and I looked at each other in the dark. I knew somehow, we were standing on the crumbling edge of something, with a long uncertain drop below. Even though we couldn't see each other's faces, understanding passed between us—of just how far each of us was willing to go, where we were capable of stopping.

I clapped his shoulder. "I'm going downstairs for ice," I said. "And clean towels. Text me if you think of anything else we might need."

He looked at me with salivating gratitude, and I felt—I don't know. Scooped away, almost. Hollow, like the bottom of a dry well. It could have been the tequila. I wasn't angry anymore. When I looked at Ceejay, I found I felt almost nothing at all.

When I made my exit, my best man was picking his way towards the sofa, towards Samantha Blonde. I crept through the door, into the blinding hall, and left them alone.

———

I stayed gone maybe thirty minutes.

I wandered long carpeted halls, blinking under UFO-bright wall sconces. The tequila bottle, now long empty, still dangled from my left hand. On a whim, I chucked it down a trash chute, listening as it tumbled and tumbled against the sheet metal walls until I couldn't hear it anymore.

I rode the elevator down to the lobby, leaning half-asleep in one cold corner. When I stumbled off, the concierge desk was empty, but the lights were still on in the vestibule and lower halls. The all-tile lobby was an empty diorama, a museum display with no gawking tourists and velvet ropes. Fatigue sank its claws deep in every bone. I sat on a faux-leather sofa in front of a bank of televisions, all playing the same late-night rerun of a cop show I'd never seen. The sound was off, with no subtitles.

I thought, more than a little guiltily, of the Samanthas' mysterious, toneless accents. Of them draped across my friends' legs and laps, of Cliff and Samantha Black on the loveseat in the half-darkness. Of Samantha Blonde watching me across the room, taking my measure, drinking me up with her dark strange eyes...

What did you like about her? I could hear Heather asking.

When I told her about Philly, she didn't cry. I didn't know what that meant at first. She shut her laptop and looked at me carefully, as though seeing me under a certain light for the first time. When I finally finished talking I was shaking, but Heather had barely stirred. Then she asked me a few careful questions, most of which don't matter now, but answering them cut me in two all the same.

But the worst of them all was: *What did you like about her?*

I gave her the truth. She'd wanted me. It was so simple it was almost stupid. But somewhere between twenty-nine and thirty I'd forgotten what it could be like—to be *coveted* like that. And across that hotel bar, this complete stranger had *wanted* me with her eyes, like she'd opened up a menu and thought, *That'll go down just right, I bet.*

But there was more to it even than that. This woman who could never have a name, who couldn't live in my head except as a shadow on the wall, she'd looked at me just like Samantha Blonde had looked at me, as though whatever madness was going to carry on between us represented some universal constant, fixed and unchangeable, like gravity, like the positions of the stars.

Inevitable. And at the time, I'd even believed it.

Heather listened to it all. Her face barely moved—the only thing that really betrayed her hurt was her right hand, twisting my ring on her left finger back and forth. But only when she was sure I was really finished did she put her piece in, choosing her words like she was picking them out of a box one at a time.

I know how it must have felt, she said. *Really—I know. And the best thing is, it was easy. Wasn't it? You say Yes one time—and it's done. The rest is momentum. But I don't want us to love each other like that. I'm greedy. I want a life with you. I want a house, I want kids. All of it. Complicated things, difficult things. Things we'll have to choose every day, or they'll fall apart. Or we'll... fall apart. Do you understand?*

That at the end was the only time her voice failed her, but it was enough. I swept down upon her, letting her wrap herself around me, whispering pale promises into her hair as she trembled in my arms. I still didn't understand at the time that this wasn't forgiveness, but a confession as well. But once she'd stopped shaking against me, she pulled back to study my face, eyes narrow and challenging.

So, what's it gonna be, boy? Yes, or no? Yes or…

I pulled my phone from my pocket and swiped it off Airplane mode. Heather's name appeared under messages, and I typed with slightly shaking thumbs:

I CHOOSE US

Now it was after three. But to my shock, an ellipsis appeared beneath my text almost immediately. It flashed there a moment or two, then Heather's pinged in:

I CHOOSE US TOO

Nothing further arrived. I stared at the phone screen until it went black. Then I was up and on my feet again, blinking under the lobby lights, weaving toward the elevator.

———

My key card didn't work the first three ways I tried it. I tapped it, inserted it, flipped it around—each time, the little light flashed red, accompanied by a muffled electric buzz.

But finally, finally—it admitted me. I pushed the door open as quietly as I could. After the brightness of the lobby and the hall, the suite was solid dark. I couldn't even see the shapes of the furniture, much less any of my friends.

"Ceejay," I whispered. And when no answer came: "Samantha?"

I moved further into the room. The door clunked shut behind me, snapping off the last of the light. Nothing moved. The heavy curtains over the balcony door were closed tight.

I fished in my pocket, clicking on my phone's flashlight. Shadows jumped and squirmed away from the wide beam. Beer empties lay strewn around the coffee table and piled on the TV stand. A few wet spots gleamed, from the table and the couch cushions, left over from minor spills. I winced as my bare foot struck a crumpled can, sending it bumping along the thin carpeted floor. In sudden panic, I swung the light wildly.

Nothing leapt out at me. Both bedroom doors stood resolutely shut. Behind one of them—a low throaty sound. A moan.

I shook my head, almost laughing out loud. Then just as quickly as it had been born, the laugh died in my lungs. The bed springs creaked once, heavily; the door rattled in its frame. The sound—*the moan*—came again, softer and higher, an animal whine of stifled discomfort. And another voice answered it. Even lower, even hollower. The hollowest sound I ever heard in my life. It sounded like, like—

like something being born in reverse

I can't say why I opened that door.

Even now, I can't explain it, even to myself. Every nerve sang at me with shrill fire, screaming at me, pleading to turn around. To go back out into the hall, into the light—into the safety of loneliness. But there are fixed constants, I think, in the universe. Like gravity. Like stars, rotating overhead in exact paths.

They burn; they die. They go supernova—and explode. Things are what they are, and do what they do. A is equal to A, even if it only lasts an instant.

And in that instant, I was stupidly, apocalyptically brave.

I gripped the knob and twisted; the door glided open on silent hinges. There lay the massive king-sized bed, and two dim figures, lit only by whatever light slashed in through a gap in the blackout curtains. Ceejay lay on his back, head pointed away from the door, arms stiff at his sides. Astride him rose the shape of Samantha Black.

She was—

I blinked. Slowly, slowly, she turned at the waist toward the open door, toward me.

—she was *outside of him.*

The head that twisted to face me had stopped being, precisely, a head at all. From a spot between her eyes a wide split opened, and half her nose and half of each lipsticked lip, upper and lower, flapped limply on either side. This crevasse widened the further it ran down her body. Bare breasts folded away from the center line—she seemed to open like a winter coat, legs splayed to accommodate the widening spread of her naked flesh.

I couldn't see Ceejay's legs. Samantha Black shifted her weight, then lowered herself down along the length of my friend's body. His head tipped back, his lips parted—I heard another breathy, keening sound that was half a groan, half a sob.

From inside the split of her being, Samantha answered his call. It shook her entire body, this rattling hollow moan of triumph—triumph and something else. *Welcome*, I thought, dizzyingly. That's what it is. She's welcoming him.

There came a wet soft sucking sound. Ceejay stopped making noise.

A little more of him slid smoothly out of view, up and inside.

I didn't scream. Back then, I didn't think people really screamed like that, not when they're confronting true solid horror. In that moment I only stumbled against the door, knocking it hard against the wall—the sound that came out of me was little more than a bark of surprise. Mostly I just felt breathless, like I was the one being squeezed all over.

Then the rest happened almost too fast to see. The slit down the front of Samantha Black—*the mouth, the maw, the (doorway)*—yawned impossibly wide. Then Ceejay was gone. For a moment her flesh bulged all over like a snake with a fresh meal. I thought I saw it squirm, an elbow or knee pressing out from inside. Then came a sound like eggs breaking and her skin went smooth again.

She rose, slowly, off the bed. I hardly noticed her nakedness. Her skin zippered closed, not even leaving a seam. Her eyes focused, finding me in the dark. The two halves of her mouth flowed smoothly together, just as she opened them to speak.

"Manny," she said. "A wonderful party."

One hand rested on her sealed-over midsection, mirroring Samantha Red.

I think I did scream then. But mostly, I was running. It's true that fear makes time go liquid, heavy and thick and molten as wet sap. So when I turned from the doorway and saw Samantha Blonde climbing over the back of the sofa toward me, nimble as an octopus slipping past a shelf of coral, it seemed to happen all in slow-motion.

Her spreading smile was the gleam of a cold and distant world. Her voice was a dark cave, a wound in flesh: *"I have waited. I am wanting now very much."*

Then she was beside me, as though the distance between the both of us had somehow broken apart. Then she was breathing her name in my ear again, low and hollow and lovely all in some impossible, unnamable way.

It wasn't Samantha; it wasn't any kind of word at all. It was—

————

IT WAS
moon cold as cream lancing off a black ocean
stars dying inside with nothing but vacuous space between
the bite of emptiness—the hollow yawn of solitude
warm wet lips pressing against my wrist in the dark
a voyage long and lonely and ending at last
AND THEN

————

—and then my senses at last returned. And it was already over.

There was no lingering, no savoring. There was only the physical act of it, performed briskly and without any ceremony to accompany the deed. One darkness slid inside another like changing reels at the theater. I felt

Samantha Blonde's slender weight settle over my entire body—and then it was like being pushed under warm water.

I was *encompassed*: I felt moisture and tightness and pressure constricting every inch of naked skin, and heard, somewhere, what sounded like a sigh. Then a pulse, constant and rhythmically perfect, like the beat of a heart.

Then—nothing more. I (we) stood up, and we (she) left the hotel, vanishing into the night as though she (we) were but one small piece of the greater, devouring darkness.

And now it's later on. How long, I can't begin to discern. I'm only aware in fleeting moments—all the rest, I think, are dreams, feverish from this warmth. I am prisoner; I am companion. I am food and lover and slave. I'm a child in a womb who'd only dreamed he was a man. I think it's been a long time. But what are years, compared to a lonely voyage across dark oceans of stars? What's the loss of myself, compared to the wide and aching emptiness of the heavens, longing to be filled?

What affection have I lost, held up against such intimacy, such adoration? If I had not known love already, I might have learned to accept this in its place.

I fill you up. Let's have a party.

But I *had* known love. And sometimes her (our) eyes open in a way that I can see out too, giving me flashes of the world beyond. And through one such open window I saw Heather. Just once, and just the back of her, sitting in a white wrought-iron café chair in the winter sun, staring out at the street while jaywalkers hustled between slow-moving cars. Even from behind, she looked older, sadder. Her hair was short in a way that suited her, the way she'd worn it in grad school when we were first going out. A narrow black briefcase rested on the sidewalk at her feet. Her left hand lay flat on the café table, a familiar diamond gleaming on the correct finger.

I hope she knows, somehow—that I was good. That I chose her, *am choosing her*, even now, at the very end, with everything I am, everything I've got left to give.

I wonder how long she'll wear my ring. I wonder how long we can each hang on.

Jacob Steven Mohr does not believe in human consciousness; his works emerge as though from the ether, fully formed and fully ominous. Selections of these can be observed in *Cosmic Horror Monthly*, *Shortwave Magazine*, *Chthonic Matter Quarterly*, *Weird Horror Magazine*, and *The Best Horror of the Year Vol. 15*. He exists in Columbus, Ohio. This is his second collaboration with Crystal Lake Publishing; the first was *Dead Letters: Episodes of Epistolary Horror*. Follow him everywhere @jacobstevenmohr.

MICHAEL HARRIS COHEN

The Better Man

FIVE MILES OFF THE highway and we're in the middle of nowhere. We're an inching GPS dot, deep in the woods, crawling a nameless road that's barely a road. There's no address, only the coordinates the bride's father texted.

Alec nurses one of his jumbo-sized hangovers. His freckled face is pale as paper. Every thump in the road has him clutching his head.

"The fucking boonies," he says. "If I'd known, I would have skipped today."

"Try listening to your voicemail," I say, skirting a dog-sized pothole. "I told you. Twice."

Though, honestly, I would have passed if they hadn't accepted my first bid. It's a long drive and outdoor ceremonies are harder to shoot. But the father agreed straight off—though my bid was high by a mile—and Venmoed half before I'd even hung up the phone. Crazy to refuse so much money for a day's work. Not a chance.

At last, the trees start to thin.

A few more doglegs and dodged craters and the spot comes into view. It's a vast clearing at the center of the forest. A perfectly mowed circle, big enough for a rave. A white pole tent rises in the mowed part, packed with tables. Next to that stands a log altar, rimmed with flowers and a bell, chairs rowed before it. It's a spread that must have cost a fortune to get delivered and assembled all the way out here, especially that circus tent.

I park on the edge of the clearing by the other cars, Benzes and even a Bentley. My rusty Ford Transit is the mutt of the bunch.

Next to us, cross-legged on the hood of a Range Rover, three longhaired men sit in snow-white robes, sharing a joint. Beyond them, more robed folk wander the grounds, stringing lights and planting Tiki torches. It all looks like a yoga retreat.

A rich hippy wedding. My favorite kind.

My pre-job tension thaws a little. I've shot a few of these around Marin. They're generally easy point-and-shoots, versus some Palo Alto jobs where the mother in-law thinks she's Bergman, shadowing me with "perfect moment" suggestions and composition advice.

As we exit the van the three hippies turn our way. They could be triplets. Same robes, same well-groomed beards. "Welcome," the middle one says, stretching the joint in our direction.

Alec is a moth to a flame, parting his bangs like he's sighted the new world. But before he can speak I say, "We're shooting the wedding video. Know where I can find Brian?"

The center of the trio points to the tent, then exhales a boulder of smoke. Alec looks like he wants to cry as I lead him away.

"I need you straight," I say.

He's my last choice for an assistant but he is my sister's boyfriend and has a decent eye. Though he never mastered the dress code. I remind him every time, "khakis and dress shoes." Per usual, he sports faded jeans and tomato-colored Converses. Worse, he's a liability if he starts drinking, which he considers the main perk of wedding videos. Still, he works cheap.

I peg Brian right off. He's in the tent directing place settings. He's an older version of the hippies by the car, though bigger and muscled like an ex-biker. He's got the same robe and long hair, just grey-streaked at the temples and beard.

I introduce myself and he mashes my hand with a sweaty shake.

I lay out my plan: wood's walk with the bride and groom; some family shots; the vows; cake cutting and toasts; first dance and after-party.

His stare unsettles me, like his eyes reach inside me and come up empty. Then his gaze swings to Alec and lingers. He smiles as he gives Alec the bear grip.

Alec makes a great first impression. Even hungover he's good-looking. Tall and blue-eyed and boyish, like the cover boy for some Midwest travel brochure. It's the other reason I've kept him on. I note the Patek Philippe shackling the father's wrist and aim for the premium package.

"We can do drone shots, too, if you like. Tricky with the trees but it'll add aerial views and a bit of grandeur. Pricey, though."

He bobs his head, letting Alec's hand go. "That'd be fine."

Not even curious *how* pricey. I decide today is going to be a great day.

I ask him where I can find the bride, and he points to a smaller tent by the trees. Red and conical, it looks like something from a renaissance fair.

Alec and I head back to the van and unzip the equipment bags. I wrap a battery belt and check the camera settings. "Shoot the grounds," I say. "Around the tent and altar. Also, some nature shots, birds and trees, establishing stuff. I'll go talk to the bride and groom."

"Roger, sir." He salutes and does a heel click. Color has returned to his cheeks. The fresh air, probably. Unfortunately, it's also returned his default, wiseass mode. I don't understand what my sister sees in him, beyond his cuteness, but then I've never understood much about relationships.

"Alec has a good heart," she always says.

So does a labrador, I always think.

My sister loves to mention his volunteer work for Greenpeace, and how he once gave away all the money in his wallet to a homeless woman with a kid.

"He's a better man than you," she's said, more than once. Which I've told her means next to nothing.

Walking toward the bride's tent I think what I always think: weddings are sad affairs. People spend a fortune to construct their dream day, for a relationship that's got a coin flip's chance of survival. Funerals are more honest. But then no one wants a funeral video.

Outside the bride's tent I voice a "Knock knock."

A soft voice from inside: "Come in."

I pull back the flap and enter. The bride touches up her makeup in a mirror. I see her before she sees me. She's a knockout. Blond braids pretzel the back of her lacy gown. She's one of those cat-eyed, thin-waisted women who model for lingerie catalogues. She catches my eye in the mirror. I stride forward, stretch a hand.

"I'm David. For the wedding photos and video."

Her hand stays locked on the mascara brush, avoiding the shake. Her eyes hold mine in the mirror, then drop. She heaves a sigh.

Christ, a diva day...

Then I realize she's not ignoring me. She's upset, maybe on the verge of a breakdown. Her mascara brush quivers in her hand. Her lips tremble. She rocks slightly on her stool, but when she whirls to face me her eyes aren't nervous or upset. That's not it. She's scared.

"David?" she says.

I nod.

Her eyes grip mine. Her voice lowers to a hoarse whisper "Can you help me?"

"That's what I'm here for. We make memories last forever."

I bury my hands in my pockets and inwardly wince. The line is on my business card, but it rings corny out loud. She searches my eyes like she lost something in them.

"These people... my fiancé..." Her voice cracks. "They're not..."

"Who's not what?" a voice chirps behind me. I jump and turn. A tall woman bares chalk-white teeth. Her long hair is shiny as tar, slicked back and ponytailed. She crosses past me, reeking of patchouli, and sets her hands on the bride's shoulders. "Nervous, Gaia?"

Gaia? I groan inside. New age names turn my stomach

The bride's eyes crinkle into a quick smile, her mask of fear vanished.

"Cold feet, I guess." Her voice is steady, perfect features poised in the mirror.

The woman introduces herself as the mother. Her eyes give me the once over like a I'm a moldy sandwich, then she returns her attention to her daughter.

"The groom isn't here," the mother says. "But he'll arrive soon."

Fuck. If the groom is a no-show I'm out half my fee. It wouldn't be the first time a wedding went south due to last minute bail outs.

We exit the tent and there stands Alec. He sways a little. The smell of fresh dope and alcohol bloom around him.

Christ. Of course I can't say a word in front of the clients. I introduce the mother, who gives Alec the up and down, then a wide smile. His boyish looks melt the iciest types. He smiles and totters and holds her hand too long. I vow to never hire him again, though I've vowed that before.

I tell them we'll do some shots just with the bride.

"Well get the couple's shots later," I say. "When the groom arrives."

The mother nods, though she still hasn't taken her eyes off Alec.

We shoot Gaia walking a path by the tree line. The light is perfect. She's dappled in sun. I shoot her spinning and her white dress billows like a bell. It's a two-shot that'll kill in slo-mo. Clients love slo-mo.

Checking the shots, I catch something in her face. Her eyes are damp, overly bright. I've seen loads of nervous brides but she's different. Her jitters make *me* nervous.

She studies Alec, hunting for something in his vacant gaze. There's a connection there. I can feel it. "I want to talk to *you*," she says.

"Alec?" I say.

His jaw drops, his eyes glassy as soap bubbles. "Sure. We're here to make memories for always."

The idiot can't even get my cheesy slogan right. *What if she smelled the alcohol? What if she reads him the riot act and fires us before I fire him?*

"We don't want to lose the light," I say.

She nods but her eyes stay locked on Alec. He smiles. A stoned and stupid smile I want to slap right off his face.

While they're off talking, I flip on my camera to check footage. In the shots, she glows like a pre-Raphaelite painting. She looks perfect. A white-gowned fairy, floating past trees.

I study her eyes. There's something I missed before. An intensity. *Determination?*

When Alec finally returns he sits next to me and doesn't say a word. "How's our bride?"

Alec stares at his hands. "What are we gonna do?"

"We'll keep shooting and hopefully the groom will show. The more shots we have, the more we can charge if they cancel."

His gaze shifts from his hands to me. He looks scared.

"We have to get her out of here," he says.

"Take it easy. They said the groom's coming. He's just late."

Alec stares at the ground. "You don't get it," he says. "Gaia said she's been kidnapped. She said they're forcing her to marry against her will."

I start laughing. "Come on. She's just freaking out. I've seen a groom rip off his tux before the ceremony and jump in a river. I've got footage aplenty of brides puking pre-vows. People say crazy things before a wedding. It's stress."

"This is different. She's *super* freaked. She says these people are dangerous."

"Getting married is dangerous," I say.

"You don't believe in love at all, do you?"

"Sure I do," I say. "Just not its durability."

He doesn't stir. He just keeps staring at the ground, like he's drilling a hole with his eyes.

"Something in her face," he says. "Like a bad dream."

When he says it, I realize that's exactly how it feels. Something is off. The robes. This place. The *vibe* of these people. A part of me wants to pack up and split, but that'd be insane. Financial suicide.

So all I say is, "Time to wake up. Go grab the drone."

Alec shakes his head and marches back towards the van. I decide, once and for all, that I'm done with him. After today, he can go save walruses or dish out grub in a homeless shelter, for all I care.

I settle in the main tent and order a beer. As the cold beer soothes my nerves, I decide what I'll tell my sister. How I care about her but not at the expense of my business. How she might want to consider dumping him as well. I'll extol the merits of single life. Lonely but far less complicated.

A dreadlocked fellow sits at my table. "Dude, is that a 5D Mark III?" he asks.

He's pointing at my camera. I shake my head. "Mark IV."

"Awesome. You shoot anything besides weddings?"

I consider telling him about my stillborn feature film, but I'm not in the mood. I just want to drink my beer and quietly stew.

"Nah," I say. "Just weddings."

A grin splits his face. His eyes are intense and too large, like he's on something stronger than pot.

"This union is gonna be nuts. Just wait. You can get all Herzog on this thing. You know, *Herzog*?"

"Yeah, he's great."

"Great? He's a motherfucking *genius*."

Camera buffs and film nuts go with the job. He drones on about *Fitzcarraldo, Aguirre,* Kinski. I tune him out and finish my beer.

Close to dusk, the guests settle in the chairs by the altar. The string lights flick on and the Tiki torches are lit. I set a tripod camera for a constant wide shot. The rest we'll shoot handheld.

I check my watch, 6:45 and the wedding starts at seven.

Where the hell is the groom? Where's Alec?

I pan over the crowd. The light is perfect, a soft glow, filtered through the treetops. The white robes of the audience glow amber. Beautiful people made more beautiful.

Music kicks off. The wedding march, tastefully done on cello. Still, no groom, no bride, no bridesmaids, though no one looks concerned. Half the crowd stares off into the woods, the other half whispers among themselves.

The wedding march runs to the end. Then the clearing is silent, except for the squeak of folding chairs and the whispers.

The music restarts, the cello saws through the march, though no one is marching. No father of the bride. No bride.

Abruptly, the father comes tearing up the aisle. The crowd stands with a collective gasp, heads turning, searching the clearing and the woods. My gut flares.

He did it. Alec stole the fucking bride.

I keep shooting. I want to hide behind the camera. None of this will make the clip anyway, if there's a clip. My contract has a no-show fee if the wedding aborts, but it's only half, which means I won't get another dime. No drone shots or webpages. Zero extras.

Goddamn Alec. He finally lost his fucking mind.

The crowd murmurs, all eyes on the woods. More hippie guys, young and old, an elderly broad with a massive, diamond broach, her husband even older, a wispy-haired mummy lost in his oversized robe, all of them are on their feet.

The cello grinds on in the background.

I decide this is the strangest wedding party I've ever shot. Not just the missing bride, there's something weirder, a Lynchian feeling I can't pinpoint.

Then I realize what it is. The crowd isn't shocked. No handwringing or tears. No looks of disbelief. They're all... eager. Palms pressed together, eyes sweeping the trees at the edge of the clearing, they're waiting on something to emerge from the woods, like everyone's holding their breath. Cricket chirps volume up. Bird calls whistle from the pines, shrill taunts or warnings.

Suddenly, one of the triplets from the joint-circle shouts, "Over there!"

All heads pivot, following the line of his finger. I zoom the spot. Nothing.

Trees. Moss-coated rocks. I pan left. Then right. Then I snag a flash of white, a movement in the brush. The bride.

She staggers through the trees and underbrush. Her dress is filthy and mud-stained, its neckline torn. She struggles like her body is a heavy thing. Her arms stretch behind her back, as if her wrists are bound.

Jesus... Alec was right... she's in danger...

I'm suddenly desperate to see him, to set eyes on his stoned and goofy smile.

Then a terrible thought splinters my head.

Alec is a fuckup, but he wouldn't...

I search the woods. Trees scroll my lens. No sign of him.

Maybe he's passed out in the van? Overstoned and snoozing. Maybe she ran off on her own, wandered the woods, then changed her mind and turned back?

I zoom out and swing to the father. Like the rest, he's locked on the sunset-brushed woods, watching his daughter.

Why isn't he running over to her? Why doesn't anyone?

The father turns and looks right at me, face stuffing my frame. His eyes dance with joy. Overjoyed.

What the hell?

I lower the camera and there's an immediate grab of my wrist—the dreadlocked, film buff. He smiles and twists my arm back. Sharp pain shoots my shoulder.

"What the fuck are you doing?" I squeal.

"You need to film her," he says. "You need to shoot everything."

His free hand reaches inside his robe and, like a magic trick, a hunting knife appears in it. My mind goes weirdly clear. He whips it to my throat. Sharp metal pricks my skin like something hot.

Leaning in, he doesn't smile anymore. There's a speed freak certainty in his stare, like cutting my throat would be easy as stubbing out a cigarette.

My head hollows. My legs liquefy. I manage a swallow and a careful nod. I lift my camera. His knife lowers and sticks at my back, the slightest pressure there, like it's only the point of a pencil.

I try to steady my hands as I focus on the bride. I try to ignore his mouth breathing near my ear, his breath like rancid fruit, ignore the knife's tip a half inch from my spine.

She's halfway across the clearing, nearly to the mowed circle. Zoomed, she bites her lip, forehead furrowed, like she's straining. Stare fixed, braids askew, her eyes lock on the altar, arms still behind her back as she lumbers forward.

Then I see she's pulling something.

Thick rope circles her wrists and stretches taut behind her. Something heavy drags the ground after her, though the grass is too thick to see it.

The crowd starts clapping. Not applause but a slow pulse in time with her plodding steps.

The film buff lets out a high-pitched giggle. "She did it," he says. "She bested him."

At last, she reaches the mowed part. She's close enough that I can hear her grunts. A flash of red catches my eye. Converse sneakers.

Alec.

His legs raise off the ground, ankles bound by the rope she drags. My eye bulges at the viewfinder—*What the hell?*

My camera follows her as she reaches the chairs toward the back. The guests bow as she struggles up the center aisle. Alec's head bobs the rough ground. His hands flop behind him. My ears crack with the sharp claps of the crowd, my heart beats a quick counter-rhythm.

I zoom Alec's head. There's a bloody spot on his scalp. His mouth dribbles blood, eyes closed. Maybe he's breathing. Maybe he isn't.

Alec, what did you do?

She's halfway to the altar. The crowd's rhythmic claps grow louder.

A hazy feeling floods my head. *I'm shooting a dream.* But the camera is solid in my hands. The bite of the knife at my back a constant pressure. This is real. It's happening.

I should do something... clock the film buff with my camera. Help Alec...

But I keep shooting. Frozen.

I picture a scene: Alec leads her through the woods. He stops and turns. A crooked smile tilts his face. He paws her dress, tears the neckline. She gropes for a log and, like a golfer, swings upward, catching him square in the mouth. Another swing slams into his skull and he's out cold.

The clapping becomes deafening as the bride reaches the altar. In front of it, she unwraps the rope from her thin wrists. Alec's legs flop to the ground.

I zoom: Blood smears the lower half of his face and coats his chest, but even zoomed, I can't find the wound, can't tell if he's breathing. I think he is but the image shakes, my hands wobble. My heart sprints like a runaway horse. My head spins. I'm afraid I'll faint and fall back on the knife.

I bite my lip till I taste blood and tilt up to the bride. Her chest heaves. Her features glow savage in the twilight, eyes boiling. Stepping up to the altar, she turns and beams at the crowd. She bobs her head in time with their thunderous claps. She raises her hands in the air. They're blood stained.

The father's voice booms and echoes through the clearing as if its amplified. His language is guttural and strange, a wailing tuneless song, a soundtrack for this nightmare.

"The vessel." Hot sour breath at my ear, knife point jiggling at my back. "You're unlucky, bud. It had to be the *better* man. And now it's *coming*," the camera buff roars. "At fucking last."

My legs buckle and shake, ready to give way. But it's not my legs. It's the ground. Throbbing, vibrating. The altar bell sways and rings, a dull tone like a spoon against a jar. My mind contracts to a single word: *Earthquake.*

I drop the camera, the neck strap bouncing it to my chest. People jiggle in their folding chairs. No one stands or runs or screams. Time slows, as the ground by the altar crumbles.

Gotta get out!

The knife pokes my back, the camera buff's putrid breath at my cheek. "Keep filming. Don't miss this!"

He jabs the knife through my jacket, piercing my lower back, breaking the skin with a pain like a lit cigar. I scream but no one turns. All are transfixed. I raise the camera, tears blurring the image, my mind crumpling.

The earth cracks and a hole spreads before the altar, dirt sucked down like a giant drain has opened.

A sinkhole.

I'll die here... in the middle of nowhere... buried alive... never found...

The father's voice rises to an earsplitting volume. Then abruptly he stops.

As suddenly as the quake started, it stops, too.

A silence fills the clearing.

No birds, no crickets, only my heartbeat thumping my ears, and the raspy breathing of the film buff. My legs quiver, as if the tremors echo there. My back sings with pain from the knife.

Like hijacked pilots and bank tellers in robberies, do the job and you'll wake up tomorrow. Don't think. Just do the job.

My camera pans the sinkhole, records the edges of this dirt wound, wide as a truck. Then there comes a blurred motion, as thousands of bugs scurry from the hole in black and brown waves, beetles and ants, then worms and snakes, all bolting for the forest, for escape.

I hear my pulse in my ears, my panting breath.

Then there's another sound from the hole. A skittering like a thousand crumpled newspapers.

My brain squeals *Run!* But I can't. My legs lock, rigid as fenceposts.

I don't want to see. I want to squeeze my eyes shut, but my camera eye refuses to close, bound to look, to record, as a thing emerges from the crater.

It's long and segmented, a giant snake, no, not a snake, it moves on legs, thousands of them. It's a centipede-like creature, the thickness of a man's bicep, and as long as a bus. It's an impossible thing, a jungle nightmare.

My camera is a shelter, a barrier, reducing this madness to the tiny window of my viewfinder. My mind sputters as I run the camera over its sleek black skin.

I'm grateful the world is dimmed, that I can't see it clearly, though it's still too much, even in twilight, *too much, too much.*

The creature slithers to the altar, to the bride, and her head tilts to meet it. Elation spreads her face, as she pulls Alec to his feet. His chin lolls against his chest, blood dribbling his mouth. The bride's mother and father grab onto his arms holding him upright.

Alec's head snaps up.

He's alive!

His eyes pop with pain. His mouth stretches in a scream that doesn't arrive. Instead, he emits a toneless wail. I zoom his gaping mouth. A bloodied stump wriggles within. He stares right at me, eyes shrieking as his mouth can't.

She cut off his tongue. He tried to help her and she cut off his tongue.

His face distorts as the nightmare insect approaches him. It slithers up his belly. His chest. I'm zoomed on his face, recording the terror in his eyes, as the thing forces its way into his mouth, stretching it impossibly wide.

It seems to take an eternity for it to fully enter him. But it does. All of it disappears inside him as his body bucks and convulses, held upright by the parents.

My stomach twists and acid floods my mouth. I squeeze my eyes shut.

When I open them, he's crumpled to his knees. Eyes glassy, mouth still stretched like a gaping cavern. Though the creature is gone, all of it somehow within him.

The bride kneels before Alec and kisses him.

I frame it perfectly. The money shot.

Then my legs finally give. I crumple to my knees, nothing left. The film buff crouches by me, knife at my back. "Shoot it!" He shouts in my ear.

I raise the camera, heavy as a cinderblock, but I keep filming.

"The devil," I say flatly.

The film buff whispers at my ear. "The devil is a fairytale. This is older. And its time has come."

A train horn sounds in the distance. A signal from another world, impossibly far off. A world now unreal to me. Then everything goes black.

I watch it again and again. Rewind and watch.

My fingers skitter on the keyboard as I cut the images from two cameras into something coherent.

I am not the same man who last sat in this editing chair.

TV news blares in the background. I'm half listening, waiting to hear something that will pull my whole attention: A slaughter somewhere. An emergency broadcast ordering evacuation. A town overrun by... something. Some*things*.

But there's nothing. Not yet. The news runs its normal course—political scandals and distant wars—not a ripple of this thing.

Though I know there will be.

I thought they'd kill me at the wedding. Chase me in the woods and slice my throat. Bury me in a shallow grave or burn me.

But they let me go. They want their wedding film.

And they want more.

The film buff walked me to my van. He hugged me. *Really* hugged me, long and with feeling. I drove out of there on that cratered road, as if transported to another planet. My van's wheels spun like my mind, turning over his last words.

"We can't wait to see what you cut together," he said, hands on my shoulders. "And what follows. There'll be loads more to shoot—and you're our Leni."

I watch and think of Leni, of course, Leni Riefenstahl, filming the dark power's rise. Like her, what I've shot has never been recorded. Like the Nuremburg rallies or the moon landing, I'm the first. The only one.

I'm going to cut a fucking masterpiece.

There's a hum in my blood. My mind feels wider than ever before as I return to the last shots, the images filmed after I blacked out. I view them over and over, frame by frame. I watch Alec as he changes in slow motion.

After the kiss, Alec spreads out on his belly. His limbs and body elongate. There's no sound as I slowly scroll forward, but I've watched it enough at regular speed, my mind overdubs it. Sounds like snapping branches as his body extends into something else, no longer fully human. His arms and legs elongate and bend in impossible ways, and dozens more limbs burst from his chest and belly, fully formed, raising him off the ground.

Though his head remains the same. His blue eyes spread wide with pain and terror, aware of all that is happening to him.

He can't even scream.

The bride raises her dress and mounts him, as if he were some nightmarish horse. Her expression is fierce and dogged as she settles on his oddly curved back.

Then the Alec-thing skitters off the altar and over the ground, carrying the bride towards the hole. Its movements are abrupt and jerky, then smoother, as it seems to gain confidence in its newly formed limbs.

"It needed to be part human to mate," the hippie said. "It needed a good man. For their union."

I freezeframe on the bride's face, just before they descend into the earth. Unlike Alec, there's no terror in her face. Her cat eyes are wide. Her lips part in a smile of exhilaration and ecstasy.

She's more beautiful than any woman I've ever seen.

"Soon Gaia will couple and breed." The hippie's dilated eyes glitter full of moonlight. "Her endless litter will roam the earth. Millions of ravenous spawn, and you'll shoot it all."

I feel it. The shift in things. In me.

History needs those who won't look away. Like Leni. Like me. Those who have the eye to record the end of eras. Not better men. But men like me.

Michael Harris Cohen has published stories in *Conjunctions*, *The Dark Magazine*, *Pseudopod*, *Apparition Lit*, *Litro*, and numerous anthologies including *Catapult's Tiny Crimes*. He's a recipient of a Fulbright grant for literary translation, and fellowships from the OMI International Arts Center for Writers, Atlantic Center for the Arts, The Djerassi Foundation, The Jentel Artist's Residency, the Künstlerdorf Schöppingen Foundation, and Hawthornden Castle, among others. He's won F(r)iction's short story contest, judged by Mercedes M. Yardley as well as Mixer Publishing's Sex, Violence and Satire prize, judged by Stephen Graham Jones, which was published as his first collection, *The Eyes*. His most recent collection is *Effects Vary* from Cemetery Gates Media. He lives in Sofia, Bulgaria with his wife and daughters, and teaches creative writing and literature at the American University in Bulgaria. Find him online at Michaelharriscohen.net.

THE END?

Not if you want to dive into more of Crystal Lake Publishing's Tales from the Darkest Depths!

Check out our amazing website and online store or download our latest catalog here.

We always have great new projects and content on the website to dive into, as well as a newsletter, behind the scenes options, social media platforms, our own dark fiction shared-world series and our very own webstore. Our webstore even has categories specifically for KU books, non-fiction, anthologies, and of course more novels and novellas.

Readers...

Thank you for reading *The Joining*. We hope you enjoyed this anthology. If you have a moment, please review *The Joining* at the store where you bought it.

Help other readers by telling them why you enjoyed this book. No need to write an in-depth discussion. Even a single sentence will be greatly appreciated. Reviews go a long way to helping a book sell, and is great for an author's career. It'll also help us to continue publishing quality books.

Thank you again for taking the time to journey with Crystal Lake Publishing.

You will find links to all our social media platforms on our Linktree page. https://linktr.ee/CrystalLakePublishing

Follow us on Amazon:

MISSION STATEMENT

SINCE ITS FOUNDING IN August 2012, Crystal Lake has quickly become one of the world's leading publishers of Dark Fiction and Horror books. In 2023, Crystal Lake officially transitioned into an entertainment company, joining several other divisions, genres, and imprints, including Torrid Waters, Crystal Lake Comics, Crystal Lake Games, Crystal Lake Kids, and many more.

While we strive to present only the highest quality fiction and entertainment, we also endeavour to support authors along their writing journey. We offer our time and experience in non-fiction projects, as well as author mentoring and services, at competitive prices.

With several Bram Stoker Award wins and many other wins and nominations (including the HWA's Specialty Press Award), Crystal Lake Publishing puts integrity, honor, and respect at the forefront of our publishing operations.

We strive for each book and outreach program we spearhead to not only entertain and touch or comment on issues that affect our readers, but also to strengthen and support the Dark Fiction field and its authors.

Not only do we find and publish authors we believe are destined for greatness, but we strive to work with men and women who endeavour to be decent human beings who care more for others than themselves, while still being hard working, driven, and passionate artists and storytellers.

Crystal Lake Publishing is and will always be a beacon of what passion and dedication, combined with overwhelming teamwork and respect, can accomplish. We endeavour to know each and every one of our readers, while building personal relationships with our authors, reviewers, bloggers, podcasters, bookstores, and libraries.

We will be as trustworthy, forthright, and transparent as any business can be, while also keeping most of the headaches away from our authors, since it's our job to solve the problems so they can stay in a creative mind. Which of course also means paying our authors.

We do not just publish books, we present to you worlds within your world, doors within your mind, from talented authors who sacrifice so much for a moment of your time.

There are some amazing small presses out there, and through collaboration and open forums we will continue to support other presses in the goal of helping authors and showing the world what quality small presses are capable of accomplishing. No one wins when a small press goes down, so we will always be there to support hardworking, legitimate presses and their authors. We don't see Crystal Lake as the best press out there, but we will always strive to be the best, strive to be the most interactive and grateful, and even blessed press around. No matter what happens over time, we will also take our mission very seriously while appreciating where we are and enjoying the journey.

What do we offer our authors that they can't do for themselves through self-publishing?

We are big supporters of self-publishing (especially hybrid publishing), if done with care, patience, and planning. However, not every author has the time or inclination to do market research, advertise, and set up book launch strategies. Although a lot of authors are successful in doing it all, strong small presses will always be there for the authors who just want to do what they do best: write.

What we offer is experience, industry knowledge, contacts and trust built up over years. And due to our strong brand and trusting fanbase, every Crystal Lake Publishing book comes with weight of respect. In time our fans begin to trust our judgment and will try a new author purely based on our support of said author.

With each launch we strive to fine-tune our approach, learn from our mistakes, and increase our reach. We continue to assure our authors that we're here for them and that we'll carry the weight of the launch and dealing with third parties while they focus on their strengths—be it writing, interviews, blogs, signings, etc.

We also offer several mentoring packages to authors that include knowledge and skills they can use in both traditional and self-publishing endeavours.

We look forward to launching many new careers.

This is what we believe in. What we stand for. This will be our legacy.

Welcome to Crystal Lake Publishing—Where Stories Come Alive!